Praise for *Saint Glinglin*

"Consider what you get here: references to and satires of mythology and Freudian psychology. Varied narrative styles, including soliloquy, interior monologue, verse, and third person. A lot of laughs. Discussions of serious philosophical issues which are thought-provoking even when hilarious. All in one slim volume."—*Austin Chronicle*

"Like all his fiction, it is so blissfully fizzy that the reader may scarcely notice its complexity."—*New Yorker*

"Wondrous."—Bill Marx, *Boston Phoenix*

"Replete with characters just this side of lunacy yet touchingly human. . . . The plot is fantastical but interwoven with enough threads of reality to keep the reader turning pages."—*Library Journal*

"A carnival ride of surprises and pleasures."—*Kirkus*

"Queneau's funny, philosophical nonsense is addictive."—*Publishers Weekly*

"Sometimes hilarious and sometimes—as in its central story of sons driving their corrupt father to his death—as powerful as Greek tragedy. . . . Queneau's play with language begs for comparisons with Joyce, and the undercurrents of ancient and modern mythology (particularly those cooked up by Freud) are perfectly integrated. This, in short, is literature."—*Booklist*

Works by Raymond Queneau that have been translated into English

Saint Glinglin

Raymond Queneau

Translated from the French
with an Introduction by James Sallis

Dalkey Archive Press

Originally published © 1948 by Éditions Gallimard; copyright renewed © 1975.

English translation and introduction © 1993 by James Sallis

First hardcover edition, 1993
First paperback edition, 2000

Library of Congress Cataloging-in-Publication Data
Queneau, Raymond, 1903-1976.
      [Saint Glinglin. English]
      Saint Glinglin : a novel / by Raymond Queneau ; translated with an intro-
duction by James Sallis.
    I. Title.
    PQ2633.U43S313 1993   92-29479
    843'.912—dc20

ISBN: 1-56478-027-9 cloth
          1-56478-230-1 paperback

Partially funded by grants from the National Endowment for the Arts, a federal agency,
the Illinois Arts Council, a state agency, and the French Ministry of Culture.

Dalkey Archive Press
Illinois State University
Campus Box 4241
Normal, IL 61790-4241

www.dalkeyarchive.com

Printed on permanent/durable acid-free paper and bound in the United States of
America.

Contents

Preface

Raymond Queneau

It was in 1933 that I began writing this book. I always thought there would be five parts: the first three were published in 1934 under the title *Gueule de pierre*. Not until 1938 did I take up the fourth part, published in 1941 under the title *Temps mêlés*; it was preceded by a "monologue" and a suite of poems (included now in *Bucoliques*). The fifth part had to be called *Saint Glinglin*. Under this title, I've joined to the unpublished text of the last part a heavily modified version of the two earlier volumes. Almost all the names of characters are changed, the theatrical form which I initially gave *Temps mêlés* is abandoned, etc. *Saint Glinglin* is therefore a work almost wholly new, and, this time, finished.

If I've changed the names, it's often quite gratuitously, because "it works better" (at least, I imagine it does: thus Mulhierr and Shantant become Paracole and Catogan). Sometimes I've had other reasons: thus Kougard became Nabonidus. That, as everyone knows, is the name of the last king of Babylon (Herodotus called him Labynetus): this name suggested itself accordingly for the principal character in *Gueule de pierre*.

Finally, I'll make no excuses for having everywhere printed: *esscuse, essplication*, etc. This exclusion of the letter *x* (save in final position) reveals no particular taste for "spoken language." The reader will easily discover the symbolic significance, above all if he notes that this letter is preserved in the book's last word, which rhymes moreover with its pronunciation: "le beau temps fixe."

Introduction

James Sallis

Poorly known among English-language readers and writers despite several excellent translations over the years (these principally by way of Barbara Wright), Raymond Queneau is a direct precursor to much that is most interesting and influential in modern continental literature, from surrealism and *le nouveau roman* to the contemporary experimentalism of OuLiPo and such writers as Georges Perec or Milan Kundera.

Editorial director of Gallimard (where he became a conduit for writers as diverse as Boris Vian, Chandler Brossard, and Henry Miller) and editor of the massive *Encyclopédie de la Pléïade* (an attempt to provide a *summa* of all man's knowledge), Queneau was a true polymath, a man of letters the like of which we're not likely to see again, quintessentially original, quintessentially French, a man whose intelligence and interests—he wrote widely on mathematics and linguistics, was a student of philosophy at the Sorbonne, painted seriously, wrote popular songs and screenplays—were as pervasive as his influence.

Queneau's career spanned some forty-five years until his death in 1976, and included at least six volumes of miscellaneous writing, eighteen novels, and thirteen volumes of poetry. Among the latter are two profoundly original works. *Chêne et chien*, subtitled a novel in verse, tells the story of Queneau's life, often humorously, often movingly, and in doing so evolves a kind of personal mythology. Like Cendrars's "La Prose du Transsibérien et de la Petite Jehanne de France," it is a major work, a point about which contemporaneous literature, and the age itself, must revolve. *Petite cosmogonie portative* takes as subject the entire universe, recounting in its six cantos, in a mulch of street slang, neologisms, puns, mythic imagery, juxtaposed poetic and scientific diction and technical terms, the origins of the world and of life therein, up to the invention of artificial intelligence.

These poems, alongside immensely popular novels like *Zazie in the Metro* and obscure ones like *Les enfants du limon*, form the richest, if also far the most idiosyncratic, body of work produced in France, or anywhere else, in our time.

Queneau's first novel, *The Bark Tree*, a brilliantly original work, was published in 1933. It had begun, playfully, as a translation of Descartes into spoken French, and makes use of widely diverse narrative modes—letters, soliloquies, telegrams, catalogs, interior monolog and stream-of-consciousness, indirect discourse, dreams, even narrative from a dog's point of view—in its investigation of what lies (the pun is one Queneau would have liked) behind appearances. Replete with parodies and pastiches of Plato, Parmenides, Hegel, and Heidegger, this is hardly the dry stuff it may sound. In Queneau, slapstick and comedy are never far off. One character, hauling everywhere Plato's *Apology*, turns out to be interested only in an obscene photo secreted therein. Another, dying, strikes the pose of Socrates drinking hemlock and, in purest Parisian street slang, delivers a final discourse on the soul's nonexistence.

Plots are important to Queneau. Things *happen* in Queneau, all sorts of things, and they often happen with the language as much as with the book's events.

The texture and movement of his novels are those of the imagination, making his work a clear precursor to the sort of circular, self-referential, reality-skeptical books we've taken to calling postmodern. In *The Bark Tree*, Pierre le Grand, asked if he is a novelist, replies that no, he is a character. In *The Flight of Icarus* a character escapes its book and, much like Gogol's nose, roves all about Paris having adventures, pursued by its desperate author. And in *Les Enfants du limon* Queneau himself appears briefly as a character.

Queneau also experiments widely with narrative strategies. *Exercises in Style*, perhaps his best-known work, consists of the same "story" in ninety-nine versions ranging from anecdote to reportage to haiku to philosophical treatise. He often squeezes syntax and language until they take on almost unrecognizable shapes. And in an otherwise "realist" novel may include, without explanation, what is clearly a demon.

But always the plots—the complications, complicities, coincidences, reversals, concealments and uncoverings—are primary.

♦

Saint Glinglin retells the Freudian myth of sons killing the father;
not too surprisingly, its composition coincided with Queneau's own
psychoanalysis, which became a major theme of *Chêne et chien.* It also
tells of a town, Home Town, where it never rains, and where there
are no fish, and of how the town's mayor falls into a petrifying spring
and becomes a statue that's set up on the town square but soon dis-
solves, of how one of the mayor's sons brings on a year of unending
rain until fish are aswim in all the taverns, of how another son marries
a famous foreign-film star (who swims almost nude in that same town
square) and becomes mayor himself, and of the sister hidden away in
an abandoned mill where she speaks with worms and insects she has
given her brothers' names. There's nothing quite like it anywhere.

The novel falls into seven discrete parts, three of them narrated
in first-person: Pierre's diarylike musings on his sojourn among
Foreigners, his vertigo and great discoveries; brother Paul's interior
monolog on the horrors of the countryside and the civilizing effects
of girdles and bras; sister Hélène's autistic soliloquy on her beloved
insects and later life among Foreigners. Another section, alternating
viewpoints, is written in near-biblical verse.

Critic Allen Thiher has described *Saint Glinglin* as "an intellectual comedy whose scope of reference includes most of Western
anthropological thought and the myths that this anthropology has
highlighted in its attempts to understand the nature of culture." But
whatever else he is doing, and perhaps especially at the moments he
becomes most serious, Queneau has fun. Intertwined in the biblical
verse of the third section is a playful substructure in which each of
the twelve sections has its own zodiac sign and internal references.
Anthropologist Dussouchel, pursuing his researches among the
natives of Home Town (and particularly in the vicinity of young
Eveline's legs), is subjected to folkloric kicks in the rear and scientific
gobs of spittle.

For Queneau saw science and literature much in the same light:
as games offering marvelous opportunities to make all sorts of
connections and play out the consequences of arbitrary rules, but
offering no essential knowledge of things in themselves. It's little
wonder that he had so much fun with Hegelian classification in
Pierre's meditations on the lives of fish, or that he became so active
in later years in the Pataphysicians' "science of imaginary solutions"
and in the extravagant game-playing of OuLiPo.

◆

Asked why I set about translating Queneau, my stock reply these last months has been: I didn't step backwards fast enough when the line was drawn.

After all, I had my own work to do, and *any* translation is difficult, even one whose writer doesn't create his own universe and language in each book.

But Queneau is probably the single writer most responsible for my love of contemporary French literature. And whenever I conjure up visions of the man of letters I aspire to be—poet, novelist, essayist, editor, critic, and commentator—it's Queneau who first comes to mind.

In *Saint Glinglin*, as in most of his books, Queneau served up a lifetime of problems to the translator.

For many years he was a crusader for demotic, spoken French as opposed to the literary, and though he later abandoned this crusade, its influence persists in his dialogue, in the way he fractures syntax, for instance, separating morpheme (or framework of thought) from semanteme (or concrete data). Similarly, he has a penchant for phonetic spellings (he'll often write *spa* for n'est-ce pas), and for the Francification of English words (*ouateurproufe* for "waterproof," or raincoat). And if none of these possibilities seems quite satisfactory, well, there are always neologisms and portmanteau words. Lots of them.

*X*s do not exist, for instance (save, unsounded, in characters' names), in *Glinglin*. For "existence," we find *aiguesistence, eksistence, ogresistence, eggsistence* and so on. Sometimes these variant spellings make a linguistic point: that the *x* in "existence" is pronounced *gz*, not *ks*. Sometimes they are conceptual puns, *aiguesistence* in Pierre's meditation on fish recalling (as in *aigue-marine*) that prefix's derivation from the Latin *aqua*. And sometimes, too, they're there for the simple fun of it. For whatever else it may be—and it can be, it was, many things in his work—art is, first of all, artifice and play.

Queneau's preface to the final version of *Glinglin* pointed out that the *x* was eschewed throughout the book expressly so that it might chime in symbolically at the very end: *le beau temps fixe*, good weather of everlasting excellence. The same practice has been followed here. The names were a more difficult decision. Some of these, in purest Queneau fashion, are marvelous puns; but I've chosen to retain the original forms.

Of the book's myriad other puns, and flurries of wordplay of every sort, I've tried where possible to find rough equivalents. The most frustrating have been passages throughout the novel in which people are conversing and one, by way of puns, is responding to a different chain of concepts than the other, who nevertheless carries on, intends. These are rather brilliant in French, and their corresponding wattage in English is a sad thing to see.

But the translator knows that various shades of compromise are the best he can hope for; and one begins this task (unless he's to go mad) accepting that the aim is not so much to translate as to recreate the book in a second language. Which is precisely what I've spent a great part of the year doing. It's my way of trying to give something back, and I hope very much that Queneau would approve. I am at any rate fairly convinced that what you hold here is, in its own idiosyncratic way, as much *Saint Glinglin* now, and here, as Queneau's was there, and then.

The title, finally. In French, when one says I'll love you till Saint Glinglin's, it means that his love will last forever. And when one says I'll do something-or-other on that fictitious saint's day, well, don't hold your breath: it'll never happen.

Saint Glinglin

1

Fish

How strange a fish's life must be! . . . Glittery, walleyed. . . . I've never been able to understand how such a life is possible. The aguesistence of life in that form reduces me to tears quicker than anything else in the world. An aquarium stirs up in me whole potfuls of red-hot pincers. This afternoon, I went to see the one they're so proud of here in the Foreign Town's Zoological Garden. I wandered in that upside-down world until officials finally turned me out.

Captivity underscores the strangeness of this life. I stood watching one animal, striped with black, swim monotonously up and down. Since these beasts as far as I know never sleep, I suppose that even now, at the late hour I'm writing this, my zebra still sloughs aimlessly back and forth, utterly unoccupied. Even to eat, it doesn't have to stop, nor to reproduce. And this latter activity, we're told, it pursues so impersonally as to forego any need to interrupt swimming.

Whatever does it think about, my fish? Naturally, I don't ekspect that it should reflect, that it abandon itself to rational activity, construct syllogisms and refute fallacies, no, of course not, but I do have to wonder if my fish has any interest at all in what passes on the other side of that thick glass dividing it from the human world. Common sense says: no, my fish doesn't think, its intellectual activity amounts to nothing. And that's precisely what I find so savage. It's not possible to have human relations with a fish. I think fishermen tell true stories. But one seldom meets such people in my Home Town, and I know them for their stories only: legends and far-off hearsay. Outside aquariums, this animal is restored to life. We're able then to make some sense of its aguesistence: it comes and goes in the

river (I've seen some rivers in the Foreigners' country), glides among
grasses beaten down by the current, awaits its prey, lets itself be
drawn to the lure. Yes, one can still understand freshwater fish. But
saltwater fish? sardines? herring? cod? The sardine's truly stupefying.
At Foreign Town's cinematograph into which I recently strayed, I
saw piles of them, innumerable and nautical, laid out scale to scale.
For all that, a sardine's an individual. But the cod! the herring! Tears
come to my eyes. Papa! Mama! It's truly terrible, truly savage, the life
these shoal-fish lead! Just thinking about it drives you mad. Coming
into the world in choirs by the millions, voyaging out all together,
this brotherhood of herrings, into the limitless ocean, snagging its
fins and falling into nets everywhere. That's a herring's life. And the
one who finds itself in the middle of the shoal? Millions of the same
species swarm about it and so it happens one day, though it can't tell
day from night, so it happens that one day vertigo seizes the chief
herring. Yes, vertigo. And what will our herring's destiny be then?
Oh, it's just too dismal! Papa! Mama! It's just too savage, the shoal-
fish's life.

This is becoming insufferable. My scales are all ragged. Salt splits my
gums. The ocean tosses rag ends of its tide against my window. I am
so very alone in this town where drudgingly I study their foreign
language. But solitude's the least of my concerns. It bothers me not
at all. My Home Town provided a grant to allow me to acquire
thorough knowledge of this language. Professor of gibberish, that's
the only role my father believed me capable of playing. I don't want
to disappoint him; I'll prove myself deserving of the honor he
worked so hard to obtain for me; I acknowledge his efforts and am
thankful; but why does my father think me a fool? I'll be professor of
gibberish, so be it. I'll do what I must and hold my tongue, but I can't
help having other concerns, concerns bearing on the science of life.
Life! I'll dedicate my life to the study of life! I vow it, here and now,
before my window overlooking one of Foreign Town's quadri-
lateral streets. I get up, I take in that street with a wave of my arm,
and I say: I, etc., life. And then I'm calm. It's said and done. My
eggzistence has meaning now, and I realize that my action has
restored something of that sense of life we have when young and
bursting with promise, able to make anything of ourselves, in short:
able to construct ourselves a future. It seems to me that a star has
risen which will guide me to the very heights I long for. And within
me there's a new pride. It's to the summits of the science of life that

I must make my way, not to this doggerel patois of Foreigners we know only as Tourists, and deal with rarely. What's the use of speaking to them?

Today I returned to the aquarium. I saw the moray eels. Each one is alone in its cage. They are ferocious. They eat meat. In imperial times they dined on slaves, journalists tell us. They differ remarkably from other fish at every turn, and this ferocity sets them apart still more. Ferocity, you see, is one of the cardinal categories of man's life in society. This is fraught with mystery. That ferocity should deliver some fish from the atrocity of their species' communal life, is a shocking thought. The moray eel seems to be an autonomous individual by very virtue of its ferocity!

There is, to my mind, another dismal case: the ray. This fish's anatomic construction breaks my heart: head on its back or belly like that, you really can't tell, it makes my skin crawl. Its gills look to me like eyes. And those eyes, carried beneath it! that nose! and small, cruel mouth. I wept with sorrow trying to make head or tail of this horrific creature, as the apparition rose towards the water's surface, flapping fins as though they were wings, suddenly become some aquatic bird, a mirror-image, beplumed albatross. No. It's not possible, the ray's eggzistence. With eyes placed like that, flying in the water, accomplishing nothing. No.

Here's what happened. I began too low on the scale of living things. The abyss is so deep. A monkey's life, one can accept; a cow's, easily enough; a bird's, fine. But with all the animals what I can't understand is the way they're forever unoccupied, forever unmindful. It's unfathomable. This morning, I received two letters, one from my father and the other from Paul. The first wrote me: "Our town prepares for the Festival. I regret that you won't be here to take part; there hasn't been one grander for years and years. I'll be making sacrifices which will again guarantee my wealth and fame.

"I hope that you are working ardently and proving yourself worthy of the scholarship I took such trouble to secure for you. It's most fortunate that I was able to get you that distinction, thereby assuring you a position at once lustrous, distinguished, and new: official guide-interpreter-dragoman of Home Town. Isn't that wonderful? What a prospect, my boy! What gratitude you owe me! Without me, what would you be? For me, what must you do? Make yourself worthy of my great name. Work."

So be it. The second wrote me: "Thanks for the two-wheeled means of locomotion you sent. I know now how to operate it and amaze the populace quite without meaning to. Everyone says that this year the Festival surpasses in splendor any seen before. It's terrible that you can't be here. But that's not what's important. Jean is making curious discoveries; he's on the track of something truly strange. We're waiting to be sure before telling you this ekstraordinary tale. The velocipede serves me well." A discovery is a discovery; being on track isn't a discovery. My brothers? children.

I live truly as an alien in this Foreign Town: wholly lacking contact with its populace. I know only (and these barely) the boardinghouse keeper, the professor, and the guardian. I have no understanding at all of the migratory patterns of their public transport, but I get about on my own by means of birotation. My bicycle carries me from where my landlady keeps watch to where my professor teaches and from there, most often, to where the guardian reigns. Thus do I roll about Foreign Town, abuses I don't understand from bus drivers and admonishments from vigilant policemen with eyes peeled to the regularity of traffic my only contact with the swarming crowd. Whatever communications I have, I provide myself, for myself, by myself. I see no women—real women, that is. Chastity is essential to my concentration. That's how one Foreigner conceived, for instance, the law of apples falling. I don't want to lose in my own seed the very seeds of my future glory. My life is dedicated to life, I've taken that oath. I consider life among lobsters. Of course it's dreadful. But to itself, to the lobster, it seems OK. Or so we must believe. I decide to write my father and relate to him these thoughts on the lobster's life. I know, of course, that he never has such thoughts himself, but I'm eager to keep him apprised of my progress.

At first glance it seems there's not much difference between the life of fish and that of crustaceans. The day before yesterday I watched a lobster as it strolled among turbot and sole. They seemed all to belong to the same world. But, reflecting on it, I came to perceive significant differences between these fellows. A lobster's something quite different from a fish! The sole, as I've come to believe, isn't so far removed from man, after all. But the lobster! Living in a carapace, wrapped in its own bones, as it were—how radically this must alter the way it views life! With the whole of the sea about it at every turn; moving its claws; watching others pass as it lies in wait for prey: here, indisputably, begins any consideration of the lobster.

As for fish, I continue to find them the dogs of life, aguesistence's cows, devoid of character. The lobster's ogresistence, for all that, is no less agonizing. What is life for it? Silence, shadow, and seaweed, ferocity at the end of its claws, this rapacious armor? How we must wonder about life, thinking of the lobster in its osscurity. And how does it die, should it evade ending up plunged into the hot water of a household cook-pot? Does it pass away of old age, this lobster? And does it go gently or rage against that death, pincers stiffening arthritically, encrusted already with annelids? Does it suspect its defunction, this lobster? Would it not prefer to be a manta ray, for instance, with eyes on its belly and white wings? Would it not prefer being able to clamber up trees and gobble down fruits like its toothed, swift colleague the crab in coconut palms? Yet in saying that an animal is one thing or the other, I don't mean to pass judgment. Not even benevolently. But only to determine what awareness it has of its eksistence.

I haven't received a letter from Home Town. I've been hard at work. Yet the streets seemed to me so dull as I returned home tonight. I thought of my father, my mother, my brothers; then of a cheetah seen the other day at the zoo. Strangely, it deserves, I think, a kind of knighthood. What a plunge from cheetah to lobster, though the latter does also wear armor.

I imagine only man and cheetah remaining in the world. Together they tread earth's surface, proud, free. And for them, we can believe, it might always be so. But now imagine man and lobster, sole survivors of a global cataclysm. Flames clutter the horizon. This eggzhausted man divests himself of shredded shoes, raveling socks. He steeps his bloody feet in the sea to find some ease there. Just then the lobster arrives and grabs hold of his toe. This man who's forgotten what it is to scream stoops toward the surface of the water and says to the lobster: "We are the only two living things on this devastated earth, lobster! We're the only living things in the universe, we're left alone, the two of us, to hold off universal disaster, shouldn't we work together, lobster?" But that disdainful animal turns its carapace and heads for other oceans. How could we ever know what a lobster dreams of? And what can we make of its incomprehensible hatesistence? The image of this infleggsible, imperturbable lobster thrusts its unintelligible claws even into the human sky. Out over dim housetops beyond my open window, I think I see it suddenly rear up on two menacing feet, opening and closing its great claws as though to cleave the very constellations.

I've made no progress with the foreign language. My professor has been of little use, and I know now that I'll return to Home Town no more bilingual than when I came, perhaps a little less. What will my father say then, and the whole town with him? If I hadn't other, more pressing concerns, this would bother me terribly.

Should animal life be a perpetual happiness? Lately I've been going to the aquarium to watch the sole and dorado. I stand watching them impartially, objectively. And I have to note that these fish don't seem to me particularly happy: they give no such impression. That designation, then, is one we can't really apply to life of the maritime animal sort. Such life is a stranger to happiness. But to misery? Conger eels, turbot, and sole can't provide my answer. So I refrain from wasting time on them and make my way to an unfamiliar section harboring tropical fish. Some come from the Tropics of Cancer and Capricorn, some from the seas of the West Indies. Some have plumes and whiskers, others have the faces of dogs or foreshortened bodies. Millimetric fellows, absolutely transparent, whizzing about at breakneck speed. Larger ones who indulge in all kinds of ornamentation: stripes, dots, colors. These tiny fish push my thoughts in a direction more confounding than the first; suddenly it occurs to me that, deprived of any possible coherent view of the world, these minuscule beasts (or so I imagine) manifest, in their own way, every sign of gaiety. Their sudden, absurd turnabouts, the flashes they describe in water, so quick as to appear senseless and random—these fitful trajectories reflect a joy we can only call tropical.

The discovery of elements of humanity in these beasts' behavior, or to make my point more strongly, discovery of a genuine vitality corresponding to the human image of life, had given me solace for the anguish each visit to the aquarium inflicts upon me, when, making my way out, near the eksit I noticed a feebly lit corner where a glass cage seemed to be slumbering. I had no idea what was there. I went over to it.

It's a good thing, in its way, that I did: in the interests of life science. I might easily have bypassed that terrible vision. The isolated vessel contained a number of white worms: they were fish, of a sort: cave-dwelling fish. Deprived of sun for eons, they've lost their eyes. They've lost even the memory of color, and their fins are nothing

but stubby vermiform appendages. In them, the sea's silence and
osscurity are a phosphorescence, an echo. Only deep in subterranean caves where pockets of pure water stagnate can there be such
silence, such mineral osscurity. Yet it is possible to live even there.
These are living things, but *such* living things: corpse white larvae
presuming to the name of fish. Their ancestors, as one eggsplanatory
placard tells us, were legitimate fish quick of eye and fin, dressed out
in color like all those touched by light. But now dark's costume has
transformed them, and here they are. They live! They live! Some
might take this as a testimony to life's raw power, to its suppleness
and perpetuity. But for my part, I wept before these cave-spawned
and -sequestered aquatic things, before the atrocious life they must
lead. It's all but impossible, imagining it: to be born there, to endure
and eventually die so: osscure, blind. And to breed that way. What a
bottomless mystery, this stubborn insistence to go on even in such
hopeless, miserable conditions. Yes, miserable, they have to be
miserable! But what if they still have a kind of . . . I wouldn't say
thought, but suppose there's still . . . I wouldn't call it conscience . . .
but what if, still, they do have some way of transcending themselves?
Yes, eggzactly: some way of transcending themselves. There's
nothing here that resembles human life. These things, this life they
lead, they're perfectly inhuman, perfectly incomprehensible; and
for all that, still they must have some sense of that life: blind,
osscure.
  Blind . . . Osscure . . . I wept for good reason.

My mother wrote me. Jean is making lengthy ekscursions into the
Bare Mountains, that rugged, savage range no one dares. Absent for
days at a time, he may have made his way as far as the Petrifying
Fountain, perhaps even to the summit of Rock of Ages, the highest
of the mountains. This greatly disturbs my mother. She's afraid one
of these times he won't return. But my father, of course, offers no
reproach. As for me, I must work and prove myself worthy of this
great honor he's bestowed upon me. And really there's nothing I'd
like more, but this strange language seems so unsuited to me. I make
no progress. My professor blames me and bemoans himself. Have
rumors of my inability already reached as far as Home Town? Has
this simpleton written them? Possibly even my landlady is a spy. Ah!
to be rid of this obsession with the outlandish words Foreigners use
to esspress what they believe to be thoughts; and of having to see
them again, these Foreigners, as Tourists, with their muddleheaded

questions, their piddling concerns, their asinine curiosities; and of this talk of theirs, of having to lather my spit into the globulous vocables of their hyperpatois! Fie! Misery! And suddenly I remember, but why this memory? of a winter day. Wind roared behind the windows: alone in my room I initiated myself into Springtime; I would soon be eleven. It was almost night. My father entered brusquely, watched me for a few moments during which his eyes seemed to me made of stone; then, saying nothing, very softly he shut the door and went away. I stopped my play and sat thinking, realizing that in later years I'd become.... Enough. That memory's more troubling than happy, a kind of magical portent.

When I return to Home Town, I believe that my father and his administrators with him at first will judge me severely, for my knowledge of the foreign tongue is certain to strike them as deficient, although few among them, save Le Busoqueux the tradesman, are themselves knowledgeable. But their opinions in this regard are of no consequence, for I'll have other goods to present them, treasures dredged from the very depths, treasures for whose discovery I dared the most secret caverns, came to know the lobster intimately and swam with the sea's innumerable sardines. My meditations on life—that's what I'll have for them. And then, then only, will Home Town be proud to be what it is, my birthplace.

Only when I lost my old knowledge of life, life as mankind comprehends it, did I see clearly the objectives of my research, objectives evident most purely and penetratingly in the case of cave-dwelling fish. Today, I went back to see them. It occurred to me, even if they do transcend themselves, how very inhuman that transcendence must be! But is that really possible? I stand watching them closely. The tank that contains them isn't very large. A horizontal lamp lights them, feebly as it must. The water looks stagnant, as it also must. They're there, four, no more. Though perhaps others hide themselves more completely from the light. They're not much to look at. Most of the time they are immobile. When they do bestir themselves, it's with a kind of whitish flow, a pale wind that barely disturbs the sand; then a few "steps" further on, they're still again. I wonder when they eat and what. Yes, what would they eat? And the lobster, what does it devour? fish, I suppose; giving again an illusion of entry to the lobster's world, since man also consumes fresh fish. But these ghostly things? What could they possibly eat? Some grass or herb devoid of all color like themselves? Maybe they don't eat at all? Or perhaps something lacking any nourishment?

There's only a month left, leaving me wholly indifferent to all this. Life, and not its grotesque translation into a barbarous patois— life itself underscores my efforts: my whole being strives to understand. And remarkably enough, these impassioned efforts derive from recognition of the very incomprehensibility of animal life, of its inhumanness. How could I hope to render the universe intelligible in a series of interdependent concepts, a system, of a sort, when a lobster's sense of life, or that of cave-dwelling fish, eludes completely every enterprise of human intellect? The only soundings we can take of that life are those of Terror, Silence, Gloom. And for the cave-dwelling fish, perhaps, we must add Decoloration.

Two A.M. strikes. Out my window I catch sight of a brightly lit room across the way. Its shutters are closed. The room is lit very late, like my own . . . Light dies out . . . Was it only a mirror?

My father wrote. I kept his letter in my pocket. I didn't read it right away. The better part of my day was spent in the Gardens. I thought mostly of the crayfish and of its kinship with the lobster. How is it that the crayfish seems to have a more "acceptable" eksistence, in much the same way that river fish seem "closer" than sea fish? Does the ocean, then, give mystery to their eksistence? And by contrast does the life of the river fish in some ways resemble that of the human community? This deliberation occupied me the whole time I pumped up my tire on Imperial Route number seven.

But the letter's there. I recognize my father's writing and the postmark of Home Town. I open it. I read it. There, it's done. He didn't much care for my dissertation on the life of the lobster; not only didn't he much care for this dissertation, he in fact detested it, and detests it still. There's nothing at all to it, he thinks, nothing but foolish ramblings, unbecoming stupidities. "I took great pains to obtain this grant for you," he wrote, "and here you are, doing everything you can to make a hopeless mess of all my efforts on your behalf and of your own future as well. Imagine! Home Town gave you its trust, it supported you for an entire year so that you could learn the foreign tongue in the very country where it arose, and instead of studying, you pass your time there rambling on incoherently about a lobster in a glass tank filled with salt water!"

It's true, that's what I've done. I don't deny it. That's eggzactly what I've done: lobster, glass tank, water, salt, it's all there. Father's absolutely right. I cry out to you across sea and lands and brooks separating Foreign Town from our Home Town, I cry out to you in a dutiful voice: he's right! But I'm not ashamed. I take the liberty of saying this, respected father, but for once, I fear you're not entirely right. It's your eldest son who boldly tells you this. My researches are not frivolous. They're a step forward for the human spirit, supposing, of course, that man's spirit like his body is biped and thereby capable of steps. I'm convinced of it: herein is the purpose of my life.

I must make him see this. I'll reveal to him in detail the life of cave-dwelling fish. Then his own intelligence and impartiality will bring him round to the importance and beauty of my discoveries. But that's not all. While he is pleased with Paul—calm, intelligent, and industrious—Jean on the other hand rather troubles him. What has he been up to since I left? Again and again he returns home eggzhausted, haggard, starved, after a whole week in the Bare Mountains. Am I responsible for this transformation? I can't answer this. There's nothing I can say. Do I myself know the reason for this transformation? I have no idea. Shrouded in dust, hair in disarray and hands delicate as ever, fingers slender and whitened by the mountains' chalk, mouth a bit twisted to the right like that of a man who's suffered greatly, Jean goes by in the street below my window. I get up. I stoop, I see him, weighed down by fatigue, dragging flayed espadrilles along the pavements of Foreign Town and vanishing beneath a streetlight just as a patrolman's footsteps sound. He wasn't alone.

I responded like this:

We call cavernicoles those creatures living in the osscurity of caverns, among them fish. The "habitat" blinds and discolors them. They resemble larvae. I have no idea what it is they feed upon, and I cannot see how one could remain unmoved even by the simple fact of their aguesistance. For my own part, just thinking about that algaesistance makes me dizzy. Yet going further, past this initial, purely sentimental response, one comes to understand that the aversion is something more than merely affective, that it in fact betokens another, separate reality, which is to say, the Inhuman. I want to make him understand that life is not something wholly assimilable to man's comprehension, and that whatever ethical or aesthetic values one may apply to it do not pertain to all its forms, still less to Life-in-Itself. Going on at length about this, I came up with a letter of some siks pages. Plus four pages to my mother and four to Paul and ten postcards for the family (I hadn't forgotten the most unpleasant: my vile old bitch of a grandmother with crooked, greedy fingers, confined to her small farm not far from the town and near the mountains). Then I posted them all. I kept my appointment with the professor. I ate lunch. I attended a lecture and about three-thirty made my way to the Zoological Gardens.

The problems posed by the behavior of mammals seem to me of little real interest. They're variably stupid, sympathetic, pretty or disgusting, yet each shares a line of descent with man. Even with birds, nothing is profoundly alien. The mystery of the screech owl is a human mystery.

Perhaps I've thrown myself too deeply into the abyss for these first encounters. Perhaps a slow, gradual descent would have been preferable. I could have sought among apes whatever traces of the human survive, then among dogs, cats, elephants, raccoons, on down to the platypus; then among birds. With reptiles, I would sense the gaps ever widening. Fish, though still vertebrates, are definitely distressing. And with invertebrates, true anguish begins.

But this route would take too long. It's not the eclipse of the human I seek across species, but the dawn of the Inhuman.

I walked across the Gardens largely at ease before diverse beasts, seals or vultures, pumas or pelicans, cats or penguins. The hummingbirds fascinated me, but I couldn't afford to let this winged curiosity turn me back towards contemplation of birds. Largely at ease in the presence of beasts, I've said—far less at ease in the presence of humans. I'm filled with defiance towards those who are there: Foreigners. I don't trust them at all, they don't seem to me at all honest. So how could I ever rush headlong into a study of their language, devised for who knows what fraudulent uses?

For two days I've made no progress. I went to the Museum where thousands of stuffed animals and millions of insects jostle one another's elbows. But this mob didn't interest me. Meanwhile my inquiry to an attendant about where to find restrooms brought a response in my own language. That was most odd. For who among Foreigners ever bothers to study our native tongue? A future Tourist? Or perhaps I heard him wrong? This fellow, furthermore, had a self-important air quite at odds with his position and civil function. I avoided his gaze, so arrogant that it frightened me, and soon fled; but he may have been innocent of mysterious intentions which I attributed to him without going so far as actually to imagine what they might be.

Tonight it's raining; word from Home Town is not good. Work at the foreign language, my mother tells me over and over, for the whole of siks pages. And earn the grant, she adds. Finally, in a postscript, she mentions that Jean's behavior seems to her more and more peculiar, but that his father (mine) overlooks all this. The letter has a disagreeable effect upon me. I wonder why.

Study the foreign language! is the only advice she has for me. I imagine that I hear all of Home Town whispering behind her: study the foreign language! But I detest it, this foreign tongue. I hate it. I want nothing more to do with it. Still, it would be terrible to return home without having earned the distinction afforded me, to hear grumbles on every side that I'm nothing more than a bungler and idler and that my father is too taken with conceits of celebrity and gain. Ah! how they'll egzult, his enemies, the Paracoles and Catogans! Ah! how they'll stamp their feet with joy at the situation! How they'll slaver with satisfaction!

Although I tell myself this at least daily, I can't work up much real dread; for despite the opinion of my father, who seems to me unable to grasp the situation fully, I'm confident that disclosure of my researches to my fellow citizens will sweep away such miserable defamations and win them over.

All the above was written upon receipt of a letter that utterly disconcerted me. He doesn't see any reason at all for puttering about and racking one's brain over these inconsequential, puny beasts. The time I've devoted to them has been stolen from essential things, from training for my career as guide-interpreter-dragoman-officer. He advises me not to breathe a word about these esstravagances to my fellow citizens, for "you'd soon see how they'll laugh at you." Finally, if I do persist in these follies that can only bring dishonor to the family, he will be forced to deal severely with me. Though he doesn't say in what fashion.

So there it is. I don't understand anymore. It's all too much for me. How has it come to this? And how can he go on deceiving himself about the significance of my researches? How can he even talk about "dealing with me severely"? Is what I'm saying so difficult? But for him, there's more to it, I think. Can his will be thwarted? By whom? For what reasons? Or more to the point, how? So many shadows drifting together in my head, their multiform images of Home Town curious omens. Maybe the landlady has her own reasons for smiling when, passing by her, I absurdly imagine that she knows what she can't possibly know.

✦

I return to the insect. As with the lobster, I must first speak again of man, for the insect in some respects does parallel man. As for the ant, which with its three pairs of legs and tracheal respiration is an eccellent eggzample of the arthropoid, its social life tempers the inhumanity of its eksistence, although from another perspective this collective life seems crushing. I was looking for something else, and discovered it with the lobster and cave-dwelling fish: the ineksplicable horror of certain aspects of life and their utter illegitimacy in the eyes of superior beings, wolf and ocellated lizard as much as man or cormorant.

The more I think of it, the more I'm convinced it's the ocean that gives the life of the beings inhabiting it this inhuman aspect which dismays me so much in the lobster's case and so little in the ant's. When one compares, in fact, the oyster and snail, one oceanic, the other terrestrial, well, the latter's an animal lacking any mystery, its bearing by no means incomprehensible. Is this because it shares certain characteristics with the tortoise? Its rustic nature predisposes us to find in it a vague humanity. Whereas the oyster . . . a kind of catarrh, the rude nature of its disinterest in the eksternal world, its absolute isolation, its malady: the pearl . . . if I give it much thought at all, my terror starts up again. This living being, LIVING! alive, ALIVE! indefinitely stuck on a rock, immobile, imperturbable, savage, opening its beak to reclose it cruelly around luckless animalcules and wretched algae. Such is its life. They multiply, these oysters, they're even (I'm ashamed to write) hermaphrodites; in a word, they live. They even die—horribly! Snails, at least, are cooked before eating; oysters are devoured alive.

The mussel's an even better eggzample than the oyster, still more terrifying at first thought. Considering this sticky little mess whose collective stupidity clings to piers and boardwalks, you have to wonder if it's alive in the same manner as a cow. For there aren't degrees of life. It's not a matter of more or less. Life shows itself completely in every animal. The mussel is as perfectly, as fully, alive as cow or man. That the mussel, that a mussel, might have, perhaps not a conscience, but some way, still, of transcending itself: this plunges me anew into depths of anguish and uncertainty.

And the sea slug in the great deep? Comprised uniquely of a sort of bowel, it subsists in the total, homogenous gloom of oceanic

depths, dragging its pale, tormented form across the reddish sands of that abyss, far from human menace, free of fear. . . .
Free of Fear. I'm astonished at the thought.

For some time I stood gaping. At that moment, incontestably, I had a flash of vertigo. I've spent much of my day analyzing that moment without success: which is strong testimony. I thought it over this afternoon while making my way along the insipid route between my lodgings and the high school, where there was a conference on Foreign Town's history from archaic times to our own. Gradually I came to understand that what I had discovered was only a simple universal law, but since I myself had discovered it, the commonplace became intoksicating. I was eager to make him understand this. At first by telegram, immediately after by a letter penned on a bench beneath the eye of a police constable who bore a striking resemblance to Choumaque, the tradesman, but was more athletic; this made me recall how, when I was twelve years old, Choumaque had the habit of saying: "This boy here may have a foolish look and flat feet, but he'll become someone," to which my dear papa always responded: "It's true that he has a foolish look, but he doesn't have flat feet," and now he would have to add: "Yes, he has become a vertigenial someone."

The fact that I have this vertigo completely changes the situation. How can I deal with my reasons for being here before resolving that? I'll return to Home Town incapable of speaking the foreign language, incapable of receiving Tourists graciously, unable to vindicate myself by telling of my researches since they've come to nothing. Thence: catastrophes. But wait! This vertigo having an incontestable subjective reality, my father has no choice but to take my word for it, and I'll justify my ignorance of the foreign tongue by reason of my vertiginosity! So will I become the first of a new breed of Urbinataliens, having taken the most difficult, the most arduous and passionate of paths, one plumbing the very depths of life.

I then reached a turning point, a decisive moment: I had discovered a category that united oyster, lobster, and man: Fear. I know that, in a sense, this is banal. It's a truism that the two fundamental instincts are those of self-preservation and reproduction, and fear is obviously one manifestation of the first of these. The wayward path I've followed has brought me round to familiar turf. For fear produces angziety, and angziety is precisely that high sign of humanity whose disappearance so disturbs me. The oyster is ankshus, the lobster, the codfish are ankshus, and by that, come closer to man. Their inhumanity is humanized, their life is justified, their acresistence is legitimized. Between man and lobster, between lobster and oyster, there's this single connection always, this bridge, this solidarity: Fear.

But that's not where my discovery lies. My discovery, my vertigo, begins with the notion of living beings who fear nothing and have nothing to fear but their "good death," beings who need fear neither the voracity of other living beings nor bacteria's undoings, beings who are beyond fear, beings such as cave-dwelling fish and sea slugs of the great deep. For those subterranean waters, though clear, are an equivalent of the ocean's miry deeps. And don't tell me: they must have *their* microbic maladies, the sea slugs of the great deep, *their* cancer and tuberculosis, these cave-dwelling fish; and furthermore, what about oceanographers' eel-pots and spelunkers' nets? What about them? I'll just put them between parentheses, evils and hecklers alike, and go on with my description. This astonishing, unsettling discovery! Perhaps they preserve the traces of old fears, fears from a time when their ancestors swam between oceans, eyes alert and gills aflow, fearing the fishhook or pike, others from a time when forebears dwelt in algae close to the surface of seas where oceangoing junks evolved gastronomically. Perhaps they preserve these traces in their albumin! But they're no longer torn by such angziety and fear, now they live alone and outlandish within the impenetrable gloom and perfect silence of the water. Nothing of man approaches them there, sequestered as they are by those pits, those gulfs. Their life is no longer our life. But for all that, it's life. It evades us. The absence of fear seems to us an absence of life itself, but still it *is* life—down there far, far beneath us.

Absorbed in all the thoughts floating about my skull since that ekstraordinary breakthrough two nights ago, I arrive late at the professor's home. I don't know my lesson and have forgotten what I already learned. Evidently there's no hope that I'll someday gain fluency in the foreign language: that's what my professor thinks. I think the same thing myself. He's written to my father to advise him of this. So be it. At one time this disclosure would have crushed me. Now I envision the consequences with the greatest detachment. My letter of yesterday drains the situation, I think, of all power. Anyone can teach tiny children to mouth barbarous words, but who then might enlighten them, however feebly, on the opaque mysteries of profoundest life, save a certain Pierre Nabonidus? Under these circumstances, all things considered, I decided that it was futile to continue studies that upset me. I informed the professor, the municipal council, and my father of this: three official letters. I'll stay here a few more days, then return home for the Festival. These sweeping decisions made, I saw stretching before me a long afternoon, free and clear. It had been ages since I'd felt that way, not since a day two years or so back when, departing at dawn on bicycle with my young brother, I looked out before me on a wide road softly lit by an early sun. Where was my brother at the moment I was recalling that? Was he again in the Bare Mountains, wandering alone?

Meditating thus, I took a stroll through the streets of Foreign Town. I was drawn to its center, which I knew scarcely at all. At first, I walked along without giving much attention to my surroundings; but gradually I began to think that, as I walked by them, people were not only talking about me, they were also alluding to my situation, or to the questions that concerned me. It was difficult for me to try and defend myself. In fact I hardly understand the foreign language at all, and what's more, I had no idea how these people could have learned the particulars of my acridsistence, or that I was leaving; yes, they knew even that. Also, it seemed to me ekstraordinary that so many coincidences could follow with such rapidity, for I passed at least five groups whose small talk, caught on the wing but unsnared, seemed to bear knowledge of my affairs.

It was with considerable chagrin that I reached the city's navel. Disheartened, I watched automobiles revolve in a ring around the obelisk before being thrown into radiating streets by centrifugal force. I was myself without direction, irresolute. I spied, opposite me, an official-looking building; at length I managed to make my way across circling traffic to it. It was a museum, or rather *the* Museum, national and universal. I entered, noticing with displeasure that the principal staircase had an even number of steps.

Why do I go on about this at such length? All the same, I continue. In a hall devoted to glassware, to glass trinkets actually, I was assaulted by doubt regarding the moment's reality, and by a radical self-doubt. I stood immobile, mechanically regarding my face in a kind of funhouse mirror; I noted the rather vacant look that people always attribute to me, augmented now by this deformation giving my image a lurid softness. I stood there telling myself: there's nothing to it! Nothing to it! And I thought of my return to Home Town, which is to say, to my father. And I had to restrain myself for a time then as a guard prowled nosily around me. I had already noticed how curiously all the functionaries of Foreign Town bore a striking resemblance to notables of Home Town, as though they were carbons charged with preserving the marvels of that distant city. This one closely resembled Le Busoqueux: that same look of an old man well on the road to dessication, that symmetry of wrinkles, that mournful gait. The presence of this burlesque image disgusted me. I hurriedly left, though without leaving behind there the contagion of those doubts.

The day approaches when I'll leave Foreign Town—without regret, I would say, if only I could be sure of this: that it's appropriate to boast of my meditations on life. But I hesitate. I haven't been able to overcome my misgivings in this regard. The Foreigners who surround me plunge me into apprehension, seeming as they do to know all about my concerns. Those overheard conversations still upset me terribly. A general malaise weighs me down. I fled to a large park in the suburbs and there I once again set about dreaming of those beings who live in the gloom and silence of deep waters. I'm only interested in rudimentary forms, sponges, worms (earthworms have such a lively appearance about them), flagellates. And hasn't this challenge lain in wait for me from the first, by the way, the riddle of this unicellular infusorian? Hard as it may be to scale the abysses separating man and lobster, I'd be far harder put to try and bridge the limitless faults opening between bacilli and wistiti.

I contemplated this on the ocher of a dying lawn littered with empty cigarette packets, used bus tickets, and other debris; my bicycle waited faithfully nearby. And I said to myself: this autonomous cell in a homogenous habitat on which it feeds, I see this cell in the watery deep, I see it vaguely unfolding in that habitat of water. Blind. Silent. Deaf. It lies there and, if it transcends itself, must apprehend itself as a unity living within another unity, a unity unaffected by multiplicity, forever whole. It lives on, blind, silent, and deaf. And without fear: for it knows no enemies. It knows only one other unity: the ocean, and not: Fear. It knows only one other unity, a nutritive unity, and knows nothing of ravenous multiplicities, even if it does ekspose itself to the consumptive activity of an equal or superior being; for me, that's a matter of little importance. I answered my many misgivings in this way. People passed who wanted to give significance to this fact: that they were there. Two men in particular went by me gabbling loudly and I believed them to be mocking me as someone who spoke their language poorly. I cared not at all what they thought, but their mocking manner annoyed me. I got up, mounted my bike, and galloped off. On the road, people stopped as I passed and I saw them point their fingers at me. I picked up speed.

So it was that I took in with one sweep of my eyes all those inhuman animals living in deep waters, the cave-dwelling fish, sea slugs of the great deeps, amoebas—I saw them all, blind, silent, and deaf, and I understood that the characteristics by which we may come to apprehend them are not those which define man, but rather those pertaining to the embryo, that their life was a fetal life, and that there were two lives: that of man and that of fetus, with two sets of characteristics, and that Life was as much Silence, Osscurity, Immobility, and Unity as it was Multiplicity, Motion, Light, and Renewal, that it was as much Repose as Disquiet and Quietness as Fear. And I saw that one was of the future and called Glory, and that the other, of the past, was called Happiness. And I understood that I was about to have a second attack of vertigo, speeding on my bicycle past the trivial menaces of a whole village alarmed at my presence.

This time, it's serious. My father, my father whom I love and whom I respect, he who is for me the standard in whose shadow I grew up, he who has defended me, guided me, taught me, he towards whom everything directs me even now as in my childhood, the master and legitimate guide who bore me witness always of his love, his affection, and his kind intentions, he who delivered me from childish diapers to conduct me towards manhood, he thanks to whom I finally was admitted to higher learning and obtained this grant to study the foreign language, he who in this fashion is more or less the indirect author of my discoveries and responsible for my vertigo, my father repudiates me. He wishes to see me no more. I am no longer his son. I am no longer named Nabonidus. My foolishness, my lunacy, my supposed vertigo, I can keep these to myself, along with my aberrations, and I no longer love them, neither Himself, nor Her, nor Paul, nor Jean, nor Grandmother Pauline, nor the family. I am a disgrace and a degenerate. My father, he who is the very image of honor, reimbursed Home Town immediately upon having this most recent and conclusive evidence that I am undeserving of the distinction the city accorded me, but like a plumb, I could still drag away in the bags of my own failure Mama, brothers, the whole family. That's what he wrote to me, my papa.

I return in three days. Today, Paul announced without giving details that he'd reveal a shocking secret upon my return. This makes me uneasy, but, he went on, "happily, preparation for the Festival absorbs every spirit. No one speaks of the past, save Paracole; and no one listens, ekcept Catogan." So Home Town sets itself into motion far from me, my Home Town, my dear Home Town. Shortly I'll reoccupy my room in my father's house, that old abode whose wrought-iron balcony recalls ancient splendors. My fellow citizens will have a chance then to judge me, and I will essplicate to them just what life is, and how there are utterly inhuman ways to transcend eksistence within the hollows of rocks, and how sleep is life, just as the riotous movement of small tropical fish is, or the incessant activity of the ant commune. I'll elucidate the whole matter for them, and they'll be forced to revise whatever ill-considered judgments they've made previously, yes, they'll all revise them, all my fellow citizens, the notables included, and Paracole himself and even my father. For if my father has judged me so severely, it must be by reason of inegzact reports deriving from who knows where. Yet when I am there, he will have to accept the truth of what I have to say. Everyone along with him will have to accept the truth of what I have to say, for truth is what I bring them, my truth, unalloyed, a truth which I saw with my own eyes and which I alone have seen. I'll arrive at my Home Town heaped with shame and dishonor, begrimed and discredited. My first contacts will be difficult, humbling; I know that first I must suffer the slings and arrows of the entire town. They hold me in disgrace and think I should feel only shame. Nevertheless I'll possess in my head, and elsewhere, untold secrets of life. Yes, that head unable to redeem the town's confidence, that head which couldn't bleat the silly vocables of the foreign language, that head carries within it the solution to a multitude of small mysteries. It wouldn't surprise me if someone over there suspects this already. The one they'll see return is not the one who left, for this vertigo has refined him.

Two more days. I shut myself in my room in order to collect my thoughts. My landlady has asked if I am unwell. No, not at all. She's beginning to get on my nerves. How have I been able to put up with her hypocritical weasel's face for so long? Couldn't she easily have sent my father false reports of my affairs? Perhaps she is paid to spy on me, for all I know. Everyone in this Foreign Town now seems to me responsible for the misrepresentations standing in my way in Home Town. And the professor, isn't he like those others who detest me from envy, hate me from jealousy, discredit me by treachery, underestimate me, misjudge me? They content themselves with insinuations. They pronounce their own language poorly so that I can't understand it and pronounce it so perfectly that I misunderstand it. Whether or not they do this knowingly, it happens often enough that I must think so. In any case, many of them seem suspect at the very least: my landlady, for instance.

I therefore remained shut away in my room to think about all this, repeating to myself over and over the very phrases that I wrote yesterday. I read aloud what I'd written yesterday. I'm every bit as satisfied with it now as yesterday. Truth will triumph over misunderstanding and this vertigo of mine over the establishment. There'll be no one to greet me at the station, no fanfare in the town, no notables, no choirs of young women, no papa, no mama. Nothing will greet me but derision and mockery on one hand, shame and dishonor on the other. That's how it will go, how it must, but the heart and its beacon only wait. Do we ever see falsehood triumph over truth?

My mother sent a letter damp with tears. The writing is blurred. I couldn't make much out of it. What does she want? To condemn me herself, or to "console" me? To caution me? At certain points I think I've deciphered a suggestion that I do this or that, but her counsel seems osscure. Behind those scribblings, the scornful wrath of my father. And I received also this crumpled note, written in crayon: "There are 25,920 steps from Home Town to Grandmother Pauline's farm. From the base to the summit of the Bare Mountains, it's a 21-hour trek, and from the Ravine of the Ancestors to the Petrifying Fountain, 13 more. If you pass by Nicomedes and Nicodemus, it's shorter. The Festival draws near. You haven't forgotten that. You'll return in time to witness a strange catastrophe. The town is uneasy and all this will end badly. We'll count together how many hours the tragedy goes on and you can call that number to mind as a talisman. For afterwards, we'll part. This Festival differs from others. I've not in vain spent so many nights alone in the Bare Mountains. Some claim that I walk on my hands, others that I bang my head against rocks in order to test the hardness of my skull, others that I howl insults at the face of the dazzling moon and challenge fates they won't name. It's not in vain that I've spent so many nights alone in the Bare Mountains. This summer differs from others. All this will end badly. But we'll count together the hours which separate us from the denouement. Don't forget that Paul's the one who dwells in the midst of the town, just as he came into the world between us. I've put him on to many things I don't want to write here, but he's not shaken. We'll be together for a while, then you'll rejoin Home Town, and I'll leave eventually to return with a companion you can't possibly imagine. For it's not in vain that I spent so many nights alone in the Bare Mountains. JEAN."

I went again to the Zoological Gardens. The Aquarium was closed. Supreme proof, final spitefulness of that town which has seen my fate awaken and my vertigo come of age.

So here's my packed-up baggage, the landlady paid with funds from the grant. Comedy! In just two days the Festival begins, the Festival of our Home Town. In two days begins Saint Glinglin. I'll be there.

2

Springtime

At 6:00 A.M. Home Town began stirring. A growing clamor announced the populace's eager waking. On the Esplanade peddlers and hawkers were setting out their wares. On the Great Square, earthenware and porcelain for the Festival of Midday were lovingly displayed. Already, cafés overran the sidewalks, and in groups, by omnibus, by cart, Countryfolk began arriving. At 6:30 a brass band strolled through the town playing "Cloud-Conqueror," Home Town's traditional anthem, in B-flat minor. The waking became universal.

Robert, surfacing with a yawn from his dreams, hearing the music in the distance, opened his eyes and peered at the clock. In the adjacent bed, his brother still slept ostinato. He listened for a moment to the rhythm of his breathing, then turned his attention to the clamor in the streets. The Festival was well underway, no doubt about it. He got up, barefooted and in his nightshirt, to pee, after which he went back to bed and, sitting there with hands on knees, thought: what a good start the Festival is off to this year! Everyone in town said so! Never had there been so many stalls, they said, or so many plates and dishes! Or so very many Tourists! And Countryfolk had been turning up in throngs day after day, chief among them in Robert's eyes his uncle Obscar, the viticulturist. He was a fool, of course, that good fellow, but of an ineggzaustible generosity; Robert was to meet him at the station this morning. Which thought made him look again at the time; seeing it, he promptly fell asleep.

When he woke again, the clock showed eight. His brother stood, soap bubbles bursting around him. Eyes open, Robert lay silently for a time, watching with interest and methodically noting each motion: Manuel emptied water from the shallow basin, leaving a large pool around it, then set about combing his hair, delicate business. At long last satisfied, he bent his face towards a mirror, caressing his cheeks.

"It's grown back since yesterday?" Robert asked.

"Well, finally up and about!" Manuel responded.

He had shaved himself the day before for the first time.

"When are you planning a return engagement?" Robert asked.

"Who knows? It does come back in quickly, you know, once you've started."

"So pretty soon you'll have to start shaving every day?"

"You're a pain in the butt. You'd better get up."

Robert was silent. He witnessed further stages of the fraternal toilet.

"Come on, are you getting up or not?" bawled Manuel. "If you're late, I won't wait for you."

Robert leapt up, threw water on fingers and face, and in a jiffy was dressed. He caught up with Manuel in the kitchen in the act of heating coffee.

"Make some toast, Robert, I'm starving."

"The old man's not up?"

"Not yet. Look at this, you used up all the sugar last night. There's more in the pantry."

Robert sliced bread without responding; then he buttered the slices.

When the coffee was ready, both sat down to breakfast.

They'd almost finished when the door opened. A whitish being appeared, face ashen, eyes glazed.

"Good morning, children," it said.

"Good morning, Papa," the children responded.

"Is there coffee for me?"

"No," Manuel answered. "I drank what was left of yesterday's."

"You'll have to make me some, then."

"There's no time, I'm off to meet Uncle at the station."

"And Robert, you can't either?"

"I'm going with Manuel, Papa."

The father sat on a stool, heavy-assed, arms hung down.

"Ah, that's right, Obscar gets in this morning," he said in a crestfallen voice, holding head in hand. "Therefore, there's no coffee."

Manuel and Robert got up.

"We're off," the older said.

"You're just going to run off like this?" the father asked with hangdog concern.

"You got pretty drunk yesterday," Robert said with great serious-
ness and a certain admiration.

"Pah!" said the other. "Oh well," he added, yawning.

"So we're off," Manuel said. "Don't forget to make coffee, OK?
You always say it smooths out the bumps. We'll be back by ten, wait
for us, OK?"

"Right, I'll wait for you, yes indeed," he said, getting up and going
back to bed.

In the street the two brothers walked at a good pace towards the
station. Behind the walls of houses Home Town prepared itself with
discreet ardor, scarcely showing at all its aguesaltation. At 9:12 the
train pulled in. The uncle, shoes beribboned with dry mud, stepped
down from a third-class compartment full of Countryfolk with their
loud talk and high laughter. Everyone made for the celebration at
once. Then Manuel caught sight of, shrouded in solitude, suitcase in
hand, Pierre Nabonidus. He abandoned the uncle (who was being
looked after, after all, by Robert) and, bumping into this other
voyager, ekscused himself.

"What a surprise! You've come back for the Festival?"

"Hello, Manuel. I never imagined you'd be the first one I'd run
in to!"

"You've had a good trip?"

Pierre shrugged. "Travel's a drag. But tell me, what have you
heard?"

"Oh well, nothing much, really," Manuel answered, restrained.
"From all indications the fireworks this evening are going to be
spectacular."

"You know that I've had to renounce the grant?"

"I heard."

"What did you hear?"

"Well, you know how it is, no one talks about anything but the
Festival."

"Not about me?"

"Hardly at all."

"But then what do they say about me?"

"Nothing much. That the grant's history, so what, not much else.
Just what did happen?" Manuel asked with sudden indiscretion.

"It's quite simple. I made some discoveries over there. And
because of this, you understand, I had no time to spend studying the
foreign language. I eksplained this at length to my father. Besides
which, I plan to give a lecture."

Manuel couldn't get over that. "A lecture! You?"
Pierre smiled. "So long, I have to go! I can't talk for long just now.
I'll see you again during the Festival."
"Absolutely!" Manuel responded enthusiastically.
"You haven't seen Jean today?"
"He's off in the mountains. As of last night, he still hadn't
returned."
Pierre, without comment, again took up his solitary way and his
suitcase in hand.
Manuel, spellbound, turned back towards the uncle and his
baskets.

Nabonidus (which without a given name signifies the mayor of
Home Town) sat wearing a floral dressing gown. He inspected
minutely the mechanism of a tommy gun, for by custom Home
Town's premier town councillor possessed one. Then, minutely, he
cleaned it. Bent on a task he'd never entrust to anyone else, he
appeared to be wholly absorbed. Yet he was no less attentive to
noise from outside and remained alert. Finally he heard what he
waited for: a certain footfall in the corridor. He cried out twice:
Paul; the person belonging to that name partly opened the door, no
doubt to ask why he had called. Nabonidus didn't give him time.
Without looking at him, he asked: "Where are you going?"
"I'm going to see if everything is in place."
"There's no need. I've put Quéfasse in charge of that. You're to
stay here."
"It would probably be a good idea for me to just give it a final
once-over."
"You want to go out, right? You want to go meet Pierre at the
station? Well, I forbid you to meet Pierre at the station, you hear
me?"
"But. . . ."
"You are perhaps going to tell me that you have no intention of
meeting Pierre?"
"No. . . ."
"I insist that he see no one before me. Understand?"
"Yes, Father."
The door was reclosing.
"Jean hasn't yet returned?"
"No, Father."
"Very well."

The door reclosed. Nabonidus listened to the direction of his steps to be sure his son had obeyed him. Still attentive to comings and goings, he resumed his polishing. When he heard a knock at the street door, he didn't stir. He heard the old maid open it, say "Hello, Monsieur Pierre," the other voice ask, "My father's there?" then an approach in the corridor. A knock.

"Come in," Nabonidus said, settling into his absorbed-in-tommy-gun pose.

An entry.

"Hello, Father."

"Hmmmm," Nabonidus responded, still in his pose.

A silence.

"I arrived by train this morning, and was met there." Then: "You're not too angry? You understand, don't you, that I had to come back? It was useless to stay there. I was wasting my time." Then: "You see, I was never cut out to be an interpreter. That's not my calling. The grant complicates things, I know that. But finally. . . ."

Nabonidus, finally, rose. He was fleshy and square. Rough hands hung at the end of his arms. He looked sharply at Pierre. No parental flame smoldered in that regard.

"Father, did you get the letters I sent?"

"What of them?"

"I know you don't accept this vertigo. But you'll soon see that I'm becoming ever more vertiginous, Father. Life, that's what I've begun to understand: life's two faces! Luminous life, osscure life. By observing the cave-dwelling fish. . . ."

"Are-they-ed-i-ble-these-cave-fish?" Nabonidus articulated in a leaden monotone, heaving himself in slow steps across the floor.

Pierre looked sadly at the powerful mass rearing up before him; with distaste, he noticed the oil staining paternal fingers. He recoiled. At the end of his retreat his head struck the wall. He groped behind him for the doorknob and went out. The door reclosed. Nabonidus followed.

Pierre had already climbed three stairs.

"Where are you going?" Nabonidus cried.

A ferocious look told him he wouldn't be answered.

"You'll have to leave, boy," Nabonidus said gently. "There's no place in this house for people with vertigo."

Pierre went back down the three steps, paused by his father without turning his head, put his hat atop his head where it belonged, bent to pick up his suitcase and left.

Nabonidus went back to his verification of the tommy gun's readiness; his movements betrayed no trace of nervous tension.

Zostril, Saimpier, and Choumaque sat and, all of them drinking, set about gossiping.

Zostril, the deputy mayor, otherwise a manufacturer of fertilizer, put his glass on the table and said: "It's curious how on Festival days one gets thirsty early."

Saimpier, the tinman, rested his glass on the table and said: "Drinks don't taste the same on a day like this as they do other days." He breathed, a bladder deflating. Zostril lit his pipe.

"There'll be good weather," he remarked with assurance, watching his match flare up.

This remark was truly superfluous, for there had been no bad weather since the cloud-chaser was installed. But these things were always said from time to time: a custom perpetuating for no good reason memories of the good old days when meteorology still mattered.

Choumaque, the tradesman, rested his glass on the table and said: "So, your dishware is ready?"

The others nodded.

"I've sunk 15,000 turpins into it this year," Zostril said. "All of it fine porcelain."

"Then you'll be sure to retain your standing," Saimpier said, bitter and envious.

With the tinnery he "lost" paper "money."

"I'll be wasting 2,750 coffee cups," the fertilizer-fabricant said forcefully.

Choumaque whistled in admiration. "I can manage a thousand. That's plenty, for me. I have no desire to be mayor."

"This year," Zostril said, "his display is colossal. He's half ruined himself."

"Well," Saimpier said scornfully, nose in air, "he does have to offset the dishonor his son's brought him, you know."

"Don't use so many big words," Zostril whispered.

"You've heard that he returned today?" Choumaque asked.

"No!" Saimpier said.

"Oh yes."

Zostril hastened to intervene. He considered himself well-informed. "Not only have I heard that, I'm certain of it. He arrived this morning."

"What will he do with himself?" Choumaque asked.

"It's quite sad, that whole affair," Zostril said. "A young man who had such a fine future before him. Before him, mind you, not behind."

"Eggzactly," Saimpier said. "Before."

"Just what has he been up to in Foreign Town?" Choumaque wondered.

"Pah," Zostril essclaimed thoughtlessly: "a spree."

"He came by it honestly," Saimpier affirmed. "I have the distinct impression his father's running after his future daughter-in-law."

"Maybe a young woman's behind it all," the tradesman said. "After all, he's never seemed the crafty sort."

Leaving it there, he embellished his silence with a deep draft of ambient air: "Here's to that young man."

"Yes, a woman has to be at the heart of it," the deputy mayor agreed, scratching nervously at his chest.

He was fearful.

"We really don't have any idea why he's returned," Choumaque contended.

Zostril was silent. The other continued:

"It happens that I've heard something else, myself, something that has nothing to do with young women."

"Boys?" Saimpier asked.

"Of course not! It seems that Pierre Nabonidus has made a discovery over there, in Foreign Town."

"A discovery!" the others eksclaimed.

"Yes, a discovery having to do with fish."

"Well now, that's peculiar," Saimpier said.

"And how do you happen to know this?" Zostril asked jealously.

"I heard it from his brother Paul. It's a secret. I tell you this in confidence."

"Ah, so Paul told you about it," Saimpier said thoughtfully. "If Paul told you, then. . . ."

"And what about the youngest?" Zostril asked. "You think it's normal, spending night after night in the mountains like that and days doing who knows what?"

"Nabonidus indulges his every whim," Choumaque said.

"It's more or less official, Paul and little Eveline Busoqueux's engagement," Zostril said.

"Pah! She seems to have eyes only for the father," Saimpier remarked. "The father who's always giving her the eye," he added.

"So you've noticed, have you," Zostril said unsmiling.

"Speak of the devil," Choumaque said.

Nabonidus entered the café, tommy gun under one arm.

"I still have time for a drink, no?"

"We have to leave in ten minutes, that should be enough," the others said.

"I'm devilishly thirsty. Saint Glinglin's Day always grabs me early."

"It's 11:30," Zostril pointed out.

"You've already been to the Square?"

"I went by around eight," the deputy mayor responded. "Everything looks good. They're all talking about your amazing display."

"Almost 400,000 pieces."

"Ho, we've never seen the like of that."

"Even Grandfather Bonjean's display, fifty years back, can't compare with that," said Choumaque, who pretended to know the whole history of Home Town. "His amounted to no more than 200,000 pieces."

"Well," Nabonidus said, "Paracole and Catogan won't be able to say much. Do you have any idea what they've brought for the Festival?"

"Nothing of much interest," Zostril said. "I saw that this morning."

"So! These pissants who want to make trouble for me because of the grant! I'll squash them with my dishware!"

"Bravo!" cried Zostril, whose own lot was bound intimately to the mayor's. "Bravo! it makes me happy to see you step on such bugs."

"Thank you, Zostril," Nabonidus said.

"We must drink to the occasion," Saimpier proposed, not to be outdone servility-wise.

The four officials called for a bottle of sparkling fifrequet, clinked glasses, drank, and belched.

"It's time now," Choumaque said.

"Let's go."

Nabonidus picked up his tommy gun and left, followed by Choumaque and Saimpier. Zostril brought up the rear, carrying in hand an elegant golf club.

Machut, Marqueux, and Mandace gathered around a table already sticky and, all of them gulping down small bowls of fifrequet, set about commenting on events.

Machut, who practiced butchery with great virtuosity, rested his goblet on the table and said: "It's funny, you know, but when it's Festival time, I'm always thirsty at the crack of dawn."

Marqueux the cellophane merchant (Home Town didn't use much of it) rested his glass on the table and said: "I think what you drink is always better on a day like today. It has more taste somehow." He clicked his tongue.

Machut lit his pipe. "Looks to be great weather," he declared with conviction, ekstinguishing his match in a puddle of fifrequet.

This declaration was absolutely unnecessary, since with the cloud-chaser balanced atop its mast the weather was always good in Home Town. But people still used that esspression from time to time; it was a popular formula which never fell into disuse. Mandace, the importer (although Urbinataliens had little appreciation for anything of foreign origin), rested his glass on the table and said: "Your dishware is in place?"

The others nodded affirmatively.

"I take part only as a matter of form, myself," he continued. "I wouldn't even go, if it were up to me."

"You do well to retain your standing," Machut said.

"I think an offering of a hundred ganelons is plenty, given my position," Marqueux said.

"To be sure," Mandace said.

"Everyone can't ruin himself like the mayor," Marqueux added in his defense.

"His dishware this year is incredible," Machut said.

"Well," Marqueux said, pulling at his mustache, "he does have to patch up his reputation a little, after the story of the grant, you know."

"Apparently he got back this morning," Machut said.

"Who's that?"

"Nabonidus's son: the one who had the grant."

Mandace, pretending always to know everything before the others, said immediately: "He got in this very morning. Bonjean's son saw him getting off the train."

"He spoke to him?"

"Yes, it seems he is planning a lecture."

"What: a lecture?" fretted Marqueux. "What could he possibly have to say that calls for a lecture?"

"He'll speak of his discoveries," Mandace essplicated.

"That's all I know," Marqueux said, pulling at his mustache. "Perhaps he's invented something?"

"Right, he's invented something and he's going to give a lecture," Mandace affirmed, perpleksed.

"That doesn't clear things up very much," Machut said.

"It certainly doesn't," Marqueux said more strongly.

Mandace, angered, kept silent.

"It astonishes me that he should have become an inventor," the other repeated, "since I remember well that my son, when he was in class with him, always called him stupid."

"That's true," the butcher confirmed.

"An inventor needs a good head," the cellophane merchant went on in a low voice.

"You've got to admit they're a pack of weird kids, those sons of Nabonidus," Mandace said.

"Haven't you always wondered why the youngest spends so much time at the rural postman's?"

No one, alas, really had any idea. Mandace was fascinated, but it was all quite beyond him.

"It's completely inessplicable," lamented Machut. "There's no way we could figure it out."

"Even when he's drunk, Sahul never says anything about that," Mandace said.

"In any case, there's something fishy about it all," Marqueux said. He nodded his head in emphasis.

"And why does he spend so much time wandering aimlessly in the Bare Mountains?" Machut asked. "Tell me: does that make any sense?"

"It'll all come to a bad end," Mandace proffered somberly. "I have my own ideas on the subject."

"Oh?" Machut said.

Mandace didn't go any further, since he was lying.

There was a silence.

"Who do you think will come out on top at the Springtime this afternoon," Marqueux asked, fleeing ignorance, settling on speculation.

"Rosquilly has a good shot at it," Machut said.

"Bonjean too," Mandace said. "He's a true connoisseur, and clearly in the running."

"Bonjean's at the top of the heap," Marqueux said. "You have to give him that."

"Speak of the devil."

Bonjean entered the café accompanied by his country brother

and two of his sons. Mandace, hoping to elicit information from Manuel, harpooned the quartet.

"Bonjean! Over here! There's plenty of room!"

Everyone took seats noisily.

"Well," Bonjean said, "I could really use a drink. When Saint Glinglin comes around, I'm dry from the minute I wake up."

"We're not here to let our throats crack, that's for sure," the uncle said, ordering fifrequet for everyone.

What a hick, the three merchants thought.

"Your stuff's all set up?" Bonjean asked.

"Yes," the others said.

"We'll get to that when the time comes," the uncle said. "Don't fret over it now."

"The mayor's put together an essposition like nothing seen since your grandfather's," the butcher said.

Machut was proud of his Home Town; he knew its history in precise detail, petty details most of all, and egzercized that avocation by stuffing his chatter full of egzamples and anecdotes from the locality's annals. There wasn't a pig here whose pedigree he didn't know.

"We'll see, we'll see," the uncle said, whom last year's Festival had rather disappointed.

"Well, Manuel," Mandace asked, "you've seen Pierre Nabonidus again?"

"No, Msieu Mandace," Manuel responded. "He's probably getting ready for his lecture."

"When's his talk scheduled?" Marqueux asked.

"A quarter to twelve," Machut essclaimed. "We're late for it already."

"We've got to get going," Mandace said.

The three merchants wiped their mustaches and hastily got up.

"See you soon," Bonjean cried out to them.

"Right," they agreed, leaving the uncle to pay for the drinks.

"Well, now that they're gone, you want to tell me what's going on?"

"Stay calm," Obscar said. "You always did have a tendency to go off half-cocked."

He laughed a little, as he did every time he used citified esspressions.

♦

On the Great Square the dishware was laid out, complete dinner settings by the hundreds or similar collections of special pieces. Banners announced the names of proprietors, who now awaited the Festival's commencement at midday. The displays were variably impressive and differed greatly among themselves as much by quality as by quantity. Among them the crowd circulated, appraising objects impartially, never hesitating to criticize harshly those displays stingily or shabbily stocked.

Bonjean, Uncle Obscar, Manuel, and Robert mingled with the throng. One of the first participants they came across in their course was Machut the butcher. He had by him only a stack of plates, some plain earthenware, and a complete set of tiny teacups.

"I heard that one of your plates is cracked," Bonjean said with suspicion.

Such an allegation immediately attracted the attention of all who heard it, and a circle formed around Machut. He began protesting violently.

"Absolutely not, what do you take me for? Telling stories like that! And just which one is it that's cracked, tell me?"

Bonjean pointed. Machut turned the plate over and over. "That one! Cracked!"

It wasn't.

"Good, good, it's OK," someone said.

"You don't have much set out this year, Machut," Bonjean said osstinately.

"But look at these teacups," the butcher went on. "Aren't they splendid? A wedding present from my aunt. They come from the Foreigners, actually. Over there, they're as good as sundials. You see one and you know it's five in the afternoon."

Not caring much for travel stories, the swarm moved on. The following displays offered nothing of interest: dishware of the common domestic sort, though in quantities sufficient to avoid drawing public scorn: a great deal of earthenware, a little porcelain. Farther on was Zostril's lot. It stood out immediately by the number and homogeneity of objects: 2,750 porcelain coffee cups stacked in a heap close by him. And not one of them was cracked, as verified by the urban guard that very morning. Admiring murmurs crowned, as much as the cups themselves, their owner, who, with an elegant gesture, leaned on his golf club. This object intrigued people.

"What is that thing?" someone asked Zostril.

"A gift from my friend Mandace. It's imported."

"What's it for?" someone asked.

"It's quite the thing over there. You never know with those people. But apparently they use it to make holes in the turf."

Robert and Manuel longed terribly for one just like it. But the neighboring stall finally drew them on; it was comprised uniquely of ancient plates, all of them ekstremely rare. Le Busoqueux had taken great pains with their presentation. They weren't stacked but set out individually on the ground. Some of them bore traces of restoration, but given their historical nature, this certainly was no reason to disqualify them. Robert and Manuel lingered, looking at imagery of a humorous, even scatological, character. They laughed loudly. Mandace had put out only two vegetable plates and three sauceboats; he was without opposition this year. Further along, Choumaque drew attention with a set of dessert plates illustrated with a rebus. But people had already seen that the preceding year, and Rosquilly's collection was even more complete, these amateurs decided. Finally, at the farthest end of the square, before a fence built especially for the event, they came across the mayor's display. It described a parallelepiped rectangle one hundred meters long, ten meters wide, and five meters tall. One saw there more than 5,000 plates, 12,000 coffee cups, 20,000 teacups, 7,000 soup bowls, 300 ewers, 250 dessert plates, 1,200 round plates, 1,500 oval plates, 2,000 salad bowls, 4,123 sauceboats, 20 pastry saucers, 350 sugar basins, 7 butter dishes, 12,000 coffee pots, and at least 317,000 eggcups.

The mayor, Nabonidus himself, walked back and forth before this heap, head haughtily erect, chest puffed out and held high. He was there, alone, as custom prescribed. Outfitted in hunting clothes, he wore huge leather boots polished to such a shine that they gleamed in the sunlight, and held at his side a fine-looking tommy gun no less dazzling than his Moroccan leather. A great silence crouched about him. People stood stock-still, gaping. Holding back murmurs of approbation and hiphiphurrassments of enthusiasm as well as strident sarcasm and hootulations of rancor. Robert, Manuel, and their elders mingled with the introspective congregation, sharing communal feelings imposed on the population by the imposing presence of the mayor, the stupefying marvel of his display, and his tommy gun's savage polish.

Meanwhile, animation grew by the minute. On the balcony of Town Hall, urban guard Quéfasse got ready to give the signal which officially began the Festival.

By a minute till noon the tension had become tangible. People moved to and fro, choosing their places. At the first stroke of noon on the municipal clock, Quéfasse began blowing into a balloon of gold-beater's skin, a flaccid shred which grew ever larger, little by little transforming itself, passing through various strange forms until it became finally a kind of dirigible and rose, erect, into the sky. Quéfasse puffed away for all he was worth until his cheeks were full and eyes bloodshot, brow knotted with effort. As the fifth stroke of noon sounded on the clock, the balloon at last attained monstrous dimension and everyone fell silent. No one coughed, no one whispered, no one so much as murmured or sighed. The crowd watched, immobile and mute, the ballooning of the gold-beater's skin, wondering which of the two would burst, Quéfasse's head or the thing clenched in his teeth. At the clock's tenth stroke, anticipation took on physical form; skulls emptied themselves of intelligence, spinal marrow poured into codpieces, and consciousness shrank to bright daggers of light. It hardly seemed possible that a common balloon of gold-beater's skin, even an official one, could attain such stupefying volume. Sinews creaked beneath the skin.

The twelfth stroke of noon fell into the abyss of the past. The balloon burst. The Festival began.

Zostril raised his golf club and with a single vigorous blow smashed at least 203 plates. Pieces of the display shot off vertically, reaching apogee in scant seconds. Proprietors and visitors alike hurled themselves shrieking onto crockery and porcelain. Some smashed salad bowls with their feet; others got hold of a large soup tureen, hurling it into a pile of fruit dishes and demolishing the whole lot with great commotion. Sauceboats and butter dishes were flung into the air and crashed back to earth in pieces. Specializing in the destruction of saucers, a few connoisseurs methodically shattered them against their heads. Some juggled, then suddenly abandoned their show of deksterity; plates seemed for a moment to hang immobile in the air, then took a nosedive and crashed in pieces to the ground. Still others sat down brutally on great oval plates. One fantasist forced his head into a sugar bowl and freed himself with a blow from a coffee pot. Bellowing, Le Busoqueux trampled his collection underfoot. Manuel pounded away at Choumaque's rebus. Beneath Robert's ardent feet, Machut's teacups had long since become little more than powder. Keen cries mikst with the general hubbub and howling. And finally, joining the eggzaltation, came the *tac-tac* of a tommy gun.

Nabonidus himself destroyed his dishware. He mowed down every one of the 65,750 porcelain pieces (not counting eggcups) that he'd carted in; and the butter dishes leapt and the sauceboats burst and radish dishes broke into pieces and stacks of plates took wing; second by second the pile of debris grew.

In less than ten minutes, there remained not a single object of crockery or porcelain which wasn't in pieces. Little by little proprietors and visitors stopped roaring. A few diehards still searched for plates that might have escaped destruction, to smash them. One heard only the cackle of the tommy gun hammering away at the heap of bits and pieces. Fragments crumbled, crumbs were atomized. A cloud of dust rose into the sky. Then the firing stopped.

The Festival was over, the whole square covered in a stratum of debris at least ten centimeters deep. There were only five wounded: two by Nabonidus with his firearm, one by Zostril who, swinging away at his plates with the club, had cracked the head of a foolhardy Tourist, two others whose eyes were cut by scraps of pottery.

"So tell me, Papa, where are Machut's precious cups now!"

"Ah, my children, what a blow I've dealt Mandace's wretched sauceboats," Bonjean responded gleefully. "One feels quite oneself again after a thing like that."

"What's nekst?"

"I could sure use a drink," said the uncle, who had worked hard.

Machut and Marqueux rejoined them.

"Let's go wet our whistles," the latter proposed. "This dust can give you a miserable thirst."

"Well," Machut told Bonjean, "your job's set for the nekst year."

"So it is," this one responded. "And yours as well."

"So it seems," replied that one.

"That was well worth bothering with," said the uncle. "Especially the mayor's lot."

"Yes, but that cursed tommy gun of his kept everybody away from *his* dishware," Bonjean remarked.

"True," repeated Marqueux. "It's not at all proper, such a trick! He demolished everything himself, and that's not right!"

Mandace joined them.

"You agree?" he asked the other. "It's not civil, smashing it all himself like that."

Mandace's face went up and down: "That would be my opinion at this point."

"It's just no good, doing that," Marqueux insisted. "It's even in defiance of the populace, you might say."

"That sort of thing can't be allowed to continue," Machut said, suddenly menacing.

"Don't let it get to you," Bonjean told him.

"And his kids?" asked Machut abruptly. "We haven't seen any of them."

"Not even the young one," Mandace remarked.

This mystery enhanced their thirst.

"We're going to Hippolyte's right?" said Marqueux.

" 'K," said Bonjean. "You kids coming?"

"Right behind you," they responded.

"Funny guys," remarked Uncle Obscar.

There wasn't much room at Hippolyte's, of course. And it was a clamoring zoo in there. They finally found places at the end of a long, two-tiered zinc table occupied by a family of Countryfolk.

"Fifrequet for everyone," the uncle bawled.

"And for you boys?" Bonjean asked.

"I'd love a fifrequet," Manuel said.

"Well, then, go ahead and bring us a bottle," Bonjean told the waiter. "And be quick about it."

"Now we'll have to wait an hour," grumbled Mandace, who kept running his tongue over his upper lip and poking with it at the hairs of his mustache.

"So tell us, Manuel," said Marqueux. "What's this we hear about Pierre Nabonidus, what's he up to?"

"He's up to giving a lecture, Msieu Marqueux."

This one thought it over.

"That's ludicrous," he finally decided.

"And do you have any idea what he'll say?" Bonjean inquired.

"No, Papa."

"Oh! Don't see how you could help asking. Sticking my nose in things like that's what keeps it long."

"Buffoon," said Uncle Obscar, paying for the bottle of fifrequet.

While his father vindicated his title of mayor by pulverizing dishware, Paul pedaled swiftly eastwards from Home Town, mounted on a contraption with two wheels sent by his brother from Foreign Town.

He took Important Boulevard, then, passing down Perpetual Avenue, came onto the Outer Way which led to the Bare Mountains, Home Town stretching and thinning along it into a wretched suburb. Paul stopped before one squalid house, long and partitioned by latticework into a half-dozen small dwellings. Kids wormed all about; dressed for the Festival, they'd momentarily escaped their shabby habitual picturesque. Opposite, a bar spilled its benches and zinc-covered tables into the street, and peculiar airs having nothing to do with the Festival of Midday began pricking at his nose.

From every kitchen window gushed the fumes of brouchtoucaille. Before one of them Paul stooped.

"Sahul's not back yet?" he asked.

Without interrupting her stirring of a pot, old lady Sahul responded: "No, he's not yet, returned that is. He left at five, just as you told him, and here he is, still not back. If only he was here eating brouchtoucaille with the likes of us, Msieu Paul. The poor man, well, it ain't game to make him work s'hard, Msieu Paul, and on Saint Glinglin Day, s'more. At five he got up, he's taken his mule and gone. So here he's missed out on the dishware Festival already and still he's at it and not eating brouchtoucaille with us."

"My brother's not back either?" Paul interrupted.

"Ah, no. That's a whole new notion, going out like that into the mountains. In my time, one never went there, not ever, in the mountains, you have to have courage to go there all the time that way. You have very strange notions, all of you. I don't say this to annoy you, you understand."

"I know as much, Madame Sahul."

"Your brother, the one who got the grant, he was supposed to show up today also, right? Sahul told me that yesterday."

"He's back, but I haven't seen him."

"How has such a thing come about?"

"My father didn't wish it."

"You're not telling me the truth," cried old lady Sahul, stopping to stir the brouchtoucaille.

"But I am. I don't even know where Pierre is, or what he's doing."

"Oh! that must make you sad, Meussieu Paul. And Saint Glinglin's, of all days, that it should pass like this! Tell me all about it, Meussieu Paul."

"I'm sorry, but I don't have time, Madame Sahul."

"It's very unfortunate, that."

"Will you give Sahul a message for me?"

"Why yes, boy, of course I will."

"Tell him to meet me at Hippolyte's. I'll go by there after Springtime. Got it?"

"Yes, Meussieu Paul."

"Tell Jean the same thing. And above all, that he's not to return to the house before he's seen me. If you'll esscuse me now."

"What a tale, what a tale," sighed Mama Sahul as Paul spun off westward.

By the time he reached the Great Square, the Festival was over, the tommy gun had stopped its chant, and the crowd was beginning to evacuate the premises, trampling pieces of crockery and porcelain underfoot. Plunging into that mob, he dodged towards his father; he found him surrounded by notables.

"That's the most formidable destruction of dishware that's ever taken place, I don't mean just in Home Town," said Le Busoqueux, "but on the entire surface of the planet, if there is such a thing."

"It's nothing compared to your remarkable selection of rare plates," Nabonidus responded politely.

"You're poking fun at me," Le Busoqueux simpered.

"Well there you are," Nabonidus said, catching sight of his son. "I haven't seen much of you."

"I was over there," Paul responded, pointing across the square.

"Well I didn't see you either," said the notary, who happened to have been in that area.

"I trampled some of your plates, nevertheless."

Paul lied, natsureally.

"Good, good," said Nabonidus, smiling. "I hope you enjoyed yourself."

They set out towards Hotel Cyclops, a chic spot, the inn for Tourists. They had hearty appetites for lunch which, today, meant a plate of brouchtoucaille. This is how brouchtoucaille is prepared in Home Town: take cabbage, artichokes, spinach greens, eggplants, lettuce, mushrooms, pumpkins, gherkins, beetroots, turnips, kohlrabies, tomatoes, potatoes, maize, and coconut; pick, peel, clean, wash, cut, chop, crush, grind, sift, stew, drain, wait, scour, dilute, sublimate, solidify, clarify, classify, assemble, and cook partly in water, partly in olive oil, partly in walnut oil, partly in suet, partly in goose grease. Then prepare the animals, mammiferous males and winged females. Slaughter them, skin them, behead them, section them, spread them, spit them, and roast them. In a large cook-pot prepare a sauce with oil, garlic, vinegar, diverse mustards, egg yolks, brandy, pepper, salt, pimentos, saffron, cumin, clove, thyme, bay leaf, ginger, and paprika. Throw into it equal parts of the animal and vegetable components. Stir and stew and when ready, serve on a large ancestral plate that you've taken care not to wash since the last Festival.

♦

The women waited.

While men participated in the Festival of Midday, the women prepared brouchtoucaille. Common celebrations began only with the Springtime games, in the afternoon.

So the women waited.

Madame Le Busoqueux hosted Mesdames Zostril, Choumaque, Nabonidus-mother and Nabonidus-espoused; plus Mesdemoisselles Eveline Le Busoqueux and Laodicée, her cousin. In short, all the upper-crust females of Home Town.

These women waited.

Toasting their husbands, these finest flowers of the Urbinatalien elite gulped down fifrequet to offset the nokshus effects of powdered porcelain. Brouchtoucaille cooked over a small fire in the great familial cauldron. The twenty-seven blows of one-thirty sounded.

"The men won't be long," said Madame Le Busoqueux.

"I hope not," grumbled Grandma Pauline. "I'm starved."

When she was hungry, this old lady could eat doorknobs. The young women looked at her, frightened, and shivered when she repeated: "I'm starved."

The young women stared at her teeth, transfiksed.

"They won't be long," said Madame Nabonidus without conviction.

"We might have a bit of port," proposed Madame Le Busoqueux. "I know this seems a little touristy, but Mandace managed to sell a bottle to my husband. Just a taste?"

"Bring it on," growled Grandma Pauline.

And the women sipped away at their port. Not too bad, they decided.

"Hrrouin," interjected Madame Nabonidus-mother.

This reduced the others to silence. The old lady lived on an isolated farm at the edge of the Bare Mountains. This didn't much reassure them.

"My dears, it will be most unfortunate if he does not win."

"Of course," said Madame Zostril thoughtlessly (she thought).

"My son is mayor," articulated the ancestor.

Again there was a stunned silence. A fly fell, unconscious, into Madame Choumaque's glass of port.

"Oh! how disgusting!" she cried. "A fly!"

"I'll get you another glass."

Madame Le Busoqueux hurried to fulfill her civil promise. The old lady looked scornfully at the tradesman's wife. A fly, lifting it with her fingertip, a fly, crushing it against the table, a fly. So? What degeneration in this generation! Taking advantage of the distraction furnished by the domestic insect's demise, the young women got up and began whispering to one another over by the window.

"She scares me," said Eveline.

"Me too," said Laodicée.

"She probably eats small children!"

"You're terrible, Eveline. Tell me, is she going to be on our backs the whole day?"

"Of course not! Don't be ridiculous."

"Dining with the Naboniduses always means putting up with her."

"Ah, it's just too much, too much!"

"If she wanted to drink a lot, that would be nice. Then she'd go sleep in a corner somewhere."

"Right, that's it, we'll tell Paul to make her drink."

"That could make her mean."

Both of them paused thoughtfully.

"Look over there, the Bonjeans are going by," said Laodicée.

"You saw that, Manuel Bonjean looked at us," said Eveline.

"He's so fine."

"He dresses terribly."

"Hrrouin," someone said suddenly behind them. "What are you looking at there, my dears?"

Eveline stammered a few desultory words.

"You're thinking about your sweethearts, aren't you," said the grandmother, flaring her nostrils.

"There they are!" cried Eveline, pointing her finger convulsively at the group of gentlemen advancing resolutely towards them, namely: Zostril, Choumaque, Le Busoqueux, Paul Nabonidus, and the mayor.

"There they are!" cried the old lady. "They're here! Now we can eat brouchtoucaille!"

She trotted off towards the lavatory.

"She scares me, that filthy old crow," said Laodicée.

"Look how chic Nabonidus is with his tommy gun," said Eveline.

"He looks great."

"He must be strong, big as he is."

"Paul's seen us."

"He's not as big as his father."

"But wait, Jean isn't with them."

"Maybe he hasn't come back from the mountains."

"Whatever could keep him away from the Festival?"

"He's really very elegant in those boots like that."

"Listen to me now, why isn't Jean there?"

"You'll have to ask Paul. Ah! Nabonidus's coming in."

She left the window. Shortly after, the men entered, speaking loudly and laughing.

"Mesdames, mesdemoiselles, greetings."

Tongues loosened by fifrequet, they were all ready speakers.

"We'll drink a toast to the ladies," they declared, seeing the bottle of imported port.

"So, Madame Le Busoqueux my wife," cried the tradesman, "the brouchtoucaille's ready? We're incredibly hungry."

"Well said, Le Busoqueux," said the elder Nabonidus as he entered. "I can't wait, I'm starved. I would take a small glass of port, though."

"Monsieur Nabonidus," said the women in chorus, "it seems you've been magnificent."

"Siksty-siks thousand porcelain pieces," announced the bootlick Le Busoqueux.

"Three hundred and seventeen thousand eggcups," emphasized Zostril, no less an ass-licker.

"I'd love to smash dishware," whispered Eveline.

"Hush, be quiet," cried her mother. "How dare you say such a thing? A well-bred young lady simply does not speak like that."

"It's shameful, saying such things," scolded her father.

"We'll speak no more of it," said Nabonidus indulgently.

He looked at her on the sly as he lapped up the last of his drink.

"Mon sieur Nabonidus," one of the women asked, "who do you pick as the winner this afternoon?"

"Bonjean's got a good chance," answered the mayor. "He has intelligence and imagination; and a great suppleness of the wrist, don't forget."

"And Rosquilly?"

A debate ensued. Paul and the young women gathered near the window and began speaking in low tones. Some moments later, a mule covered in dust slowed its trot before the tradesman's house.

The rider waved his hand, then, spurring with both heels, disappeared.

Eveline remarked that this was the rural postman.

"What's he brought?"

"I wonder," responded Paul.

"It was to you he made a sign, wasn't it?" asked Laodicée.

"Me? You're imagining things!"

"OK, Paul, don't get upset!"

"Who was talking about the postman?" asked the grandmother, gesticulating.

"No one," Paul answered.

Whereupon it was announced that the brouchtoucaille was ready.

It was in a spirit of inesspressible enthusiasm that Nabonidus gave Bonjean, in the name of Home Town, the Grand Prize of Springtime. Not wanting in any fashion to diminish previous prizewinners, one would have to say without egzaggeration that never had such success been more deserved. Never before had anyone carried to such perfection the finesses and subtleties of play. Even Bonjean's adversaries were forced to acknowledge his unquestioned superiority. In a few brief words, Nabonidus retraced the history of the Grand Prize from its establishment to present days. The cheering and applause crested, and the brass band worked at unknotting the opening measures of "Cloud-Conqueror."

"That's that, then, let's celebrate," said the uncle.

"Ah! Papa, always the same silliness," muttered Robert.

It was difficult to get close to the winner, from whom fanatic Tourists were begging autographs. The uncle saw Machut and Marqueux making their way towards him, dragging their women behind.

"Hey, your brother: what a triumph."

"That's it, though, let's go celebrate," said the uncle.

The other two agreed.

They had difficulty removing Bonjean from his admirers.

"Great, Papa, you've outdone them all," said Robert.

"That's right, Papa," said Manuel, "you're an ace."

"Come here and let me embrace you, my sons," declaimed Bonjean.

Emotion pricked at his eyes.

"That's it now, let's celebrate," said the uncle.

His brother embraced him.

"To Hippolyte's, then?"

A thick crowd was already swallowing fifrequet there. It greeted the winner's arrival with eksultant hurrahs. The uncle ordered several bottles at once. Marqueux and Machut realized suddenly that their women were lost in the crowd.

"They'll find us all right," said the cellophane merchant, who was miserably thirsty.

When they'd finished celebrating the triumph, they set off for the fun fair. Everywhere one heard people bellowing and the bray of the merry-go-round. Battered and rebattered songs bored into ears, along with the cries of women and the heavy laughter of men; and behind all this clamor, the monotonous, almost unremarked noise of the crowd's stirring feet.

"Let's go have a little fun," proposed the butcher, and the others followed him, faces flushed, in a playful mood.

Bonjean wanted to throw darts, but almost put out the eye of the patron, who carried her years with a great air of sacrifice. Marqueux tried to grab the darts from her but she cried out, and the current bore them away. At the shooting gallery, the uncle distinguished himself with remarkable scores, but the others, confounded by drink, were only ridiculous. Mandace went by, behind him his wife who, drunk, wanted to play Chapanese billiards, tapping balls into Jinese vases, like a man. Robert and Manuel tried out the cork gun without managing to knock down a coveted pack of cigarettes. Then the group paused a moment: should they go see the world's smallest giant, the human trash can, or the woman tattooed all over her body, entry to which was forbidden minors?

"We owe it to ourselves," the uncle proposed.

"You're right," said the others, leaving him to pay for everyone.

"The minors can't go in," said the cashier, pointing to Robert and Manuel.

"Nonsense," responded Bonjean, pushing his children ahead of him into the booth, "this is a special day."

Wanting to assure himself that it wasn't just painted on, Marqueux ekstended a wet finger to the caravel adorning the back of the befigured person. The bharker stopped him, but laughed. Also, there was no way to verify the ekstent of the woman's tattoo-ing, for you could only see the arms and head and back and the calves of the legs. The rest was disappointment.

"Their story about not allowing minors is just a come-on," said Bonjean.

Robert and Manuel concurred with paternal opinion, the chubby, colorful calves of this stout person stirring within them no evil thoughts whatsoever.

"It's alive! it's alive!" someone shouted a little further along, a grimy individual who directed the attention of Townspeople and Countryfolk alike to a poster depicting this woman descending from moon to earth, endowed, the bharker said, with a pair of silken wings like those of a bat; this zoological peculiarity did not hinder the person so constituted from smoking her pipe and playing cribbage.

The group chose to forego these turpitudes; on the other hand, it was ineksorably drawn to an apparatus sure to provide ekstraordinary thrills to connoisseurs of the same. One crouched in a cockpit which, having cast off slowly, soon began spinning at a furious rate according to the poster, then, at full speed, broke away and shot through a tunnel and dumped its contents, at last, onto a smooth incline.

"Well, one would certainly get his money's worth there," said the uncle, reshaping his hat.

The young men were inclined to agree.

"Oh no," said Bonjean. "It makes me want to vomit, that thing."

"Care for a pick-me-up?" Machut suggested.

Putting about, the group steered itself towards a bistro. En route, the champion of Springtime decided to play the lottery. While Papa did everything he could to reverse his bad luck, Robert and Manuel took the opportunity to buy themselves marshmallows.

They started swallowing the glutinous things.

"Ah! I've been looking for you," Paul said, tapping them on the shoulder.

Paul was their elder by two years; and the mayor's son.

" 'Severybody having fun?" asked Robert, to make conversation.

"Have you seen Pierre?"

"When his train got in," Manuel answered.

He licked at gluey fingers.

"Not since then," he added.

"You didn't see him again?"

"No. Why should I have seen him again?"

"No," Robert confirmed, stuck on his sweets. "He did say he was giving a lecture," he added haughtily.

"He told you that?" Paul asked, surprised.

"You, kids!" cried Bonjean. "Get over here!"

He was put out. He'd lost forty turpins in two-ganelon pieces.

"Papa's calling us," Manuel said. "We have to go."

Paul vanished into the crowd.

"What did he want?" Marqueux asked Manuel, intrigued.

"He doesn't know where his brother is."

"No good will come of that affair. No good at all."

"Let's go wet our whistles," Bonjean proposed. "It's got me all upset, that swindle."

They rejoined the ebb and flow of the crowd.

A little farther along, cries drew them ineksorably towards the source.

A compact mass of Urbinataliens, Countryfolk, and Tourists surrounded the seesaws. On one of them two women sat; whenever one rose, her skirts flew up as well. At each tipping, male onlookers let out a shout of glee at this vision.

"Just look at that," stammered Marqueux, affected.

"How crude, those women there," said the uncle, whose rural morality disapproved of such provocations. "And with two hundred watching!" he added scornfully.

A skirt fluttered high.

"Nice," said Marqueux, his voice choked with emotion, "very nice."

The Bonjean boys stole looks underneath and reveled inside. The champion watched them with a stern eye.

He seconded his brother.

"True enough, they're crude women. They give kids bad ideas. You: get your hands out of your pockets."

The two women curtailed their flight bit by bit, skirts leaping up less and less and finally not at all. The male crowd drifted away, pleased at having so plentifully and freely feasted its eyes. The seesaw stopped; both women jumped to the ground. Marqueux and Machut recognized their wives.

People talked for a long time about this wonderful fun, until finally it was turned into a song to be accompanied by bagpipes, hurdy-gurdy, tambourines, and canastanets.

Nabonidus, accompanied by notables, toured the Festival to oversee its production and be seen a little by his people.

On Perpetual Boulevard the gentlemen's arrival was marked by a respectful commotion in the crowd. Curious Tourists and austere Countryfolk pointed fingers: there's the great man over there in the straw hat.

"A damned shame," said Paracole, who was playing Chapanese billiards with Catogan. "I hate seeing them flat on their faces before that great boor."

"Pah, they're all cowards," said his companion.

"The grant is a scandal. An utter scandal. Well, it won't do any of them any good."

"He smashed his dishware all by himself: and even that doesn't turn them away."

"Right, they grouse a little and that's the end of it."

"They have no guts, these geese."

Nabonidus approached, making his way majestically through the square. He stopped briefly before a shooting gallery and, ringing the bell with each shot, earned a small ribbon the proprietor gave him, touched, amitst acclamations from an atmiring populace.

"Look at that," said Paracole. "What a faker! He'd miss an elephant at two meters."

"You're wrong on that count, he's a celebrated marksman," Catogan objected.

"See, you're even letting it get to you. If I weren't here, you'd be flat on your face with all the rest of them."

Le Busoqueux, who detested the populace, joined in deploring the mayoral retinue. "What rabble," he muttered.

"You need to get home," said Saimpier, whom the tradesman had greatly offended by failing to invite him to dinner.

Nabonidus came back towards Le Busoqueux. "You're tired? You're not having fun?"

"Ah, sieur Nabonidus, what a marvelous marksman you are," the tradesman responded.

"Pah! ringing the bell at three meters, so what?"

"You never fired a single shot in your life," Saimpier said to the tradesman.

The others cackled at this.

Before the merry-go-round Nabonidus suggested they take a ride. Le Busoqueux declined. That made him queasy. Astride one of the beasts, Nabonidus looked to be having a great time, and Townspeople said: he's not stuck up, our mayor, that's good, and Countryfolk added: he's not stuck up, their mayor, not stuck up at all, and Tourists concluded: truly, truly, for picturesqueness, this takes the cake.

"Look at that faker!" Paracole said to his companion, who was trying to snag with hook and line a bottle of sparkling wine. "He did this just to make himself popular: and it worked!"

"It's true all the same that he's not stuck up."

"Really, you're as naive as the others. It's no surprise that he's mayor again, with foolish folk like you."

Angered by that remark, Catogan made a wrong move which resulted in his hooking the bottle.

Nabonidus dismounted from the beast into a pool of deference and saw Quéfasse signaling him. They walked towards a quiet corner, behind a trailer.

"So what are my kids up to, Quéfasse?"

"Who do I start with?"

"You're getting senile, Quéfasse. Tell me what they're doing."

"Together, nothing, since they're not together. But separately, they're staying pretty busy."

"Don't attempt to reason, Quéfasse. It doesn't become you. Jean's back?"

"Yes, almost an hour now. He ate brouchtoucaille with Sahul. And as we speak, they're having a drink together, the two of them, with Paul the third. At Hippolyte's, of course. It's not really a proper friendship to have, for the sons of my mayor—a rural postman!"

"Keep your opinions to yourself, subordinate."

"Fgiveme please, my mayor. But on a day like today one takes the liberty of saying such things, no?"

"What on earth can they be planning?" murmured Nabonidus.

"How d'I know? They seem very ekcited. But so is everyone else, today: so that means nothing. It's Msieu Jean, going off all the time to the Bare Mountains, who's at the center of it."

"Don't try to reason, Quéfasse, you understand nothing of it, you dotard, nothing. What can they be doing, what can they be up to?"

Quéfasse shrugged to establish his ignorance. Then he blew his nose. Nabonidus's thoughts took a turn.

"And Pierre?"

Quéfasse smiled with a satisfied air.

"He's giving a lecture."

"Wha? Wha?"

"Yes. He's in the process of giving a lecture and he's even rented out the back room at Rosquilly's and it costs a half-turpin to get in, according to the handwritten poster. That's why I hurried over, I knew you'd want to hear Msieu Pierre give his lecture, and I'm surprised, my mayor, that you're not there. Why, it's a great honor to you, Meussieu Nabonidus, for there aren't many youngsters who'd be able to give such a lecture, above all on fish, or so it seemed to me, going by the first part of it that I listened to, but I was hurrying here to tell you about it, since I saw you weren't at Rosquilly's, and

I thought it would please you to hear Msieu Pierre address the populace."

Quéfasse, having been called an idiot, shut up.

"Let's go," said Nabonidus.

He set off towards Rosquilly's. He walked behind the trailers to avoid the crowd. Foreign dogs capered all about him, yelping and rearing up on hind legs. Quéfasse followed, warding these animals off with hardy kicks, crying "Filthy beasts!" with conviction.

In less than ten minutes everyone in Home Town had learned that Pierre Nabonidus planned to give a lecture, and this news revived memories of the grant in all those minds the Festival had, as it was supposed to, made unmindful of the city's ordinary affairs.

At the appointed hour, the hall was full as an egg and jammed as a rabbit hole. At the door Rosquilly the patron barred overflow arrivals from entering despite protests of an alcoholic vehemence. No women were in the audience, and few notables. Neither Paul nor Jean was there, but Robert and Manuel had ensconced themselves in the front row.

At siks o'clock sharp, the orator appeared. He made his way purposefully towards the table and right away began to speak. People as quickly fell silent.

The opening phrases cast themselves into that silence. What was he saying, this stupid Pierre? One could understand nothing. There were two aspects of Life. Where had he picked that up? In Foreign Town? He'd have done a lot better working hard to justify his grant. There was Life in the Light and Life in Shadow, and in the Light it was ruled by Fear and in the Shadow by Joy. That's what he was going on about. And why on Festival Day did he decide to drag the Townspeople in here and blather on to them about Life? It's right outdoors there, Life, with all its seesaws, its alcohols, and its freaks.

OK, he thinks no one understands him now. His little trip's given him a big head. So he essplains it all again: eggsimple after eggsample. He means no harm, I'm sure, but what he says isn't at all clear. What? what Life of the Fetus? It's hard not to laugh, hearing things like that. So OK, if he's here just to go on about such things, then maybe he should get paid—with a slap. And still he goes on. He goes on and even seems convinced of what he says. He claims now that life is often difficult, often severe, and you can't understand a bit of what you're hearing. And that one has tenderness in life alongside troubles and boredoms and disorders and sorrows. Because of which he believes that we were most at ease when still in our mother's belly, though it's really pretty lewd to say such things aloud.

In any case, he was drunk with ideas. One had to take it with loads of salt, naturally, and none of those grand words really came to very much. So that's how he spent his time in Foreign Town. Instead of, as he was meant to, learning their language. Here's what the public turpins went for, to let the mayor's son fill his head with outlandish notions.

OK, now he's talking about the ocean. You can't see any connection. Because of the water, is that it? There, I've got it. But what he's going on about, it's distasteful. You don't speak of such things in public. It's foul, and there are children here listening. Paracole, who has scruples, grumbles, but someone hushes him.

And now he's talking about animals more frightful than the lobster or oyster: cave-dwelling fish. Where has he got hold of all this: tell me that!

"Are-they-ed-i-ble-these-cave-fish?" someone articulated.

That brought a vast silence. Pierre peered into the audience and caught sight of his father, who had just come in followed by Quéfasse.

"Come, that's quite enough," said Nabonidus with a good-natured air.

Then, turning to the lessoners, he spoke in a lively voice: "My dear co-citizens, I thank you for the kind attention you've so freely given this most interesting nonsense that my son's been talking. I hope that it's held your attention. It does betoken, of course, a certain naïveté that I hope you'll esscuse by virtue of the orator's tender age. Thank you, my dear co-citizens, once again, thank you."

No one budged.

And so, it became an incident. In Home Town it would be talked about at least as long as the thighs of Madame Marqueux and Madame Machut. Conscious of the moment's gravity and proud to be present at this turning-point in history, the lessoners felt beat in their quotidian bosom a universal heart.

No one budged.

Quéfasse tried breaking the ice and said timidly: "Move along, Messieurs, let's move along, please."

No one budged.

And why didn't he say something, the idiot! That would help soothe the assembly. Probably it was from guilt: yes, guilt. For a

Festival Day, this was ineggscusable! What a mess, what a mess! Oh! certainly this would be remembered for a long time. It might even become, eventually, a recitative to be accompanied by timbrels, tambourines, floots, and jalopies. Nabonidus again mimed dispersal and turned to Le Busoqueux: "Ready to go, my friend?" he asked.

Then Paracole, with considerable courage, spoke up: "Why do we have to leave? It's not over."

"Eh no, it's not over," Catogan agreed.

Others were of the same opinion. People muttered. Several stood.

"Wait, wait," Pierre cried. "I'm not done. Wait, I tell you!"

"Sit down," someone cried. "He's still speaking."

Even Nabonidus stopped.

Pierre, after first opening his mouth two or three times without uttering a sound, finally said:

"I wish, in conclusion, to speak briefly about one thing: the fate of these poor fish when removed from their damp environment."

Everyone started laughing.

When they were gone, all of them, Pierre felt despondent enough to die, right there, right then.

The women remained in the dining room.

"Things aren't going well tonight," Germaine said.

"Why do you say that?" Pauline replied. "It's Festival Day. Everybody's having a good time."

"But it's scandalous what he's doing, Mother. You must think so, too."

"What?"

"He's all over little Eveline all the time. His future daughter-in-law!"

"Bah! She is not yet, after all, his daughter-in-law."

"And if Paul could see it!"

"He only has to be there. Where is he gone all the time? When one's engaged, one has to keep his eye on the future, you know."

"And little Eveline allows it! I've seen him pinch her on the chin, I have."

"Bah, so it pleases him. Nothing wrong with that."

"All the same, all the same, Mother."

From the neighboring apartment, cries of enthusiasm, "Ah! splendid greens!", alerted them that the fireworks had begun. Nabonidus senior helped herself to a small glass of trapu.

"To your health, my daughter."

Dame Nabonidus bowed her head.

"All the same," she repeated, sighing.

"Ah, splendid whites," someone cried nearby.

"He's a lothario. I'm willing to overlook a lot, but all the same, his future daughter-in-law. . . ."

"You have nothing to overlook," replied the elder. "He does as he wishes. Ah, my child, this is not a man like other men, you have to understand that."

Madame Nabonidus sighed.

"And this scandal over Pierre. . . ."

"He needs castigation, that wastrel. Give a lecture, will he, this spoiled brat who spent all his time over there chasing skirts most likely, and our money with it, and now wants to talk to us about fish! Pah! it's castigation he needs."

She finished her drink.

"Go watch the fireworks, my child. It's your husband, my off-spring, who's once again arranged for all this. He must be very proud of them."

Dame Nabonidus got up sighing and followed madame. On the balcony they rejoined their guests: a dozen notables of mikst gender; close by Eveline stood Nabonidus.

Very close.

"Ah! ah! ah!" someone cried, watching green silklike cords trail down from one of the constellations.

"Magnificent!" essclaimed Le Busoqueux.

"The finest fireworks we've ever had," Zostril said.

"Those of the fortieth year are widely praised," added Choumaque the scholar, "but they can't measure up to these."

Downstairs, on the square, eddies of crowd hailed each display. They cheered, applauded. Perfectly ordered stars pierced the dark again and again. The air was mild and still, though heavy with odors: crowd, alcohol, brouchtoucaille, dust. But it was a beautiful day all the same, and everyone breathed in deeply this precious first hour of the first night of spring.

In the sky overhead, a cloud of blue burst into new brilliance.

"What a lovely blue," Eveline said to her cousin. "That's a beautiful shade, that blue. Don't you think so, Meussieu Nabonidus?"

"Very," that one replied thoughtfully.

Eveline looked at him.

"What are you thinking, Meussieu Nabonidus?"

"That if we went up to the second floor, we'd have a better view."

Madame Nabonidus tapped at her nose and Dame Nabonidus saw nothing.

"Ah! splendid reds," cried Le Busoqueux in a feigned voice, looking foolish.

One flight up, Nabonidus opened the window of his children's study.

"We can't see them any better," Eveline remarked.

"No, but it's more peaceful."

"True, it is more peaceful. They're all making far too much noise down there. And it can be so wonderful, the calm of the night, can't it?"

"Absolutely. It calms us as well."

He tugged at his mustache and, lowering his eyes, whispered: "You'll make such a darling little daughter-in-law."

"Let's not talk of that tonight, Meussieu Nabonidus. Let's dream instead."

"Ahhh," he said, intrigued.

He added: "That's magnificent."

He meant a pyrotechnic that shelled the sky, fading downward then in whitish trails.

"You know me, Eveline," Nabonidus added, "I don't have much use for dreaming."

"Sometimes, nevertheless, you have the look of a dreamer."

"Perhaps it comes over me nowadays without my intending or even knowing it, oh, oh, oh."

That made him laugh, acting so, surprised at what leapt out. And the trembling in his chest brought on an esstension of arms, one of them suddenly encompassing Eveline's waist. Eveline trembled lightly, let out a breathy ah and concluded, after a spectacle of candles violet indigo blue green orange and red:

"And you, Msieu Nabonidus, personally selected all this loveliness?"

"Yes," he said, "Eveline," he added. And added again: "Eveline," in a lower voice, hand pressing more heavily.

Whereupon, several luminous bombs burst through the sky's dark silk. Behind them in the study, someone turned on the light. Eveline disengaged herself and turned. Seeing Pierre, she spoke his name. Nabonidus pivoted in that direction.

"What good have all these books done me," sneered Pierre.

"Look! a dictionary of the foreign language."

"What are you doing here?"

"I'll go back down," Eveline said.

"Hello, Eveline," said Pierre.

He watched her go by.

They listened to her steps on the stairway, descending hastily.

"I asked why you're here."

"To kill you."

"That makes no sense," Nabonidus said, shocked. "I am your father."

"I want very much to kill you. Sadly, I've brought nothing with me to accomplish that. I have no knife, gun, hatchet, truncheon."

"Then these are only words."

"But I did want to let you know."

"Very well, then. I stand informed."

"Yes, I want to kill you."

"And might I at least inquire why?"

"You have opposed me."

"That was pure foolishness this afternoon, all that prattle."

"Less foolish than your fireworks."

"It's the custom, my boy."

"Customs will change."

"And why is that?"

"Because the cloud-chaser is no longer in operation."

"Horrible," Nabonidus said, leaning against the frame of the French window and hiding his face in a hand whose palm smelled faintly of Eveline's perfume. This discovery having put his mind on another track, he repeated again the word: "horrible," wondering all the while how he might get rid of Pierre and return to the balcony below.

Lowering his hands, he uncovered his face and more with detachment than resolve said: "Like everything else you say: only words. Thank you all the same for informing me of this. I'll go rejoin my guests now."

"I will kill you."

Nabonidus stood and filed past weaponless Pierre. And so it was, still safe-n-sound, that the mayor rejoined his guests and the father his future daughter-in-law.

When the final blaze of fireworks died away, the guests agreed to a taste of the champagne imported by Mandace, a whispery, coruscating, heady novelty. Le Busoqueux was of the opinion that his daughter shouldn't take part, but Nabonidus poured her a full cup and Eveline, partaking, thought it wonderful.

Then parlor games were suggested, which occupied them for some time. Grandmother Pauline slept. Eveline esscused herself from playing. Host Nabonidus consented to keep her company, although he dearly adored such recreation. They sat together away from the youngsters.

Eveline set down her glass, quite empty, wanting to say that she thought it wonderful (eccelent, delicious, marvelous, and other such things; in particular refreshing, she decided), but, turning her head and seeing Nabonidus's face more or less aflame, she grew uneasy.

"Paul's not coming back tonight?"

"I've no idea," Nabonidus responded distractedly.

His eyes were fully round now, fikst to his face by dark studs of iris and flinty pupil.

"I don't understand why he's not here with us tonight."

Nabonidus appeared not to hear. He grasped Eveline's hand. Eveline was afraid one of the youngsters was coming. But it was Paul who entered.

Nabonidus let go of her hand.

Paul smiled.

"Where have you been?" Eveline asked. "I haven't seen you all evening. And we could have danced."

"I'm looking for my brothers and sister."

"But you don't have a sister," Eveline said, laughing.

"So I was told. In which case we'll speak of brothers only."

"I don't much care for your manner," Nabonidus said. "You were supposed to be here. What have you been up to? And what of Jean?"

"Jean's gone back to the Bare Mountains. He'll depart again, with Pierre, from there. And they've taken care to see that I know what's going on as well."

Nabonidus was not a pretty sight. Now Eveline would prefer parlor games. Nabonidus's the one who wanted to be here, anyway. She slipped out and left the two men to family matters.

"Essplain yourself," Nabonidus said.

"When I say the Bare Mountains, I should perhaps say, more precisely, their border: Grandmother's farm."

"And?"

"Do you still intend to continue this farce? It's very simple: we've made a discovery."

"Really?"

"Really."

Nabonidus went to rouse his mother, who was muttering ekcerpts from malevolent dreams. Both departed. The youngsters, trembling, pretended not to notice their flight.

Paul approached Eveline: "Shall we dance now?"

"What is going on?" she asked, fingering her curls.

"We are in the middle of an historic moment," Paul replied.

She looked at him: "Oh tell me, dear Paul. Oh, tell me everything."

"No," Paul said.

He looked at her again.

"No," he said.

3

Stone

JEAN:

Day began, disaster alongside, as I started off for the mountains:
At Festival's end, the old faker had flown like a thief.
I knew where the father was headed and what he was up to.
I knew his plan, his fate and his flight, his end and his means.
I started off for the mountains in this beginning day towards the
    barren hills,
In the fresh air of dawn on the deserted road leading to the farm,
First firm step, first roadmark on the fated course,
First installment.
Pierre also, though fitfully, followed the fugitive father,
Solitude pursuing solitude
Thinking only of his personal vengeance and his death wish
As I tracked the father's spore, foot falling into footprint.
I knew where I was going, knew where I wanted to go, would go,
To the far-off farm where Grandmother lived, where was born
The illustrious, great Nabonidus, mayor of Home Town, the
    powerful and strong,
In a word, my father.
In that modest house, the last human outpost before the rock's
    dominion,
She lived with her hens and their brood, her rams and their sheep,
    her cows and caretaker.
The ground around her, already bereft, had begun to peel away here
    and there,
Prickly earth, quilled earth, biting earth,
Work's never done for those who cultivate this land.

The old woman balanced there at the keen edge of rock and
vegetation
And no one could say if she'd taken rock for plant
Or if sundered from Home Town she had fallen
For the mountain's waste without surrendering to it,
Grazing grass like a cow, aspiring to rocky heights like a goat.
The old woman lived there, border of two kingdoms, frontier of
two realms.
Coming down for the Festival, she went back up by night,
Leaving the town behind her to toss in a sleepless bed,
Taking away with her a man confounded, overcome by his fate,
His sons, the illustrious and powerful mayor of Home Town,
My father, simply put.
Alone and sustained by old ferocities, she remained on her farm,
But he fled further towards higher refuge.
Sunlight chewed at heaps of trash steaming in the yard,
The grandmother slept, sucking at her teeth.
Sodden with fifrequet from the Festival, she watched stupidly one
son of her only son.
Not a word between us, no nod or acknowledgment,
As I passed before her searching stable and house.
The ancestor bemoaned herself, she lamented and blathered,
blathered.
I had no time even to laugh at the senile fury of this old veganimal.
The father fled further towards higher refuge.
Knowing the route's rigors, I drank and ate
And left, never greeting this spiteful old dam of the shadowed
jailer.

Past the farm, the route continued over pastureland
Till it tapered at last to a narrow footpath leading to the mill
Near which a cow and goats watched over by a sheepdog
Picked at the pitiful grass this prickly earth sustained.
Just before dawn the old goat appeared in the shadows
Itself a thickening shadow as it hurried towards the mill,
Becoming at length he who governed the servile citizens
And destroyed his own goods to distract them.
Great Nabonidus, tommy gun under arm, has he come to kill
rapacious birds?
The old goat turned his head and looked at his herd of scruffy
beasts.

Three hours into morning I reached the mill everyone says is
abandoned.
The door was open and nothing, no one, refused entry.
I cried: "Are you there, Father," but without awaiting response,
went on in.
Through that tower everyone says is abandoned, I moved alone,
along,
I felt quivering there a mysterious life, a secret life,
And Sahul with me had found out about that secret, mysterious
life,
About the old goat's sealed lips, the old dam's secret trips.
I stood in the tower where was shut away a mysterious, secret life,
A life to which Paul had been able to put a name,
I stood in the tower I had put an end to.
Climbing a spiral staircase to its top, I found the door,
And entered the lair, but recoiled at the stench.
On the ground nourishments rotted, and worms nibbled at scraps
of meat,
From a heap of ordure thick fluids oozed to pool and mold in one
corner,
Vermin gnawed at a grimy straw mattress and mice danced in
ekscrement,
Through a crack in the wall that sunlight couldn't penetrate, could
be seen,
At the bottom of the valley, the lewd town pressing dry waterways
between its thighs.
Down there flowed the stream of things, the course of time for
human life.
Imprisoned here on these heights, she lived near the horizon, that
unknown sister,
Far from the life of the town, far from animal or field,
Near the saw of the ridge, near a sky carved away by the barrenness
of mountains.
But the father fled further towards higher refuge,
But the father fled for his life towards mountains rugged and sere,
Towards Rock of Ages alongside which flows the Petrifying
Fountain,
The father runs, he runs from Home Town which no longer accepts
him,
Pursued by my disclosures, his own doggedness, and by our truth.

◆

Pierre's route took him by the other house preceding the
  mountains,
He had to greet the two cripples, cloistered and clever, esscluded
and esspelled,
Unwanted occupants, two shrewd slovenly folk, careless care-
  takers,
The ekciled, camels, curs, outcasts, the canceled, the cataracted,
Blind and paralytic, Nicomedes and Nicodemus, the banished.
Merchants of the town came every eight days to leave at their
  door
Nourishments sufficient to their meager eksistence
Then fled back to town in a flash to turn this pittance to ganelons,
Presenting vouchers to the mayor of Home Town,
My father. And father of the one who now drew near the hut of the
  Nicos.
Nicodemus and Nicomedes walked in their yard, one mounted on
  the other's shoulder,
And when the blind one was perched up there, they never went
  very far,
But they liked to change about, it gave them some distraction.
On this day after Saint Glinglin whose many pleasures because of
  their ostracism
They couldn't sample, they walked the usual way,
Blind one calmly on high and paralytic calmly beneath.
When they realized a visitor was approaching,
Their tongues stirred in chorus in their hidelike mouths:
"Where do you go then, you who we thought in Foreign Town?
"What are you doing here in the Bare Mountains, you who never
  left the city down there
"Till you went off to Foreign Town to study its language?
"Why are you haunting these paths? Your brother is the only one
  who ever disturbs our solitude.
"You have no business, Pierre Nabonidus, being here, your steps
  have gone astray.
"The Bare Mountains are not for cityfolk,
"Their air isn't like what stagnates down there on your squares and
  boulevards.
"You have no business here, son of Nabonidus, this isn't your
  path."

But Nicodemus suggested that perhaps he had his reasons.
"I'm not in the mountains because I love them," said Pierre,
"I'm not here with you because a dream leads me,
"I'm not here for recreation, because everything I love is in the city
down there.
"I come to the mountains only, I tell you now, to kill."
"There's no game in these accursed stones that soak up our misery,"
Nicomedes said.
"Who flees in the mountains, then?" "My father, Nabonidus the
Great."
"But why does he flee, this strong and powerful man who rules
"Over the city down there, in Home Town?"
"He thinks he flees my brother, but it's myself he flees."
"Why does he flee you?" "Because he fears dying."
"Why does he fear that?" "Because he must die and because I
wish it."
"The fumes of the Festival, have they intoksicated you?" "He will
die because my Truth must triumph."
"What is your Truth, then?" asked the twin invalids.
"There's Life in Shadow and Life in Light, Life in Repose and Life in
Disquiet,
"A Life of the Past, a Life of the Future, a Life of the Fetus, a Life of
the Man, a Life of the Ocean, a Life of the Atmosphere,
"A Life of harsh Sun, a Life of falling Water."
"For we who know so little of Life, your words truly are riddles,
"Yet soaked with blood these words make sense!"
And Pierre went on, thanking them deeply for their hospitality.

At the siksth hour of day, I reached the Ravine of the Ancestors.
Rocks there watched over the figure of old men, heads adorned
with moss.
The sun attained its full power, stone throbbed like fevered flesh
And the wind came up, the wind that sleeps in the bowels of the
mountain.
It galloped in the ravine like an indefatigable army,
Irrefutable charge of the mountain's invisible horses,
And its breath flayed face and hands and ate away at rock and bone.
I moved through the Ravine of the Ancestors, first doorway to Rock
of Ages.
The father must have come this way, but I saw no evidence to
substantiate this

Until the eighth hour of the day.
I walked, I walked, struggling against the wind bellowing in this
    larynks
Wrestling stone, wrestling sun, wrestling waste.
At the eighth hour, against a rock I saw a wet spot dividing into
    runnels.
Air and heat had already dried this puddle into shadow.
So I knew he had followed the usual trail, since the father had
    marked that spot,
And now he had to be panting on towards the Fountain, for there
    was no other route.
And I knew it very well, I who had made these mountains my
    own.
Sure of my path and my course, I'd grown hungry and stopped a
    while
To eat bread, cheese and fruit, and drink red wine.
"Paul Nabonidus, do you hear me? here I am on the scent,
"Here I am on the road carrying me face to face with my father,
"Face to face with this father we've confounded,
"Who hid away that life we're determined to know.
"We've unmasked him, we've broken him,
"And here I am without hate walking towards him on this bare
    mountain,
"Towards him who without hate we've overthrown.
"He flees, our father! He flees across the mountains with that life he
    concealed from us,
"With that life we'll set free, for we were careful, clever and
    shrewd.
"No: you alone were the careful, the clever, the shrewd, for I did
    nothing but dream,
"While you took my dreams in capable hands and made of them a
    true vision,
"And so it is that my father has deserted the town,
"Again and again I've come into these mountains a tortured being,
    a torn being, a flown bird,
"Fleeing the town, yet when I returned there my father forgave
    me,
"Having for me every indulgence.
"But I discovered his true love, and so from my dream you've
    formed this flight,
"And put me into it, this hunt, this quest.

"I only dream."
Having so chanted, I drank a cup of wine and resumed my
    course,
Wrestling wind, wrestling rock, wrestling sun.

Pierre alone on the mountain said:
"Oh, I hate you, my father, I hate you immoderately, my father!
"And here I am, cast onto the side of this mountain like a rock,
    author who will wipe away your breath with his vengeance,
"And I am blind, knowing neither my path nor my course.
"My route is a mystery to this fatigued body heaving its way towards
    the heights.
"Death, I'm consumed by death, by desire for death,
"I want you to die, my father, yes I want you to die!
"Why were you so powerful, my father? why were you so strong?
"You stood in my way and I didn't see you.
"You protected me when I was young, my father, but now you have
    crushed me.
"You supported me when I didn't know how to walk, my father, but
    now you have stepped on me.
"You guided me to the door of manhood, my father, but now you
    have castrated me.
"You wanted me to hold my tongue, and my truth to hold its
    tongue as well,
"And in Home Town where everything was yours, I hadn't even
    myself.
"You didn't understand my truth, you humiliated me.
"You didn't listen to what I said, you crushed me.
"You were powerful and you were strong and in that Home Town
    you held in your hand,
"You were the best, you were chief, and its inhabitants licked the
    soles of your boots,
"When you spoke, people bowed down to the ground,
"And all Home Town propped up your power and your glory.
"Even the hatred of some increased your strength!
"You were my father, you wanted to make a man of me, you said,
"But really, yes really, you wanted me weak,
"I believed what you said, my father, you were chief and king, rule
    and law,
"And when I wanted to reveal to you the double mystery of Life,
"And to tell you of the aguesistence and condition of the fish,

"You mocked me, you shamed me with the uproar of your
    laughter.
"When I wanted to reveal to others the double mystery of Life,
"And to tell them of the aguesistence and condition of the fish,
"You plucked out my tongue and threw it to the swine who
    loved it.
"You made me suffer, you who, by right of office, marries all the
    women of the town.
"You who destroys more riches than anyone else, you who
    triumphs over friend and foe alike,
"You made me suffer, oh great Nabonidus my father, but you have
    not conquered me.
"You crushed me until I barely egzisted,
"You wanted to tear out my ogresistence, the very eksistence of my
    soul,
"You were strong and powerful,
"You thought that against you I could do nothing, that I would do
    nothing,
"And I thought the same.
"I had to silence my truth because of your thundering great
    mouth!
"How I hate you! Oh my father! Oh you Nabonidus the Great! Fat
    ass without a head!
"Ape arms and monkey soul,
"Filthy old goat, old elephant in mud, toad fed on ekscrement,
"Bandy-legged bull, diarrhetic ram, soul of rabble!
"You feed yourself on the pus of my wounds, you giant big-bellied
    maggot,
"Ah you'll die! you'll die! you who wants my silence! you who wants
    to castrate me!
"Ah, you'll die! Ah! I'll burst your powerful, strong belly,
"And let out guts and paunch, old pater, and hang them to dry on
    the rocks
"And rapacious birds will devour your heart and your pale liver,
"Those beautiful rapacious birds you so enjoyed killing
"Oh you that I hate so much, oh you who humiliated me
"So much that my soul was devoured
"Almost to the point of death."

Nabonidus had isolated his daughter from the world, he had
    provided for her a blissful life

Up there in the mountains at the border of grass and stone
In the solitary mill everyone thought abandoned.
He had isolated that secret mad daughter whom he loved more than
    anyone else,
He had separated her from mankind and vowed she would be
    happy.
In her carrionesque shelter high in the mill, she lived happily and
    loved only him.
The inhabitants of Home Town never scoffed at her madness, never
    mocked her imaginings,
For she prophesied.
Each week Nabonidus, the great Nabonidus, climbed into the
    foothills,
Walking into the wind which always blew across that prickly
    ground,
Towards the mill.
He listened to blissful words from the one he loved more than
    anyone else.
He listened to the senseless words spilling out of that miraculous
    mouth,
The oracles he interpreted on his way back down to Home Town
And upon which he based his life.
So it was that these two lived, the happiness of one providing the
    other's strength,
And the father's strength providing this strange and wonderful
    bliss
Whose sight simple citizens did not have to endure.
Up there in that tower encircled by wind from day to night and from
    night to day,
Up there in that mill innocent of mankind's fevers and men's
    desires,
Far from city laughter and villaginous satire, far from immortal
    stupidities,
She weaved a life of absolute, final joy, a perfect, finished life,
She warbled her chants of the future.
The refuse lying about her feet and the vermin running over her
    body
And fetid odors and rotting carrion, all this was nothing but
Further proof of her joy. So thought the great Nabonidus who
    dissimulated to the city below
The wellspring of its life.

But we took the mill by guile and discretion,
We violated this secret, and the father fled across the mountains.
She fled with him.

Crags of cinder, leprous rocks, rocks without moss,
Wind that gallops roaring through its ravines and against the
    mountain's side.
The sun all alone in that sky went about its quotidian doom,
Rapacious birds slashed the light to ribbons and picked at clouds,
Mountain bare immense and stripped pointing its teat to the sky,
Breast of stone, great mineral bosom of earth,
Rugged proud waste and perfect solitude, purity of air that makes
    the blood boil,
There proceeded daughter and father towards Rock of Ages.
At the eleventh hour Pierre caught up with me near the bridge
Which joins the lips of a yawning, dry gorge
And side by side we went the same way but not to the same end,
Following the same tracks, but a different game.
"It's his death," said the other, "it's his death that I seek. He will
    die!
"He'll die, the tyrant, the buffalo, the old bear!
"I'll throw him from the highest of these mountains, mouth open
    and chest covered with blood.
"I'll make him suffer terribly, he's terribly humiliated me, he's
    thrown me to the ground,
"But I'll throw him from the highest of these mountains.
"He was so strong and so powerful that I could do nothing against
    him
"And my heart devoured itself and hate gnawed at my chest
"And I was so weak and wretched that I couldn't right myself,
"I'd never have been able to, and I would have had to remain silent
    forever
"If
"You hadn't sapped him of his strength, my clever, shrewd
    brothers.
"And now he flees, great Nabonidus, powerful and rich.
"He flees and already he is dead, for my hatred is profound,
"And now he's become nothing more than frightened fair game, an
    amusement, a wretch!
"He flees, the one who wanted my Truth to hold its tongue and give
    way to him.

"He shamed my lecture, he shamed my thought, he shamed my
   being,
"He threw me to the ground but I'll throw him from the highest of
   these mountains,
"Heart gone bloodless and eyes empty and snout hanging open."
And I said to him:
"I seek not death, but a life, and I pursue eagerly a dream,
"But does she truly eksist, this sister who dwelled down there in the
   mill?
"I run after a dream that seems against all reason or good sense.
"Who can she be, this sister who lived down there in the mill
"Shrouded in stench, in vermin, in the corruption of things?
"I don't know this prisoner but I must ekstend my hands to she who
   was put away,
"I must wrest those hands from him, and if he should die, what does
   it matter! I care only about that life which accompanies him."
"And to me what does it matter whether she be enchained on plain
   or on mountain?
"What does it matter to me, this dream of a liberation?
"I make my way towards death, towards the death of the one who
   set himself against my Truth."
"And I, I make my way to make my way," and together we made our
   way towards Rock of Ages.
And the sun began sinking.

Birds, boulders, and winds and sun and mountains,
Against you and through you proceeded the two hunters.
"What can it be that so devours my heart?" said Pierre.
"What blight nibbles at me? What vitriol disfigures me?
"Blood alone can cleanse my breast, blood of the old bear who flees
   towards Rock of Ages,
"The old bear wild and bewildered, the old bear in flight across the
   mountain.
"Year after year I followed his commandments
"And I saw him as a man perfect and strong, powerful and rich,
"But his good sense and goodness only made me stupid and
   docile
"And when I roused from the slumber he'd prepared for me, when
   I wanted to speak, well,
"His great shaggy paw fell on me and I was forced to be still and hold
   my tongue and die.

"The one I had believed good humiliated me, the one I had
    believed benevolent crushed me,
"The one I had believed strong now flees across the mountain,
"For you have sapped his strength and destroyed his influence and
    you have handed him over to me enchained,
"And my hatred now can rejoice at blood clotting on his breast,
"This hatred which devours me and gnaws away at me even as
    consummation draws near."
They continued along this great void grilling beneath sky
And the sun began sinking, casting elongated shadows on the
    rocks.
Rock of Ages drew them on, and from its side welled the
    Fountain.
As they approached the Ravine of Birds, they saw climbing towards
    it
Two bodies.
"A scorpion uncoils in my heart. Here it is! Here it is!
"Here's the old bear heavy with years, the old potentate!
"It strains, it clambers, it heaves itself on, it thinks it knows where it's
    going, thinks it gets away,
"It has no idea it's already dead, dead of my vengeance, dead by my
    hand and hatred,
"Ah! giant of the cradle, tyrant of the hamlet, father of the family,
"Here you are, stumbling on stones, gasping, winded, dragging
    behind you nevertheless this feminine cargo.
"You will die, my father, setting free thereby my heart and my life,
    and then I'll proclaim
"My truth in the town."
And I said to him: "Yes, truly a scorpion poisons your blood,
    perhaps *that* is your truth?"
And Pierre said to himself: "It's my hatred, o that he dies!
"And if he does not die by my own hand, that somehow still I
    should be responsible for his demise!
"That he dies, the one who shamed me!"
The sun began sinking
And as they came up onto the windswept plateau just before the
    Ravine of Birds
The father turning around caught sight of us.

The dulling sun began its fall into darkness.
Nabonidus turning saw beneath him the two sons close on his trail.

"Here they are, those who chased you from the tower wherefrom you ruled town and valley.

"Those who chased you from your joy, here they are, coming on, tracking me like dogs.

"These are my sons, those I've engendered and, if they did not eggzist,

"You would have lived forever in the secret castle which gave you such happiness,

"You who provided my glory and my wealth with your marvelous utterances.

"Look at them who proceed nose in my footprint like basset-hounds,

"Once they were sweet and tiny, my sons, they were filled with respect for me, my sons,

"The first docile, the second quick-witted, and for the third I had every indulgence.

"They were sweet and tiny my sons, but they were termites,

"They undermined slowly my life and my power, these termites, these rats,

"These worms, these young tumors, this threefold decay,

"And when at last I wanted only to sink back into my comfort and rest, it collapsed, for

"They had patiently worn away walls and floor.

"The superhuman joy I made possible for you, they had utterly destroyed, these termites,

"In shadows they milled about like larvae with keen jaws

"And I the powerful and the strong, I Nabonidus the Great, I the architect and author of this Great Joy

"In which no man would ever have part,

"Men who lick the soles of my boots,

"I who had three sons submissive and obedient, they gnawed away at my strength, they undid your happiness,

"These worms, these cankers, these rats,

"And here I am, fleeing across these barren mountains with these curs snapping foolishly at my pant-leg.

"What does it matter to flee, since such is the oracle, what does it matter to flee, since you are with me,

"My past life is nothing, since you are my life, my past life is nothing,

"But these dogs snuffling at my spore, who never stop suckling their Home Town,

"Milk of their illustrious mother!
"One betrayed my indulgence and the other my authority,
"That they would disappear into these mountains, reserved for
    giants! that they would give up my spore!
"I give up the city, since you are my life, but that the city would not
    give me up!
"That these dogs would relent, that they would return to their lairs
    and gnaw at the bones I've thrown them!"
Then Great Nabonidus made game of the two human figures
    almost lost among the rocks
And fired.
But the sons were too far away for him to hit, something he, the
    great hunter, knew,
Though he fired.
His shots squandered themselves and ekspired among the cliffs.
With his last shot he took aim on an eagle soaring above him and
    killed it.
The sun disappeared behind the mountains to the west as though
    itself struck, and osscure night moved in.
She said: "Let's go!" and Nabonidus the Great threw down his gun
    and the two of them started off into the darkness.

"Ah old hunter, you're not so sure of yourself anymore, are you,
    you're just not so sure, can't see anymore?
"Your shots are feeble and fumbling, poor old hunter become small
    game.
"Have you ever seen game fire on the hunter? poor small game?
"For you're no longer a lion, my father, a lion powerful and
    strong.
"You're no longer a lithesome, savage tiger, you're no longer a huge
    bear, master of the mountains,
"You're only powerless small game, you flee like a hare and you run
    away like a squirrel,
"And stand here, aiming at us your gun of withered grass.
"You wanted to kill the hunter, little rabbit? you'd do better to play
    on the drum
"A funeral roll to accompany the death moving steadily towards
    you.
"From the side of the mountain and bottom of the gorge will roll
    echoes of your wails and moaning,
"Echoes of your lamentations, for you must die, father rabbit!

"Even the night anticipates your death, as you must know.

"Old lion, your teeth are pulled! old tiger, your claws are pulled!

"Old bear, your hair falls out by handfuls and rheumatism
  encumbers your paws!

"Nabonidus the Great, you're nothing more now than a helpless
  sparrow, a plucked pheasant,

"But I have no pity for you, I have no pity for your pitiable defeat
  and your pitiful flight.

"I have no pity for you because you've become impotent and
  crippled.

"Your futile arrows make me laugh with hatred, not weep with
  pity.

"I will not weep with pity, for you wanted to destroy my life.

"I will not pity you, my father, because you humiliated me.

"You made me suffer so greatly that my hatred cannot be appeased
  by your ridicule and helplessness,

"But only by spilled blood and your summary death.

"You made me suffer so greatly that pity can never calm my hatred
  with milky words.

"I will crush your head and spread your viscera on rocks grilling in
  the sun,

"For my heart is filled with desire for your death."

And with his final bolt the father killed the eagle soaring above
  him.

The sun capsized behind the western mountains and went down in
  glory,

Eviscerated by the peaks.

There was a twilight, and then there was night.

In darkness the father kept to his course through the Ravine of
  Birds.

I held off pursuit, not wanting to lose my way in the dark,

And Pierre, who didn't fear losing his way, sanguine in his hatred,
  nevertheless remained behind with me,

While Nabonidus in the night disappeared into the abyss.

Night of pitch, night of asphalt, starless night,

Night that in the heights of these mountains descends like lava and
  fills up to their brim the gulfs,

Night unique and total, embracing the sky with your dark flame,
  rapacious night devouring the mountains,

Barren night, boundless night, unsettling night,

Night of stone, great mineral night of voids carrying away in your
    dark folds
Those who cleared the Ravine of Birds,
Having lost his way within you, the father has fallen into the
    abyss.
Great Nabonidus, powerful and strong, hunter of sure eye,
Male of insatiable loins, master of lives in Home Town,
Great Nabonidus has fallen into the abyss erected by night.
But it's not him who dies, great and powerful Nabonidus, it's not
    Himself who dies, but only the fugitive, this impotent archer,
This small game pursued by hatred, this helpless victim, this
    vanquished ekcile.
For a long time we sought the secret of his strength and his power.
We discovered the last piece of the mystery by chance only on the
    afternoon of the Festival,
We uprooted his secret, and now he's no more than
A simple fool, a blundering hunter who fell into the abyss,
But falling into the abyss, he again becomes great Nabonidus,
He becomes strong again in the night of the abyss.
Submerged in darkness myself, I slept and dreamed,
But Pierre did not sleep and, gnawed by hatred, stared that darkness
    in the eye
And saw his destiny unrolling there.
He saw taking shape against the still night the giant of his infancy, so
    large that it overrode the housetops,
The irrefutable protector that, docile, he so loved,
The ekspert, the almighty, the great one that he loved, himself a
    stupid person, lowest of low.
Pierre did not sleep and honed the edges of his hatred
And here at last came day, darkness undone.
Colder than night, the chalky dawn spread slowly over the valley.
I who slept didn't know that great Nabonidus had been swallowed
    up in the dark
And the one who still sat awake had no idea that now blood could
    not absolve his humiliation.
And Pierre woke me and together we crossed the Ravine of
    Birds.

We set out towards Rock of Ages, from the side of which flows the
    Petrifying Fountain,
And in the harsh, thin air, we heard the death-howl of a dog,

A howl growing louder, softer, then louder again,
A death-howl that rent the sky at every turn,
And rapacious birds abandoned that scream-torn sky.
Light came up around us, and the wailing ever more dismal,
But, courageous brothers, we held to our course.
Going on a while, ears bloodied by the lamentation,
Going on a while, keen air biting at our temples,
We at length glimpsed near the Fountain our long-concealed
    sister.
Near the Fountain on her knees she howled, the father was no
    longer there.
We moved on again, the sun climbed towards noon along the
    mountain's side.
We reached the Fountain and our sister, heedless of us, went on
    with her lamentations,
Howling like a dog and weeping like an abandoned lover.
Bending out over the gulf, we saw in clear water great Nabonidus
    stretched out face to the sky
And dead.
Dully, we contemplated this disaster a long time. The sun, diligent
    falcon,
Overtook the crest of the mountain and, sweeping into the sky
    above, shone down on us.
She was silent and Pierre said: "So there he is dead.
"He fell into the abyss and the night, and I did not kill him.
"So there he is dead and my hands are not sticky with his blood.
"He's dead, thrice dead, thirteen times deceased.
"Now it's over. My vengeance is ekstinguished, though my hatred
    yet glows.
"I'll go back down, my brother, to teach my Truth. I'll go back down
    to the town to address them there,
"But here I'll return when the time comes,
"And from this water I'll fish out the great cadaver once it's become
    mineral,
"This great Nabonidus of stone, my father, yes I'll make a god
    of it,
"A god that defends my Truth, that defends my every utterance,
"And Home Town will have its god, its god of stone, and I,
"I will be master among those who live down there, I'll be the
    guardian of that Truth
"Which fell upon me in Foreign Town.

"They'll all come to me, they'll become mine, and the stone will become the man's final defeat,

"My Truth in stone, my stone of Truth."

I turned towards my sister and said to her: "Come." She rose.

"Good-bye, Pierre Nabonidus, go back down to the town with your god of stone,

"Go back down to the town with your Truth.

"You will be great among men, Pierre, you will be strong and you will be powerful.

"People will listen to you. They will watch in awe. They will believe your utterances.

"You will have disciples who perhaps will die for you.

"You have suffered greatly and now you will bring suffering,

"For you will become great and strong armed with your god of stone and with your Truth.

"You will rule the town and by virtue of this god you will make yourself venerated.

"Go back down to fulfill your grand destiny! Go back down to the town!

"Your hatred has become so great that everything is devastated.

"Your vengeance eksacted, you succeed a terrible god who did not forgive,

"Who understood nothing and punished everything.

"Go back down to the town with your heavy burden and your twofold Truth.

"Twofold is your Truth, don't forget the fish, don't forget the water of sky,

"When the deformed statue is set up, your statue, yours."

Turning to my sister, I said to her again: "Come." She drew close to me.

Bending out over the gulf, I looked again at the cadaver which water had begun transforming.

"Go back down then to demonstrate the failings of this limestone face.

"I leave this Great Man, this crude Rock of Ages, this veritable negalith.

"Your twofold Truth will melt away stone and torture rock

"And I, perhaps now I'll make my way towards the humid cities."

Turning to my sister, I said to her again: "Come." She followed me,

And Pierre went back to the town down there, the giant stone shadowing his course.

4

Countryfolk

PAUL:

Around me in all its horror stretches the countryside, this long
shroud of boredom and chlorophyll in which, endless day after
endless night, Countryfolk are wrapped. How did I ever get myself
into this . . . these filthy carpets of herbage, these doormats of
nibbled grasses, these disgusting, hairlike clumps of bushes and
overgrowth, rude erections of trees. . . . Ah, the silence of the
country . . . deformed screeches of parasitic beasts, cows clinging to
the pasture like crabs in pubic hair, larval animals that look like
roots spilling out of the earth to graze . . . the slack, malicious sound
of sawing branches, this endless rustle and rattle and hiss above, this
constant leaning into the wind until you're about to vomit . . . the
shouted speech of laborers, the patois of these Countryfolk . . . I
hate this border of green skirting our town, this runny white on
which the yolk must feed. It's only among us, within the stones of
our buildings or upon those of our streets, that life can be perceived,
truly, sharply; and from there, those buildings, those streets, that it
radiates outward to this vague countryside.

How did I ever get myself into this? . . . Yet here I am, sentenced
to the spectacle of this vegetable kingdom in all its presumptuous
innocence, coming up short again and again before bipeds and
quadrupeds whose world is bound by their appetites. What boredom! On every side a riot of vegetation, on every side an arousal of
plants, only this sullen, endless regeneration of seed.

How did I ever get myself into this? But here I am, enclosed by a
horizon where trees and the hedgerows of landowners tangle in
thickets. Within this circle squared off by surveyors and wills, I see

only the ponderous track of seasons, greedy nibbles of selfish trans-
action, a slow preparation for future digestion, the countryside's
official enshitment. Why can't I be more like the sun, wise enough
to let its rays fall innocently on lichen, on moss?

And when it (the sun) takes its daily tack, spilling night behind
itself, I long for, shiver for, the town's comforts. In the sky, in a wild
geometry, gleam planets and stars, but from this arable earth come
only vague dark shapes, pockets of ink rising towards the peaks. All
nature sinks into a horrible apathy. An overwhelming gloom. The
seed of light that makes these plants grow returns to its source, leaving nothing on the earth's surface but unsettling, shapeless shadows.
How can one not be fearful before this sudden absence of all reason,
all pretense? How can one not be terrorized before this vegetable
dullness, this heavy life without memory or ghosts, without death or
phantoms? Plunged into this idiot blackness, the sunken man no
longer knows even his own fear.

In town, every stone sparkles with the light of the human spirit,
and the night's menaces are human menaces. On country roads innumerable sufferings beset one, pointless entanglements of vegetable
nightmares; in city streets flashes the killer's sword, a sword any man
can understand, could himself, in the right circumstances, wield.
There (where I am now) suffocation and swamps, here (there
where I want to be) gutters scarlet with blood still smelling of desire
and of life. If our homes are haunted, it's by human cast-offs, sad
reflections of others like us; I sense around me here only the
shadows of shadows, grey coagulations, drab mucus, the quiet
lisping of dungheaps.

As soon as I leave habitable constructions where subsists the
odor of humanity, the very walls taking it on, I'm seized by dread
and disgust, want to vomit at natural beauties. How could anyone
ever have believed that there was any natural rapport between man
and his environment? Whatever harmonies eksist, man has created
them. The common ground, man's hand has pushed into place.
Spirit breathes only where man breathes, man liberated from
biological and agricultural constraints: spirit breathes only where
nature, put in its place, disappears. Man fulfills himself only in the
city. Here, I feel nothing but dread, domination. And I long for
those tremblings, those fevers, which only urban communities can
give birth to.

The industry of my brothers, and my father's fire, never led me
to swerve off my own middle course and the comforts of its

unquestioned mediocrity. Younger brother by birth, I never envied numero uno's privileges. First place always seemed to me submission and containment. And last struck me as little more desirable. I have no wish to stand out. The less people think of me, the more I value myself. Hypocrisy is my way; privacy, what I breathe. I want to present only a smooth surface, sleek, decipherable, keeping to myself all the underthings; and I do intend playing with that word here, just as it presents itself, though not in its sense of clothing, a usage I find rather ridiculous. Still, though, the clothed woman does present a parallel to this, my own, mystery.

It's well evident, to continue, that vegetal nature, and all that which depends on it, is devoid of any deeper nature; the roots have no particular dignity; once the dirt's cleared away, the plant is wholly eksposed, wholly revealed. It has nothing more to divulge; no more is it provocative, passive, stagnant; nor is it less. The evil stuff it secretes in darkness, now that's out in the open. Everything here is part of the same stuttering pleonasm. The great fields at noon stink of the same odor that at midnight is whitewashed by the moon. Plants don't lie, their appearance consumes all their being, just as land does the man who cultivates it. And because I don't intend to let myself get absorbed, shrewd as a crab I'll surrender my claw to whatever wants to drag me off. Then at my leisure, when I'm good and ready, grow it back.

In Home Town, I had to make some concessions to be able to nurture my thoughts in peace. In the edible world of legume and grain, what fodder to offer? Down there, each day offers welcome. The town is my life, the town is my virtue. That my secrets are influenced by current ideas and fashion doesn't imply any particular taste for progress or novelty. I have no program; in some cases, I've been able to verify man's malice; in others, a surprising echo of my own desires; in all, the track of our intelligence.

For years now, a growing mass of imports has been heaped on Home Town. We finally even got a cinematograph. One of our oldest houses was demolished (many Tourists complained over this) and in its place was constructed a hall (red seats, white screen) devoted to the projection, visualization, and spectaculization of animated images, otherwise known as moving pictures.

Every notable was invited to the opening. I was there. Among our co-citizens, those who had traveled a bit esspounded on what was taking place to the more sedentary. Nevertheless, when the lights fell, uneasiness wrung their hearts; then the film began unrolling, to everyone's astonishment. Performance over, spectators scattered with their misgivings into the night towards home; but a month later, there was no one who didn't frequent the Hometown Palace, save perhaps a few ancients, a few suckling infants, a few non-transportable invalids.

During this whole period, I must say, I never counted myself among the most enthusiastic. Grand historical productions annoyed me, vaudeville bored me, comedies and dramas weighed me down, documentaries put me to sleep. What I liked was the dark, the crowding together, the tepid odor; and for a time just sitting there, without purpose or thought. One sleeps well after this. Sometimes, rarely, an image struck me; sometimes, no less rarely, another shocked. One evening: a scientific film on plants, with time-lapse photography. The "animation" purportedly gave to the springing-up of a pea the suppleness and subtlety of an octopus tentacle, bearing in its growth some trace of deliberation. It was ridiculous. I shrugged my shoulders. All that was just science, and had little to do with man. But this vegetable seen so plainly, shown thus: what could I possibly see there but an absence. I'm no botanist, only a man who's had his natural fill of this nature sprawling everywhere outside the cities, outside my Home Town.

My elder brother, the one who's mayor, since he returned from Foreign Town goes on and on endlessly about ancient life, claims there's understanding of it, says he's drunk at the source of this knowledge. But he acknowledges this ancient life only in the wetter links of the animal kingdom. I fully agree with him. Though I'm not, myself, an authority.

As I've said, I don't have a program. I'll concede, for egzample, that there are degrees to this crushing boredom with which life in the countryside overwhelms me. Vegetable gardens, those feeble witnesses to human intelligence, seem preferable to the chaos of forests. But finally none of them can hold a candle to a city sidewalk with its streetlight. And how very much I prefer to the obliging civility of legumes the gloomy rudeness of nettles and brambles; for with the latter, one's illusions must cease. Their absurdity is all too manifest.

Flowers alone give me pause. Sometimes I see in the flower's beauty an effort on the plant's part towards a comprehensible face, a hand held out to man; sometimes I see there nothing but imbecilic intimacies of reproduction without orgasm. And sometimes odiferous esspressions of a kind of intelligence, and sometimes only cavities senselessly bedewed. And sometimes a summit, an offertory, almost an intellect, and sometimes the carnivalesque, pretentious masking of an heksistence scarcely palpable.

Anyhow, all said and done, I'm not much concerned with having an opinion about flowers, or about having sometimes this one and sometimes that one, or having these and those simultaneously. It's enough for me to be aware of my boredom. I also wonder sometimes if I don't overburden unjustly the vegetable kingdom and if it's not the abstract category "life in the countryside" alone that provokes me, casting its shadow on man and animals as much as on plants. All the same, if there were no plants, there'd be no life in the countryside. . . .

To get back to the subject of man and animals hereabouts, obviously I don't have much sympathy for them. There's not much trace of man around, and as far as the lives of cattle, cocks, and other beasts, what obvious misery to them. How could spirit ever descend here, and, once descended, ever free itself again? Rural life involves nothing more than plodding behind the course of the seasons; nothing more can thrive here; life's heart is empty, it can't bring forth an intelligence it's never witnessed. An humanity captured so in the filth of these fields and the countryside's manure piles can never overcome its limits. Held in place by the earth's inertia, it gives up, it declines and lies dormant until at last its bodies begin to rot in the parallelepipeds of their graves.

It's not that I have antipathy for Countryfolk. I pity them. But what do we have in common, they and myself? The way they're stooped, the way they always give off an air of weariness, how stupidly they go on laboring like beasts to get by! Sometimes I sense in one or the other of them a spark, and wait to see it catch, but no: disappointment; the dampness of earthbound thoughts smothers it before it's born. As even I myself am smothered by this closeness.

And how can they ever hear the slightest human call when the constant object of their attentions is defined by its very inhumanity? This greenness is inhuman. Though seasonally it is visited by wayward spirits, blind like sap, laboring and sad, sorrowful genius of the cauliflowers, impoverished god of the potato—how they must suffer this fall to the very depths of visible being! What a terrible struggle for freedom then! And I suffer and struggle with them under the worldly burden of this rustic hicksistence.

My Town, my Town, how I miss your tremors, your spirit, your uncertainties; your pleasures and your lights; your solitudes and your sanity! Ah, that this summer would die, strangled by crops, and I could return to the labyrinth where only beings stripped of all intelligence lose their way. The Town. We'll be there for the Festival. More Tourists than ever before are coming this year. Many end up staying all winter: isn't there always fair weather in our Home Town? Some even adopt this as their regular place of residence. Their presence has made it possible to open a cinematograph (in their foreign language, of course), as well as several luckshury shops, or at least shops selling fineries of which our women until then were unaware.

The disgust inspired in my older brother by the foreign language for some time led him to refuse to sanction continuing these practices. But urged by notables whom the shopowners bribed with moving pictures, he at last consented.

We then could watch films in the foreign language. I wasn't long in finding in them a wonderful distraction, an acceptable pastime. If at first we proved unable to sit the whole thing out, if halfway through we staggered up and swaggered off like novice sailors out of their depth, then where else could we hope to overcome this failing save in those very halls (there soon were many of them) where shadow and light coupled, images familiar, language mysterious. Otherwise given to keeping up appearances, to convention, here finally I could allow myself to become bewitched.

The women appearing on the screen were compared to stars, like them incredibly distant, like them revealed by a ray of light, like them without apparent blemish and forever at the summit of their beauty. Soon it couldn't help being noticed that many young men in our town, though themselves certain of the absurdity of their desire and its folly, had fallen in love with the most celebrated. Then everyone realized that it wasn't just the young men who were languishing so in doomed loves, but most of the adults and all the elderly as well.

Some Tourists, perhaps wishing to protect the morality of our Home Town from novelties they themselves or their counterparts had introduced and with which they had freely gratified themselves while in their own towns, incited a small number of Urbinataliens, among which I will mention Le Busoqueux, who had almost become my father-in-law, and Marqueux the cellophane merchant, to found a League of Friends of Springtime (implying: restricted to days of the Festival); but my brother having refused his patronage and sensible Urbinataliens having decided that the activities of such a group might imperil the commercial and touristic development of Home Town, the League quickly dissolved and disappeared, vowing to take severe measures not only against the cinematograph's ravishing images, but also against other images which seemed to them every bit as seductive. They were mocked in this regard, but whereas I don't think there's any peril in such images, I do admit their impropriety.

One day I went for a walk in Brandy Street, for years one of the most chic in Home Town, and the one most frequented by Tourists. I dawdled, wholly unsuspecting of the shock that awaited me. I strolled about at leisure, window-shopping a bit, with no idea that an unknown world was to be revealed to me. I went on about what little business I had, innocent, as the veil began tearing. The unforeseen was on the lookout for me, it lay in wait for me. Never would I have recognized my fate in this new guise. I walked by the shop of Mandace, the importer. I glanced in. In a window were displayed the latest fashions in feminine undress. I didn't dare look closer and turned away reeling from the jolts of my heart. My throat felt deliciously dry, and every drop of moisture within my body surged headlong towards the spermatic channels. My very soul stammered. My eyes were drunk with the images they'd imbibed. My hands trembled such that I had to restrain them, and suddenly I bent to the blows dealt me by this new reality. I beamed like a child, and I whispered: "Oh oh, oh oh."

Scarcely had I recovered from this when I was yet again struck, and the double blow fell, and felled me, before I saw it coming. Two themes thereafter powered my personal quest, both of them directed towards, yet independent of, women, both of them deriving more from man's invention than from nature. For I have to say that by then I had fallen in love with Alice Phaye.

The first time I saw her, I took no notice; the film was good, but she, unremarkable. Only much later did I call back to mind that production and recognize its animatrice, thereby discovering the calm, first, mute bendings, the source of this brook which has become a river, this union then unsuspected.

The second time I saw her, I remember distinctly. She had only a supporting role, but just as I prefer her. She sings in a gripping voice. In each of her appearances on screen, I discover a little more of her body, her ekspressions; her face; between each appearance stretches the night. I don't just admire her legs (which she never hid away), her hips (which her gowns traced), her mouth bright with chemical

blood, her eyes aglitter with glycerine; I also take an interest in her
role and, behind that, behind the hypocrisy, in her, for herself. So
that when at the film's end her character is corrupted (the man she
has loved himself prefers a millionairess, and she, she finally consents
to give his telephone number to her young rival's vile millionaire
father), I become indignant. These are things that I take seriously. I
think this ending degrading. So every time, I leave before the final
scene; but for a whole week, every evening brings back to me her
voice and brief skirt of some lustrous, dark material, her songs and
firm, resonant hemispheres aquiver either side of their deep equator,
her touching, hoarse voice and joyful or despairing songs and thighs
glimpsed in a longitudinal rent in her skirt, lustrous and dark as I
said above. I could watch this film forever.

All too soon the week was over, though every day swelled with
ekspectation till it seemed there could be no end. On the final night I
stayed even for that last scene, to see one more time what would soon
be gone. Then I walked out again into the night, a different night. In
those days, Alice Phaye was not yet well known; yet I never doubted
that later, with other appearances, fame would come to her here in
Home Town. And so it came about; nor did I have to wait long for
her nekst appearance. On the very evening that show ended, she
came back to me and, reborn in shadows, bewitched me anew.

I walked out again into the night, a different night, slippery with
shadow. I didn't much feel like going home; I began wandering at
random in our streets. Weighed down by the gloom that pulled at
my lungs, I hesitated to walk far or long, then recalled that the nekst
day a new cinema, a second foreign-language cinema, was to be
inaugurated. Impulsively I decided, in order to set myself a goal, to
go have a look. The street was deserted. Light from a streetlamp fell
against the building's side; and further on, when I saw what was
beneath this light, I felt my legs weaken, my throat constrict, my eyes
become wide. That night, posters for the show opening tomorrow
had been put up, and these posters, I became pretty sure, I was
certain of it, stock-still there beneath the streetlamp, standing open-
mouthed, these posters showed Alice Phaye in a close-fitting long
dress of black silk, adorned on the left leg with an embroidered
butterfly. Behind her a city burned. The outline of her legs over-
whelmed me. Our intimacy became immense. I tore her form from
the paper to fiks it within myself. I devoured it. I detached that
beauty already freed from real (to reel) presence to inoculate myself
against the real, to nourish me, to consume me.

From her emanated this ethereal image, a pure image, atemporal, not of the flesh or sordid life, and this image I had before me delivered me, wholly unsuspecting, to powerlessness: that was its purpose. Tearing at the poster with my eyes to make an image of an image, I re-created a reality for myself alone, not of this reality filling the countryside with its sprawl, but of those purer, finer realities distilled in cities.

The street was deserted, we were alone.

For me, the night was dark no more. I was overjoyed. Nekst evening, I hurried towards the new showplace and watched the film. And the image came back to life in a musical, singing; and there were those legs, those legs glistening in silk. And every night the film played, I went to watch this great scandal that Le Bu and his dying League wanted to ban. And they started looking at me oddly from the ticket booth, and I became something of a legend in Home Town, the one who goes every night to the cinema; but they never suspected that I was particularly in love, especially in love, electively in love, only that I passed my time as I wished, that I grieved for my father, that I was upset with my brother, that I misogynized and would become the old bachelor of the family since, for my brother, the best-informed forecast marriage: inevitably; as for Jean, he'd been forgotten: inevitably. In short, if I went so often to the cinematograph, it was only because I was unhappy.

Lie! I am not unhappy! Lie! Lie! But I'd prefer them to imagine this than the truth, since they've always mocked my loves. Does the fact the star knows nothing of me prevent my thoughts from being obsessed by her? How could one ever imagine that feelings of such power wouldn't reach their source; or that this ideal connection I've created wouldn't have strength and merit enough to establish perfect spiritual rapport between two things removed in space? Imagination's virulence has established between her and myself a bond from which she cannot escape. Of her many attributes, she knows but a few; doubtless she has some understanding of the desires multiplied by each of her appearances; yes, and from among the many attributes, numberless as they are, whose interplay comprises her personality, among the most important, though unknown to her, is my love.

The distance I'd established between others and myself was also our bond, and the forms of my eroticism challenged nothing but the vulgarity of the laws of nature. I was prepared nevertheless to observe those laws; it was enough, and satisfactory, for my imagined tensions to remain in the realm of beautiful idea. That star which lived incarnate in such blonde flesh and appeared intangibly on this side of the ocean nevertheless preserved its every charm, this star which, in its limited domain, in its limitless beauty drew to it such adulation and desire, increased itself, became untouchable image, the ever-increasing sum of starved thirsty regards, and, for me, finally was one with the very wellspring of my morals and my religion, this torrent of fetishism, clad in erotic armor that magnified for me now all female flesh, all female beauty.

Much feminine clothing requires little justification or commentary, although even the skins in which the first woman was dressed with care by a jealous squire set in motion this boundless bother of fur. Luckshuries like gems and lace mean little to me. The undress of years gone by falls well outside my interest. My thoughts were never founded on the propositions of old books and the yellowing of old dresses. Crinolines eaten by worms leave in my memory's recesses only skeletal remains, and corsets ribbed in whalebone are relegated to horror stories of old customs and to junk drawers stinking with neglect. Such old-fashioned things had never stirred my erotic instincts, but the astonishing novelty I'm talking about now made me understand how history's detours always come back to the main road, to the objectivity of such finery and the artifices of a divest humanity.

The girdle brings together in itself, beyond material contingencies of reproduction, the artificial and the erotic. Pages of anatomy describing the function of organs marked by vagaries of the flesh, by necroses, by future putrefaction, who would submit to them, these pages, these realities, if not for such enticements? I'm in awe of the foreign merchant who proposes for Ubinatalien hips this eksultant artifice he's invented, artifice and reality in which purity of purpose, merit of line, and seggsual geometry join in the body's service. The very material of this object is a metaphor for the elasticity of feminine flesh.

And that's how I kept going. As a result of the invasion of our Home Town by foreign propaganda and goods, I'd happened onto this revelation. Without it, I couldn't have gone on. So what would you have me do now, eksiled far from the urban source of my rapture into this brownish-green magma of rural life, far from the bright photographic images of my dreams into this three-dimensional dullness of biologic space, far from urban detachments into the swarming vitality of cowshed and countryside, what would you have me do, if not vomit?

How much more contemptible still are the attitudes of wrong-headed citizens and neighbors; that, for instance, of the one who just missed being my father-in-law, Le Busoqueux, who, steeped in the dust of cities, here would waks eloquent over the abundant harvest and overflowing grapes. He takes pleasure in what he calls "open" air, the good odor of vegetables and their physiological purity, frank country manners, the beauty of salsify, the majesty of pumpkins, the use and employment of various manures, waking to the cock's crow. As for me, I suffer and long for my return. "A-ha," Le Bu told me, "you must be truly desperate not having a cinematograph there, you who went every night." And he hinted that family life does away with any need for such ekspenses, down there, and here, with this boredom. As though he imagined I would want to take her back, his daughter. As though he imagined that the niece wasn't so bad after all. I replied that I compost them, himself and his family. He didn't understand.

And this countryside, these fields, I compost them too; or rather I would compost them if I didn't know that they fatten from ekscretions. Like dogs, the countryside eats manure, that's its nature. Pah! Nature! Pah! Pah! Fortunately man isn't natural. What a filthy life he'd have to lead if he were natural! And this countryside calls him to that, it clings to him, overtakes him, brings him down, pushes his nose into the foul mire out of which cabbages make their way. Peuh!

I wasn't cut out for life there. Happily, happily the streets are paved with cobblestone and asphalt and this unnatural purity becomes such a habit that even wretched little herbs springing up between the chinks are hunted down. Suburbs were erected for the impure as well, so that at the center of cities pure spirit could finally free itself of its biological bonds.

Soon I'll see this countryside, these meadows, these woods no more, and just now I don't know which of them annoys me the most. For if the first, carrying the imprint of humanity, thereby departs somewhat from its animality, the last smells of dark blood, of a savagery preferable at least to servility. But what does it matter? I can't be bothered with choosing favorite aversions. My life of reverie has as little interest in sylvan realities as in agronomical ones. I'll never again find myself between two such cityless horizons. Beauty is essential to me, not this carnal beauty redolent always of the animal, but beauty like a statue's, a beauty no less ordinary, yet specific.

Mold has supplanted drape. No more ample folds sublimating woman's beauty, but the form itself instead underlined, perfected as though according to rigorous intellectual principles: the brassiere, the girdle, and silk stockings evidence these laws, translating them into their particular charms. And so the nude elevates itself to the dignity of the scantily dressed. Slenderness, strength, suppleness—all heighten the strict purity of line. Art here classically restricts its means; it embraces the artificial and sweeps away all vulgarity. It celebrates the beauty of the feminine body stripped of anything rococo. Woman considered as unreal image and model of realities gives new meaning to so-called abstaraction.

Alice Phaye, I imagine, must glove her body according to strictest principle and underneath wear only that which supports her bottom, that which supports her breasts. What films of hers will be offered this winter to my greed? What new images of her will affiks themselves to my soul to go on about their phantom life there? The scandalous shop will again set out its photos of models. And like the stars, and like the models, the rich lights of realities stripped of contingencies, absolute realities, will flare up within me, realities returning to their origin, penetrating me with the fire of their passage, to the point that I concentrate within myself a bursting brilliance.

Happy the winter when she comes, mnemonic when she's gone. Then arrive the glorious days of the Festival and the games of Springtime, whose vegetable allusions I find so distasteful. Then will come the new summer, a summer without this countryside for me, perhaps. But why, otherwise, should it in any wise be better than others?

5

Tourists

Alice Phaye and Dussouchel stood before the statue and egzamined it in silence.

"It's hardly proper," Alice said finally, "especially since it's a lifelike figure."

"I think you're in the presence of an original."

"But don't you think it obscene first of all, and gruesome as well?"

"Perhaps. In any case quite striking. I've never seen anything like it."

"Nor have I. Though of course I've just arrived from Holy Wood."

"I don't mean to boast, but I know almost every tribe trampling and scratching at the surface of the Earth: this is truly unique."

"So you do agree that it's gruesome and obscene."

"We—by which I mean professional essplorers and ethnographers—we make no value judgments on the objects of our study. I would inquire into the meaning of this figurehead, for instance, but not in order to criticize it in any way."

Alice Phaye and Dussouchel circled the statue one more time.

"He was quite a man," Alice said.

"With every bit as much muscle as could be ekspected in a town where there are no sports."

"And you don't think it's touched up?"

"Perhaps a little here and there. The openings of the nose, the openings of the ear strictly speaking would have to be perforated. Hard to be sure. It all comes together well."

"When I think what this block of stone is in reality, it makes me tremble. I don't want to look at it any longer."

She moved away.

"I must request authorization to take measurements. Among
other things. Want to come with me to the mayor's? That should be
interesting."

"Thanks. I might as well be the complete Tourist. I'll go see the
mayor."

They strolled through the streets of the town, coming across
nothing of any great interest.

"We absolutely must attend Saint Glinglin," Dussouchel said.

"I leave tomorrow," Alice Phaye said.

"That's ekspress Tourism."

"I have to start another film in eight days."

Dussouchel rubbed thoughtfully at his beard. His lengthy pere-
grinations had never given him time for the cinema. Besides, he
evaded subjects whose bibliography he didn't know. So, passing
before Mandace's shop, he changed the conversation.

"Look, an umbrella," he said.

"What's so surprising about that?"

"Only that it never rains here."

He egzamined the window display: "Ah, an importer. That
essplains it."

"It really never rains?"

"They attribute this benefit to the ingenuity of one of their citizens.
It's another matter that I must study carefully, this cloud-chaser."

"But, it works? really? the cloud-chaser?"

"It's not just a myth," Dussouchel declared brightly.

He looked around.

"There it is."

He pointed with his chin.

"Ah," said Alice Phaye, looking that way.

"You have to understand that in the country, mere kilometers
from the town, it rains the same as everywhere else."

They found themselves before Hippolyte's inn.

"Do you want to go in here a while?" suggested Dussouchel. "A
Tourist friend guarantees that the place has great local color and
that the very best fifrequet is served here."

"I've never tasted it. I'd adore that."

They went in. They had to go down several steps; it was a half-
cellar. On wooden benches the clientele seemed reduced to cheer-
less gestures or talk. A drunk man slept by himself; two others fell
silent, though they'd been talking before the Tourists came in.
Hippolyte hurried over.

"A bottle of fifrequet," said Dussouchel, adding: "from the year when Yves-Albert Tranath won the Grand Prize of Springtime. That year's been recommended to me," he whispered to Alice Phaye.

The two men regarded the visitors. One of them made the following statement: "That's a good year."

Dussouchel pretended not to have heard. He turned to Alice: "Isn't it picturesque here? Not that I'm particularly crazy about the picturesque. . . ."

"The best year, really," the Urbinatalien went on.

He got up, picked up his glass and came towards them.

"We're about to meet some Urbinataliens," Dussouchel whispered.

"What fun," murmured Alice.

"May I?"

The native sat.

"You coming?"

He signaled his companion. That one got up, picked up his glass and joined them.

"My friend Catogan. I'm Paracole."

Hippolyte arrived with the fifrequet.

"What are you up to?" he cried. "You're to leave this gentleman and lady alone, you hear?"

"But these gentlemen aren't bothering us," Dussouchel said.

"Go on," said Hippolyte, "you won't say that a minute from now."

He opened the bottle.

"You'll be very pleased with it," said Paracole, "it's the real thing."

Hippolyte served Alice Phaye, then Dussouchel.

"Empty your glass," Paracole said to Catogan. "One ought not miks vintages."

"You're right," said Dussouchel.

So Hippolyte served them as well. He turned away disgusted. The drunkard slept tirelessly, timelessly.

"So," said Paracole, "you've come to see our Saint Glinglin? Don't answer: I've guessed right, I know it. I can even tell you something more: this is the first time you've been here: for I remember a Tourist even after many years: the Urbinatalien eye, eh?"

"You've never gone to the cinematograph?" Dussouchel asked.

"Absolutely not! Squander my money on chattering pictures? 'Mnot crazy. Of course, everyone here wouldn't agree. Right?"

He elbowed Catogan, who launched his laugh without preparation and brought it up short in the same way.

"Oh?" spoke Dussouchel, pursuing, although cautiously, his
ethnographic inquiries.

"Yes," said Paracole. "Right, Hippolyte?" he called to the innkeeper, throwing his words over his shoulder.

"Leave me in peace."

Paracole rubbed his hands and esspressed himself thus: "You
understand that there's not been a cinematograph in our Home
Town for long. Very well, some people became . . . well, how can I
put it, well, OK, let's just say: amorous, yes amorous, of those flat
characters speaking up there on the screen, these stars, eh? You
don't believe this, right? very well, it's true anyway. And the biggest
fool of them all was . . ."

"Shut your face," Hippolyte said.

"He's a coward," Paracole commented, then went on: "was our
mayor's brother. When a film pleases him, he goes every night,
regularly. When I say a film pleases him, I mean its star. And the one
who pleases him most, all Home Town can tell you, is . . ."

"Shut your face," Hippolyte said.

"He wants to talk all the time," commented Paracole, then went
on: "is a young woman who usually appears not wearing much, I can
verify this since I occasionally glance at the photos in passing, once
she even had a sheath of black silk with a butterfly embroidered on
its thigh."

"Indecent," said Catogan.

"Do you have any idea what he's talking about?" Dussouchel
asked Alice Phaye.

"Myself, I can't remember her name just now," Paracole said.
"Besides, no need to waste time on that. Paul Nabonidus's the one
we're interested in."

"Paul Nabonidus is the current mayor's brother," essplicated
Dussouchel.

"How do you know that?" asked Alice Phaye.

"I learned it from the Guide," Dussouchel responded modestly.

"Ah! the Guide?" essclaimed Paracole. "Don't tell me you've
read the Guide? That's one of the mayor's projects, a real novelty.
The old one wasn't worth much, but that one's really worthless."

"Shut your face," said Hippolyte.

"One has the right to essplain these things to Tourists, how the
new mayor wants to turn everything upside down, and as for Saint

Glinglin, well: that we're not certain they'll be able to see it in all its beauty."

"That would be a pity," said Alice Phaye.

"A certain pity," essclaimed Paracole. "He has a lot of foolish ideas in his head, our new mayor. So far he doesn't dare follow through on them, but he can't be trusted, all the same."

"A-ha," spoke Dussouchel methodethnologically.

"He consorts with fish," Paracole said.

"Fish, fishy, just like the proverb says," said Catogan.

"Shut your faces," Hippolyte said.

"He's afraid of our new mayor," essclaimed Paracole. "Snot-nosed kid that he is, understand, he's not easy to deal with. That drunkard you see snoring there, do you know who that is? Quéfasse, the old urban guard, what you Tourists would call the chief of police. Well, our new mayor didn't hesitate a single moment to sack him when the notion came to him."

"He's in bad shape," said the innkeeper. "He lost everything. So now he drinks day and night."

"What's that, what?" groaned Quéfasse, who vaguely overheard.

"It's been a year since it happened," said Paracole, "a year this Saint Glinglin."

"We really should say the day after Saint Glinglin," Catogan said.

"So," Paracole resumed, "I got up around noon, in one of those terrible moods, I poured some cold water on my head, and then I went down to drink a glass of fifrequet to clean my teeth. It was fine weather, still, peaceful. I listened to young birds singing. Most people were still asleep, and then Catogan came, Catogan there."

"I remember, it was the same here."

"Precisely," said Hippolyte.

Paracole went on: "We played a game of cards."

"I won by fifteen points, you weren't in good shape."

"After that, I tucked in to restore myself; I had a radish for starts, an omelette with shallots to keep going, leftovers of brouchtoucaille from the day before, a hefty slice of goat cheese to wash all that down, and then a zabaglione for dessert, and then a small coffee, well-spiked. After that, I came down to the inn here to drink another spiked coffee and that was when Hippolyte told me the news."

"Precisely," said Hippolyte. "I was the one who told him the news."

"The mayor had disappeared," Paracole and Catogan said in unison.

"Everyone wanted to know why," Hippolyte went on, "and so before long they were all gossiping."

"Didn't you tell *me* not to talk too much?" Catogan asked him.

"Shut your faces!" the innkeeper cried. "With all due respect," he added to Alice Phaye.

He came and sat at their table, having grabbed two new bottles and a glass from the bar. Quéfasse, uncovering his eyes, homed in on the movement and came toward them, not forgetting his glass.

"Ah Quéfasse! Ah Quéfasse!" Paracole called out cheerily. "Sit down here beside me so we can talk. You can tell us all about it, right, Quéfasse? You remember that day? The day after Saint Glinglin, when we heard the news. . . ."

"I remember . . . the sun that day . . . heat pressing down on you. Causing such a thirst, it was strange. No one outdoors, everyone inside. I remember. . . ."

"And then we heard the news," said Paracole.

"Yes. It was the two cripples from the mountain who came to town and brought word, who revealed that the mayor had disappeared and that his son, Pierre, pursued him across the Bare Mountains, tongue hanging, like a hunting dog."

"And who are these two cripples?" Dussouchel asked.

"Nicodemus and Nicomedes," Catogan answered.

"And what sort of cripples?"

"One is blind, the other paralyzed. These days they live near the Fountain. You seem to be well educated, you Tourists."

Catogan looked at the ethnographer with some surprise.

"Well," Quéfasse went on, "once they'd revealed that, it immediately spread through the whole town, the news was everywhere. People came out into the streets. They swarmed in them, but of course already it was becoming cooler. And then we learned that the other brother, Jean, had also taken off across the Bare Mountains in pursuit of the father. As for me, I quickly pulled myself together and hurried to the mayor's private domicile. I knock. The door opens. It's Paul. 'Msieu Mayor is here?' I ask him. 'No, he's not here,' he tells me. 'Where is he?' I say. 'I don't know,' he responds, 'my brothers are off looking for him.' 'Ah!' I say. 'Yes,' he tells me, 'my brothers are off looking for him.' 'Ah!' I say, 'I know that already.' 'Ah!' he says, 'well?' 'Well,' I say, 'why has our mayor run off like this?' 'Ah that,' Msieu Paul answers, 'ah that, he hasn't given us any essplanation.' 'Ah!' I said. And then I left."

"Because you understand," said Paracole to Dussouchel (for he thought no one ever essplained things well enough to the Tourist), "that it seemed peculiar for the two brothers, Pierre and Jean, both to go off so suddenly in search of their father. They hadn't waited, even till the nekst day, to see if he might turn up, but had dashed off that very evening. He was free, after all, to accompany his mother to her farm and spend the night there, if he felt like it, just as any good son might do, without any particular reason. The day after or the nekst day, well, by then one might start to wonder, it's true. But no, that very evening, they had run off after him."

"So," resumed Quéfasse, "they started scouring the countryside . . . searching . . . but they came up empty-handed. . . ."

"They returned that night," said Paracole, "completely eggzausted, empty-handed. . . ."

"Paul, I remember," said Catogan, "could have cared less."

"And then one day," Quéfasse went on, "one night rather, in the cool of the setting sun, people had gathered on the Great Square for some fresh air, when they saw Pierre appear from no one knows where, thin and dressed in rags. They all fell silent as he passed. They parted to let him pass. It was as though a void flowed before and behind him. My feet ached from all the running around I'd been doing, but I followed him home all the same. There, I came up behind him, for I do have, so to speak, the right to do so, and I asked him: 'So, Meussieu Pierre, any news?' He said to me: 'Yes, I'm looking for all the notables.' 'Very well, meussieu,' I told him, and I started rounding them up, all the notables, even though my feet ached so. Everyone was milling around the mayor's house by that time. Night was falling. People watched the notables arrive one at a time without saying anything. No one had anything more to say. Then when they were all there, the cripples arrived with Pierre and Paul. Me, I stood by the door, keeping an eye out. Night fell for good. The people there spoke among themselves, and from time to time to themselves, in low voices. The moon rose. It perched on the roofs, white and large, a lil whiter and a lil larger than usual. People's shadows came back to them. And then the moon sailed on and the balcony of the mayor's house was awash with light. Meussieu Le Busoqueux came out onto the balcony after a while at which point we all learned that Meussieu Pierre had become the new mayor and that the old one had fallen into the Petrifying Fountain, because there is, it's true, such a petrifying spring in the Bare Mountains, though few people have ever seen it, and that they had found and brought home what was left, the piece of stone he'd become. And that this had been accomplished with capstans and cables and wedges and such stuff. And some days later it arrived in town, strapped onto tree trunks and towed by a bunch of cows. And so, finally, it was put up right in the middle of the Great Square, like a statue, where it can still be seen."

Following this lengthy account everyone felt a need for a few moments of silence, Dussouchel at last breaking it.

"How very interesting," he muttered thoughtfully.

Hippolyte had gone for, on his own, three more bottles of fifrequet.

"What a story," sighed Quéfasse.

"But none of this essplains why you were ousted from office."

"Ah well! well!"

He tapped at his thighs with irony, bitterness and despair.

"Ah well!"

"The new mayor threw him out," Catogan essplained, "because he had brought the old one to his conference."

"A conference about fish," said Paracole.

"Yes, harking back again and again to fish," said Catogan. "And there definitely was something fishy going on."

Hippolyte, returning, opened the three bottles. He said: "There was story after story that no one could make any sense of."

Catogan guilefully said it couldn't be forgotten that the new mayor had obtained his present fine position by pushing something into the Petrifying Fountain, at which the innkeeper suggested that, at least for the time being, he keep his great trap shut. He told him this again with even more force when the door opened and two personages came in. One carried the other on its back. The whole bundle, taking to the stairs, fell.

"A pile of imbeciles," said Hippolyte, watching them pick themselves up.

Paracole and Catogan split their sides laughing.

"Nicodemus and Nicomedes," Dussouchel told Alice Phaye.

But he was overheard. Catogan looked at him suspiciously.

"They're here for the Festival," essplained Paracole in a guidely manner.

The others more or less recovered themselves. The paralytic hauled himself onto a stool, pushing another beneath the legs of the blind one, who automatically sat. They breathed deeply, in cadence, to drive out the alarm, and said in chorus: "Good evening, everyone."

They were greeted.

"There's a crowd, right?" said the blind one to the paralytic.

"Siks," said Nicomedes, "two of them Tourists."

"Two Tourists?" asked Nicodemus.

"A man and a woman," the paralytic answered.

"Blonde or brunette?"

"Blonde."

"Ah, ah," spoke the blind one. "We have to talk to her."

"They're crazy," whispered Alice Phaye.

"Don't worry," said Hippolyte, "they don't mean any harm."

"And they can tell you wonderful stories about our country and its history," said Catogan.

"Should we talk to them?" said Alice Phaye.

The two rustics approached, hopping on their stools.

"They do fascinate me," said Dussouchel. "But I'll honor them some other time."

Alice Phaye stood.

"How much?" Dussouchel asked.

"Just give them five minutes, no more," said Hippolyte.

"I'm leaving," said Alice Phaye.

"How much?" Dussouchel asked.

"Three ganelons," Hippolyte answered. "You understand, it was from the year when Yves-Albert Tranath won the Grand Prize of Springtime."

"I thought that went for five or siks turpins at most," said Dussouchel, "from what other Tourists have told me."

"He's well informed," said Catogan, suspicious of this knowledge.

"That's the price," said Hippolyte.

"Where's the blonde we're going to talk to?" said the blind one, sliding his stool forward.

"Don't make a scene over it," said Alice Phaye.

Dussouchel tossed three ganelons on the table. They went out, propelled by a forbidding silence. The two cripples fidgeted.

"I was afraid," said Alice Phaye.

"They're considered harmless."

"But many thanks for the local color."

"You haven't seen anything yet. Wait till the Festival tomorrow."

"I'm looking forward to that."

"Then you'll still come with me to the mayor's after lunch?"

"Oh yes. He can't possibly be as upsetting as his dependents."

"Don't be too sure. There's nothing to indicate he didn't push his father into that remarkable Fountain."

"You have quite an imagination for a scientist, Meussieu Dussouchel. Do you think that's what they were insinuating, those people at the tavern?"

"Without a doubt."

They lunched at the Hotel Cyclops, the only one Tourists could use, since there weren't any others. Simon Zober, the producer who accompanied Alice Phaye, was in his room sleeping off an attack of dry rot, a benign but potent malady that often struck newcomers to Home Town. Dussouchel and Alice Phaye dined alone at a small table. All the other tables were occupied: some were voyagers who'd made their way over logpiles of parallels and jams of meridians and who now ate with the impatience that always falls the day before Festival; there were also habitual Tourists who returned every year, aficionados of Saint Glinglin, infatuated with Springtime and guzzlers of fifrequet; there were even a few Countryfolk, recognizable from the specks of mud they wore with pride, for in Home Town, since it never rained, there was no mud.

Everyone concentrated on his food, but from time to time, fitfully, attentions would stray from close inspection of plates to aim covetous, longing glances at the star whom some of the diners recognized. But for the most part their prevailing hunger allowed few such imaginative scrutations. Alice Phaye, unbothered by the crowd's covetousness, was likewise undisturbed by this fickleness of desire.

She sent up some fruit from the country for Simon Zober, to slake his thirst. She didn't want to see him. Later, after some time alone, she rejoined Dussouchel. The mayor rarely received before three in the afternoon. Outside the hotel, weather was always and again beautiful. As everywhere else in the town, equally, all around.

They walked again by the statue. It stood baking in the sun, becoming fikst, eternal, impervious, and marblelike. The two Tourists refrained this time from remarking on the reproductive organs, easily visible yet tucked into the mass as though by sudden discretions of which one would have thought the old mayor incapable.

Inside, not much was going on by way of preparation for Saint Glinglin. No one moved. It was cool.

Alice and Dussouchel found the guard savoring his siesta in the great hall. No one waited, but numerous miniatures memorialized departed mayors, with the ekception, however, of the one just preceding, whose three-dimensional petrification was every bit as good, from the souvenir point of view, as the small colored surfaces consecrated to these onetime notable personages.

"Are you going to wake him?" asked Alice Phaye.

"That seems inhuman to you, I know, but in truth the human sciences do imply sometimes a certain apparent cruelty, just as do physiology, biology, and other natural sciences. Ethnography, sociology, and statistics often demand that their servants sacrifice in some particular or total fashion the comfort of their informer."

"Will it be necessary in this case?"

"No," responded Dussouchel. "We can go on in directly to the mayor's office. After having knocked several times, of course. You're with me?"

He knocked, then entered.

Pierre was working.

He was writing.

He raised his head.

"Monsieur Nabonidus?" said Dussouchel. "Permit me to present you with my letter of introduction."

Pierre covered with a modest writing pad the plans, which he was drawing up, for a municipal aquarium. His frown drew this essplanation from the intruder:

"The bailiff is asleep. . . ."

And this as well: "Mademoiselle Phaye, star, and very famous, accompanies me."

Pierre shrugged, they thought with resignation, and turned his attention momentarily to the presented papers. He returned them to Dussouchel.

"You've done well to come this year. This will be the last. And in fact you may already have come too late."

"I'm afraid I don't follow you, Monsieur Mayor," Dussouchel said politely, rather ankshus.

Pierre regarded Alice Phaye's crossed legs, which reminded him of something. But the something wasn't so striking that he chose not to respond to Dussouchel.

"Very well, since you are Tourists, I'll tell you something, though in absolute confidence. This Saint Glinglin will be the very last one. The last dry Saint Glinglin, at least. For now we will enter the reign of humidity."

"You're going to make it rain!" essclaimed Dussouchel.

"No doubt that the scientist's intellect is quick, his mind shrewd. Yes, I will make it rain. But this is still a secret. No one in Home Town is aware of my intentions. When it happens, they will raise a great ruckus, of course, which may very well carry me off. In the meantime I leave them, for tomorrow, the joys of one last Festival, according to their old customs, but by evening water will pour down on their heads from clouds newly born and burst, at last."

"Monsieur Mayor of Home Town, can you tell me how you plan to go about accomplishing this?"

"I'll hide nothing from you. I'm going to throw the cloud-chaser into the Pits."

"The cloud-chaser actually works?"

"Absolutely."

"You really believe it?"

"Absolutely."

"But don't you think there's simply some kind of coincidence between the good weather and this thing? As opposed to influence of the latter on the former?"

"Have you forgotten that formerly it rained on this town just as it does on all the others? Rained even more."

"And after the cloud-chaser, everything changed?"

"Yes, now dryness reigns."

"But this perpetual good weather, isn't it an advantage everyone enjoys?"

"Not everyone rejoices in it."

"Really?" cried Dussouchel hypocritically. "There are Urbinataliens who don't like this perpetual good weather?"

"Who speak up about it, no. But among those who don't?"

Dussouchel mentally thumbed through his questionnaire and found no interview strategy adequate to this situation. Alice Phaye was fast becoming bored, shifting weight from foot to foot; despite her dancing, she had small, rather plump feet. Pierre watched them, half-silk, half-leather, before insisting again, in the face of such seeming incomprehension:

"Yes, those who don't speak."

"And are there many of them?" asked Dussouchel, improvising.

"Numerous!" essclaimed Pierre. "Innumerable."

He caught his breath.

"Our river is sand and its bank, dirt. Our creeks are yellowish and meager and our streams have scarcely the strength to polish small pebbles. Where, where, where oh where can fish live, the fish of bygone days?"

"The man's mad," Dussouchel murmured.

"Ooh," cried Mademoiselle Phaye. "Fish?"

"Aren't you concerned?" Pierre asked.

"So it's a revolution you're setting up," Dussouchel said. "A meteorological transformation of aguesistence itself."

"A risk I must take, for Saint Glinglin."

"But your fish won't be able to defend you against the rage of the Urbinataliens, once the rain starts."

"This is true."

Pierre reflected. Went on: "If only I could persuade them . . . but no. They're all devoted to this good weather."

"None of them are on your side?"

"The guard, maybe. No one else. And I already have so much hatred against me."

Silence crashed into the room's walls. The silk of Alice Phaye's stockings became more brilliant, the line of her leg even more delightful. Pierre's eyes took refuge in the promise of his future revolution as Dussouchel, clearing his throat, resumed speech with these words:

"I will be frank with you, Monsieur Mayor, since as I told you initially, I came here with the purpose of, and with the scientific goal of, taking part in the classic festivals of Saint Glinglin. It would be most distressing to me, as a scientist, should these be in any way modified."

"I have the greatest respect for science," Pierre replied, "but as much for myself."

His eyes were fastened on Alice Phaye's ankles; they rose slowly towards Alice Phaye's own; and Pierre's tongue churned up these sounds for Alice Phaye's tympanums:

"And you, Mademoiselle, do you also desire that nothing should change in the disposition of the Festival?" Thinking of his father, he added: "For I am master here."

Alice, who thought his courtesy genuine enough, admitted: "Yes. I so desire."

"Then, Mademoiselle, Monsieur, you will take part this year in a classic Saint Glinglin, and I hope you'll take from it all the more pleasure from its being the last. After Springtime, the cloud-chaser will cease working and we'll see what we'll see."

"I thank you for such consideration," said Alice Phaye.

"Naturally," said Pierre, "this is all strictly between us."

They promised it would remain so, then Dussouchel requested a number of authorizations, permits, favors, and passes, all of them granted.

Paul, having pushed open the door, found himself behind Alice Phaye, but there was a mirror before her, and the shock of seeing her in it plunged him into unconsciousness. He fainted.

Those present stood looking down.

Pierre introduced him: "My brother."

Alice said to Dussouchel: "Really, do you think that was because of me?"

Pierre did everything in his power to summon the slumbering guard outside in the great hall; he shook a hand-bell.

Alice leaning over the fainter said to Dussouchel, again: "Do you think this was because of me?"

"It's more or less a matter of psychosociology," replied Dussouchel. "This fainting seems to be a phenomenon engendered by erotic publicity." And upon reflection: "Her films have played here?"

"Many times," said Pierre. "And Paul's not missed one of them. He went every night. Especially when they showed *The Burning of Old Town.*"

"There were firemen in this film?" asked Dussouchel.

"A league wanted to ban it," said Pierre.

Dussouchel was surprised at the acrisistence of such a group in Home Town. Pierre replied that it was indeed ephemeral, this acrisistence. And Dussouchel learned, ill at ease, that it was with some justice the film had aroused such a frenzy of condemnation. For Pierre described in detail the butterfly embroidered on Alice Phaye's black silk sheath.

"So much for the morals of lepidoptera," said Dussouchel.

Alice had time and attention for no one but Paul. She lifted the hair that hid his face, his eyes.

"We have to do something," she said. "Water, for instance, someone bring water."

"It's rare here," said Pierre. "Following my final decision, there will be more, of course. After a short time."

The guard appeared in the doorway. He rubbed at his eyes with the back of his hand, yawned, advanced cautiously.

"Water," cried Pierre, "water, a little water."

"Indeed," Sahul replied.

"For my brother!"

Sahul opened his eyes and saw Paul, whose head Alice Phaye supported in her lap.

"It can't be," said Sahul. "Alice Phaye!"

"He's seen the lepidoptera too?" asked Dussouchel.

"Oh, Mademoiselle, you honor with your presence our Home Town."

"Go get the water, then," said Pierre.

"Mademoiselle, would you sign a daguerrotype for me?"

"I truly regret," said Dussouchel, "having been so seldom to the cinema in my life. Never, you might as well say, ekcept for the occasional documentary."

"Ah, Monsieur," proclaimed Sahul, "it's marvelous, the cinematograph. And how I pity you for not having spent time in those dark halls!"

"You've seen *The Burning of Old Town?*"

"Oh, yes," cried Sahul. "A masterpiece! Mademoiselle was ekstraordinary in it. And she wore one of those sheaths. Oh, please, Mademoiselle, won't you sign a daguerrotype for me?"

"Are you going to get water or not?" asked Pierre.

"You lack authority," remarked Dussouchel.

"Let him come to gradually," said Alice Phaye.

"I'm going, I'm going," said Sahul.

"I am not a tyrant," replied Pierre.

"I think he's opening his eyes," remarked Mademoiselle Phaye.

"So you're going to throw the cloud-chaser into the Pits," said Dussouchel.

"What's that?" asked Sahul.

"Are you getting water or not?" said Pierre.

"He's coming to," said Alice Phaye.

"You could say that he's coming to you," remarked Dussouchel.

"You're very objective," said Alice Phaye.

"We always practice a bit of psychology in our profession," responded Dussouchel.

"No need bothering about water now," Sahul remarked.

"Where am I?" asked Paul.

He shook himself. His slow gaze took in his supination, the ceiling and face hovering there, then he felt again the tender soft warmth and firmness of a thigh beneath his nape. And having identified these manifestations of the beloved, he fainted anew.

"Again," spoke Dussouchel.

"It's obvious," said Sahul, "that he's infatuated."

"Despite such disrespect," said Pierre, "you are still a good friend."

"Esscuses, esscuses," muttered Sahul.

He moved away, admiring the curve of Alice Phaye's knee, the smooth tucks of silk.

"Do I still have to get water?" he asked humbly, standing at the door.

"That would seem superfluous now," said Dussouchel.

"Esscuses, esscuses, but I'm only following my mayor's orders."

"Go on," said Pierre.

The door reclosed. It reopened. Sahul pointed his chin at Dussouchel and questioned his mayor.

"He said something about the cloud-chaser."

"I'll speak with you about that as well," said Pierre. "Go on now."

"Just tell me: Water or no water?"

"I'd be happy to give you an inscribed daguerrotype," said Alice Phaye.

"When, please?"

"You can come by and pick it up at the inn anytime tomorrow morning."

"I am most happy, and I thank you, oh how I thank you, Mademoiselle. But look now, he's opening his eyes again, and if he sees you first thing, as before, he may return immediately into the darkness, so it would be better for you to take a seat and let him become aware of you gradually."

Dussouchel and Pierre sat Paul in the protomunicipal chair. Alice Phaye moved to the left and a little behind. Since they'd done as he said, Sahul left.

Paul looked at the protomunicipal table with surprise. He looked at things immediately before him, and then around him a little though without turning his head much, so as not to come all at once upon Alice Phaye, whose perfume he had immediately perceived, added over and above, and far finer than, all the natural odors of Home Town.

He rose, shakily, to return the chair to his brother, who was solicitous of his attributes.

"Please, please," said Pierre, sitting at once and taking hold of his brother, then adding solemnly: "Paul, I have good news for you, incredible news, but first get hold of yourself, OK, so here it is: Mademoiselle Alice Phaye, the star of foreign cinema, happens to be within our walls, even better: she happens to be within these very four."

Turning towards her, he concluded his speech in the following manner: "Mademoiselle" (he bowed), "permit me to introduce my brother, Paul Nabonidus."

"Charmed, Mademoiselle," said Paul.

And he was.

Charmed.

She was so great a surprise, here at his side of all places, and giving every indication of wanting to talk. They set about doing so by turns, despite the audience. They agreed to meet again, then Alice Phaye left, accompanied by Dussouchel.

"He's charming, this young man," said the ethnographer, "and he seemed, as well, quite aware of the regard in which you're held. It's a matter that I've never studied closely, this cinematography. I will admit, however, that I never imagined the art had spread as far as a region like this one, so little like our own."

"My image," said Alice, "is universal."

"Widespread," Dussouchel let himself amend.

"Universal," insisted Alice. "What woman more than I?"

"A goddess," replied Dussouchel.

"Absolutely, and one who moves. Not some occult or symbolic manifestation that comes and goes, some frozen icon, but a fluid continuity."

"Form without matter."

"Form of light."

"And of shadow."

"These atoms of time filing past, they are me."

"And here the brother of the mayor's fallen in love with you."

"How deep his solitude must be."

"Relieved by the flickers of your lightning."

"I flabbergast him."

"You cause him to faint."

They drank a cocktail at the Hotel Cyclops.

"So tell me, dear Msieu," asked Mademoiselle Phaye. "Do you really go so seldom to the movies?"

They dined together. Simon Zober, still afflicted with dry rot, tossed and turned in his close, hot room. Alice sent up more fruit. Dussouchel, thoughtful, spoke little. Alice felt quite odd.

After drinking thcoffee, since thcoffee wouldn't help them sleep, neither one nor the other nor for that matter Simon Zober, they sat a while in silence.

Alice sighed.

"How very odd," she finally said. "I have the distinct impression that I've fallen in love."

"You don't say," stammered Dussouchel, jealousy gnawing at his inner organs.

Still, he hadn't any claim on Alice. He lived simply, and on the go. He repeated himself and said: "He seems quite struck by you."

"That's another thing entirely."

"Yes. You're going to see him again soon?"

"Yes. For the Promenade tonight along Important Boulevard. Come there with me?"

"Yes. And you still leave this afternoon?"

She looked at him.

"Yes."

They drank a small glass of trapu, an Urbinatalien liqueur with a base of cedar and hyssop.

People from every provenance swarmed about.

In this vigil before Saint Glinglin, digestions were heavy and slow, as though to prepare stomachs for the impending brouchtoucaille, and the human paste oozed, thicker than usual, along the promenades. They were all there, Urbinataliens of every sort, the large and the small, the notable and the humble, the good and the bad, the for and the against, the moderate and the ekstreme, the onez and the otherz, coming and going, talking and tsilent, and then there were Countryfolk, large and small, notable or humble, good or bad, for or against, moderate or ekstreme, onez or otherz, coming and going, talking and tsilent, and then Foreigners, large or small, notables mostly and not many humbles since H. T. was far away and coming here took many ganelons and turpins, good or bad, moderate or ekstreme, onez zor otherz, coming and going among Countryfolk and Urbinataliens who spoke among themselves saying Why there's the star Alice Phaye or So this is the first time you've seen Saint Glinglin, and those who stayed tsilent being tsnobs who'd seen Saint Glinglin many times but had nothing good to say.

Dussouchel drank several more glasses of trapu while Alice daydreamed. Then they went out, leaving Simon Zober to his whimpering. In a tender gesture owing as much to the trapu as his jealousy, no doubt, Dussouchel took Alice's arm. She made no move to pull away, accepting this pressure on biceps firm from eggzercise, a Holy Wood activity unknown in Home Town. Lamps shone in the acacias. From time to time they recognized people. But a few people whom they didn't recognize, recognized them.

They didn't recognize, for eggzample, Le Busoqueux, his wife and daughter, all out strolling together on this pre-Festival evening. But the tradesman recognized them. Speaking first in a low voice to his family, he then hailed the visitors in the foreign language:

"Mademoiselle Alice Phaye, is it not? Would you allow me to allow myself to request an autograph?"

He took from the inner pocket of his coat a daguerrotype of Alice, rather creased. She was represented thereupon by virtue of light's action on certain salts; and was represented clad in a velvet sheath, legs shiny in silk stockings, a jet black butterfly adorning her left thigh.

"Oh please, please," muttered the tradesman in the dimness. "Inscribeitome! Inscribeitome!"

"I'm most honored by your request," replied the star. "From whom do I have this honor?"

"Your servant Le Busoqueux, tradesman in this town, our Home Town."

"My name is Dussouchel," said Dussouchel, little by little letting Alice Phaye have her arm back. "I'm an essplorer."

"Charmed," said Le Busoqueux, though he wasn't.

Having pocketed the autographed 'type, he nodded to indicate the two women accompanying him. He introduced them. Dussouchel wavered between preserving his intimacy with Alice, which he knew would be short-lived since she was to see Paul Nabonidus again, and his professional desire to become familiar with the native, which is to say in this case Le Busoqueux, and his almost certain wealth of mores, folktales, gossip, superstitions, and dialects. Alice, for her part, wanted to go.

She did so.

Le Busoqueux chatted on, wholly taken with the ethnographer, unmindful of the star. He asked if Home Town this, if Home Town that, touched on all topics of conversation common to Tourists. The wife and daughter made ready to go. Dussouchel closely watched all their mannerisms and the faces they made. He would have preferred being with Alice, but by the time they parted, he had learned a great deal. He listened with a phonographic ear as the tradesman's conversation grew more and more confidential. He, the tradesman, could scarcely bear his role as errand boy for those ignorant of the foreign tongue, going on, going on, he grieved for the era of Grand Mayor Nabonidus, no more than a year past, this era, just a year, tomorrow it would be one: yes. This is the first time you've come here? My daughter, Eveline, almost married into the family. That's just between the two of us, mind you. Between notables. The grand Nabonidus had eyes for her. Isn't that right, little girl? That's not so bad. These things happen. Especially among notables. She was supposed to marry Pierre.

"Oh no, Father, Paul."

Dussouchel looked closely at the daughter. A fine specimen of Urbinatalien virgin, it seemed to him. He wanted very much to essplore her. Many legscellent folkloric details would emerge from this confrontation.

He rubbed against her, breathing sweet words, while the father and mother smiled crookedly, thinking about their daughter's imminent copulation with this Tourist who had such a knowing air.

As though nothing were going on, tradesman Le Busoqueux went on essplaining things. And while Dussouchel, in fervid darkness, ran his hand along Eveline's buttocks, he poured out to a distracted ear story after story of things notable Home Towners had done in the course of their lives. Le Busoqueux was content with his station. Pierre had never put his nose to the grindstone. He had no backbone, and made no secret of it. And Eveline was every bit as pliant. Dussouchel grew ever more interested in this child. But the parents, after all, were still right there on their heels. Then Le Bu began to complain at how the star had been so misunderstood. A heady erotism sprang up about them all, and wife Le Busoqueux rubbed her body coarsely against her spouse's, mewing into the horn of his ear.

One thing leading to another, they'd all got pretty worked up, the legal couple as much as the virgin-Tourist pair, when they came upon, as though they'd been waiting for them, a group of notables taking air and stretching their legs, beautiful evening, so-so, and a touch of fifrequet wouldn't be at all bad, and other such nonsense, idle talk and phonic jackasseries. While the Urbinataliens wiped palms one against the other, they kept a sidelong eye on the Tourist who had all at once such sure knowledge of what to do with his own hands. Le Busoqueux introduced the Foreigners, and there were again collations of hands, but the natives' eyes watched, suspicious, and tongues struck from palates only the briefest sparks of words.

"I," Dussouchel said finally (in order to practice his skills), "am delighted to take part tomorrow in a traditional Saint Glinglin."
"Why wouldn't it be traditional?" asked Saimpier. "It's always that: traditional."
"We'll see," said carelessly simultaneously Choumaque.
"What do you mean by that?" Dussouchel hastened to ask with the Machiavellianism of the scientific investigator.
"Nothing."
And Choumaque shut up.
"There's . . . some question of change?" Dussouchel suggested, relishing his shrewdness.
"Who told you that?" asked Saimpier.
"Some people I met here."
"Where here?"
"In a tavern."
"That doesn't surprise me then," essploded Le Busoqueux. "There's nothing you won't hear in those foul places. But why on earth would you go there?"
Dussouchel drew back from his rudeness and replied weakly: "I'd been told to be sure to try the fifrequet from the year when Yves-Albert Tranath won the Grand Prize of Springtime."
"I have better," said Le Bu.
"I wasn't invited."
"Come and drain a bottle."
"Fine idea," said Saimpier.
Dussouchel hesitated. Obviously, being received as an equal wasn't common for a Tourist, still less for an ethnographer. What's more, thanks to this drinking bout he would be able to pursue his quest for Eveline, who now followed along discreetly, behind her father. But he was concerned about Alice Phaye. He tergiversated.
Saimpier insisted, though in a disinterested fashion since he was pretty much never invited along by the tradesman anyway. Le Buso set up a fierce clamor for fluids. Choumaque and Zostril stammered nonsignificantly. And so they came to a small square clotted with people. Dussouchel looked all around, casually, with a sweeping, inquisitive glance one develops only after numerous voyages to remote regions, and saw Alice Phaye nowhere.
He accepted the offer of fifrequet then and posted himself as close as possible to Eveline. He even managed to get her alone, thanks first of all to his own cunning, thanks then to the girl's, and

thanks thirdly to the complicity of the notables, although they didn't here practice the ritual prostitution of female offspring.

"It's known that you were with the mayor at noon," whispered Eveline.

"After lunch," corrected the Tourist, admiring her iambs, poetic esspression being little known or employed among Urbinatalien virgins.

"I'm going to marry him," Eveline continued. "You saw him?"

"It will make you happy to be mayoress?"

"That doesn't matter," Eveline replied. "He's determined to have me part of that family. I don't much like it."

"Why then?"

"Family history. The paternal" (with the point of her chin, which was graceful, she indicated Le Bu) "thinks only of his money. I don't understand it, but he seems bound to the Nabonidus family somehow. He imagines things, I think. In any case, here I am, one might as well say engaged."

She laughed.

This one wants to be someone, mused Dussouchel, she'll make a place for herself. That kind of thing didn't interest him at all. Before Le Busoqueux's door, he gave up.

And took his leave.

That Tourists were for the most part louts was well known, of course, at least in principle. Which essplained this retreat.

Dussouchel plunged back into the current of gyratory Urbinataliens. He looked, from time to time, to the right, to the left, towards ill-lit, out-of-the-way paths where shadow struggled circumspectly with shadow, but he did not see Alice among them Phaye.

The Roundabout just wasn't much of a bike trail, the ethno told himself. More and more he took to small roads. To the right, to the left, he found them, in the night, amorous. They didn't lack, at any rate, for those who put their hands under skirts and those who let them. But no Alice anywhere. Flashes of bare Urbinatalien leg couldn't arouse Dussouchel. Perhaps those of Eveline, which wouldn't be bad, might have moved him. But now he sought only Alice, not that he ekspected she'd ever reveal herself to him with butterflies on thighs of black silk, and he realized plainly, all too plainly, that he had lost his scientific objectivity.

At the corner of a wall walling in a thickening thicket, Dussouchel ran into two drunks who said Ah in unison, there's the 'bout, namely Paracole and Catogan.

He regarded them disinterestedly, judging they'd contribute little
to his folkloric researches, for one thing; or to his search for Phaye,
for a second. Well fifrequeted, they uttered a series of Ah, ahs that
left Dussouchel illitease despite his being used to natives.

"Ah! ah!" Paracole finally got out, "it's him."

"Him," said Catogan.

"The one who comes to have a Saint Glinglin."

"According to the old tradition."

"He's been taken in."

In unison: "Right?"

Taking courage in hand, Dussou inquired: "And why is that?"

Paracole guffawed: "You don't know!"

"So it would seem," guffawed Catogan.

"He knows more than we do."

"You're telling me!"

"Because the other told him."

"Because," said Catogan.

And Paracole completed: "It's known that you were with the
mayor at noon."

Dussouchel was irritated: "Wrong, wrong. I heard that earlier.
And I told them then, I tell you now, that it was afternoon."

Taking no account of this rather abstract point, Paracole asked:
"What did he tell you? He's given you a preview of the changes,
right?"

"I'm serious," grumbled Dussouchel.

For this he received a formidable, forceful kick in the butt. He
rubbed at the seat of his pants and muttered politely: "It's still Saint
Glinglin, all the same."

With a feeble laugh.

He turned around, saw Quéfasse.

Paracole and Catogan laughed themselves nearly to death.

The Urbinataliens were fascinated. Tourists were always fair
game, of course, but one held off pushing it too far, fearing censure
from Quéfasse and, thereby, Mayor Pierre's disfavor. But this didn't
prevent Dussouchel's receiving a second, then a third, kick in the
rhere: the second from Paracole, the third from Catogan. Dussouchel
endured with courage these initial phases of Urbinatalien intimacy,
which he had seen described in the Guide as not uncommon.

"So tell us, then," guffawed Paracole.

"And tell us now," added Catogan with spirit.

Quéfasse greatly wanted to let loose another boot at his buttocks, but the Foreigner was turned towards him and a foot in the stomach just wasn't proper. So he had to content himself with hawking up a glob of spit and depositing it on the visitor's shoulder.

"This is all," said Dussouchel with tact, "of the utmost interest to me."

"You don't say," said Quéfasse.

He hawked up a second time. It was a little less green than the first.

Dussouchel reminded himself of, invoking the necessary ardent faith in, his mission. He said: "These customs. . . ."

"Which are to be overthrown tomorrow," suggested Paracole.

"As you know," growled Catogan.

"Yes," said Quéfasse, "it's known that you were with the mayor at noon."

"No!" essploded Dussouchel. "No! Not before two! Not before two! I don't want such a story to get around."

"It's around already," replied Quéfasse.

"Yes, yes," said Paracole and Catogan, "it's around! it's around!"

They turned to those gathered nearby.

"Isn't it around?"

"Yes, yes," responded the others.

And, stepping towards Dussouchel, he spoke through his nose: "It's known that you were with the mayor at noon!"

Machut, Marqueux, and Mandace passed by, accompanied by their countessparts. Paracole and Catogan fell upon them to enlist their support. At first they demurred, but after all, it was only over the matter of a story, and a story well established, at that. They assented.

Dussouchel picked out Mandace the importer, since it seemed he might be more apt to understand foreign thinking, and said to him amiably: "I'm really growing rather annoyed! Over and over I've repeated to them that it wasn't until the afternoon that I saw Meussieu Pierre Nabonidus, and they keep insisting it was at noon."

"Because that's the story," responded Mandace.

"I couldn't care less about the story," Dussouchel replied. "But what of the truth?"

"It's known," said Mandace, "that you were with the mayor at noon."

A dense circle surrounded the Tourist. Bonjean stepped from among them. He was, also, equally, likewise, well fifrequeted.

"What's he want, this one?" he asked.

"Respect for Tourists," responded Mandace with his own interests in mind.

Bonjean looked Dussouchel over with a sparkling eye, essence of fifrequet flaring, for a moment, in the cornea. He shrugged his shoulders, let them fall back into place, then said to the object of public attention: "It's known that you were with the mayor at noon."

Dussouchel despaired. He opened his mouth several times in a row without emitting a sound, then bleated in a false, wild voice, the phrase spreading out from him in sonorous waves through the close atmosphere of this Festival Eve: "Have you no respect at all for the Tourists who wash up on your shore?"

One did have to wonder about that.

He repeated: "I persist in repeating to you that I went there closer to three."

"And he said to you?" Bonjean asked.

"And he said to you?" echoed the others.

"That there would be changes?"

"That there would be changes?" parroted the same.

The circle was dense with human flesh and apparel. The moon and streetlamps shone. Everyone was silent, awaiting his response. Dussouchel awaited, like the others, his response. An infant rent the circle. An infant, not a young man, little more than a baby. He had no understanding of the situation. He broke through the gaping ring only in order to speak to his father, Bonjean. This he did. He said to him:

"Oh ppa, ppa, Msieu Paul, do you know what he said? Iputmyhandonthestarsass! Yeth, ppa. Iputmyhandonthestarsass! Jush likh hi toldh youh."

"He's right," responded his father.

"If the occasion arose," said Paracole, "I wouldn't deprive myself."

"As far as that's concerned," said Catogan, "I'd prefer Virginia Flute, who's quite a bit younger."

The public dispersed, everyone talking idly of the cinematograph and its moving spirits. Dussouchel realized that he was no longer the center of attention, though neither moon nor streetlamp had stopped shining on his jacket. He stepped lightly to Robert's side and in his ear slipped these words: "Where is she?"

Robert watched him with a scientific eye, sealed lips.

Dussouchel became ankshus. He pushed ten ganelons into the other's hand. The boy's mouth opened: "Bear left on the narrow steep road along the old rampart until you come to the fence that surrounds the gravel that surrounds the Pits and on the right there's a bench and on this bench are sitting Msieu Paul and the star: a pretty sight, Meussieu, especially if you don't look too close."

"Now," said Quéfasse, "what I've never understood about the cinematograph is how they can haul a whole ocean up there behind the screen but no one ever gets soaked, at least to my knowledge."

"It's a mystery," Paracole said.

Dussouchel vanished, while Robert put away his informant's money. Night enveloped the small road, lamps were infrequent, and the Tourist walked slowly with his arms out before him. Despite his fervid desire to find the star, he took care not to bash his face in. He proceeded by small, measured steps, like one who has diarrhea. Then he caught sight of a red light: this was attached to the door of the fence that surrounded the gravel that surrounded the Pits. There were in fact two benches. His walk more assured, still Dussouchel held back in order to remain silent, and still he took small, measured steps, like those of one who has the grippe. On one of the benches, a man and woman embraced; they kissed, the man with one hand beneath the woman's skirt. This intrigued him, and he thought again of the young man's remarks: certain words took on new meaning, or else the circumstances of the lovers had changed. He stood still and watched.

Someone came up beside him. Dussouchel hadn't heard this someone. He turned towards him. And recognized the young mayor, who said to him in a low voice: "Don't you find this disgusting?"

"This fence?" replied Dussouchel appropriately.

"What can one do? What can one do?" Pierre asked with passion.

Dussouchel looked at him, a bit apart from all this. Pierre took on a studious, stubborn air. He declared: "Tomorrow, I'll make it rain, I'll make it rain."

"Finding myself in your confidence," said Dussouchel, "has occasioned considerable humiliation."

"Of course. This is just the beginning." He gestured broadly towards the lovers: "And that?"

"Esscuse me?" asked Dussouchel.

"That."

"Hm," spoke Dussouchel.

"All that's left is for me to marry them," Pierre said.

The lovers suddenly roused and separated. They looked at the two night watchmen.

Pierre approached them: "In the name," said he, "of the powers conferred upon me, I pronounce you to be reckoning from this moment henceforth partners in marriage."

"Well," cried Mademoiselle Phaye heartily, "that goes quite a bit quicker here than in Holy Wood."

"Pierre!" cried Paul.

"What a story!" cried Dussouchel.

"It's done, it's done," said Alice.

And she threw herself into Paul's arms. They embraced, and at once and anew he slid a hand beneath her skirt.

The two night watchmen moved away, having turned around.

"What a story," muttered Dussouchel, "what a story."

"Oh," said Pierre lightly, "you know, a lot of marriages start like that. Not bad at all, not at all."

As they passed beneath the light, Dussouchel turned his head to egzamine his associate. Pierre had to be about twenty-five.

"True," said Dussouchel.

"And there's one taken care of, at least," declared Pierre. He went on more seriously: "Perhaps you don't know that I have another brother?"

Dussouchel looked discreetly behind him, but already lamp, bench, and newlyweds had been swallowed by shadow. "No, no," he stammered. "Yes. In fact. . . ."

"And a sister."

"Oh."

"You don't hear well?" asked Pierre with solicitude.

He peered at him out of the corner of his eye. This was a Tourist, one of the people who, away from here, became Foreigners, one of those who spoke gobbledegook and gibberish and raised cave-dwelling fish, but he was also a man of science, just like himself who in Foreign Town had observed with the impartiality of the ray the larval development of cave-dwelling amblyopia.

"Are you ekcited?"

"Me? Me. Oh! No."

"Nevertheless, you find yourself here at an historic moment. Tomorrow, the cloud-chaser will be thrown in there."

He indicated the gloom, behind his shoulder, with his thumb.

"And then?" Dussouchel asked distractedly.

"It will rain."

"Really? You think so?"

Dussouchel was distraught, although it was true that in all the annals of science there wasn't a single case of an ethnographer marrying an actress from the cinematograph. Still, there was a first time for everything. A first cockroach, for egzample, a first bird, a first mammal; why not a first himself? One consoles oneself and life goes on, it just goes on, continuing. One responds distractedly. One walks through crowds. One takes leave of notables with vasophosphorescent words of servile civility. One goes about masked, pretending. One goes more or less to sleep. The café begins to darken out of the dawn. One wakes. The brass band makes a tour of the town playing "Cloud-Conqueror." One stays in a Tourist's bed, eyes closed, while people, native, rural or otherwise, begin ekserting themselves. One yawns. The café finally emerges, managed by a busty, big-bottomed girl. Dussouchel watches her, disillusioned. As he laps up his coughee, she goes on about her business of bowls and breads. The brass band goes by again and Home Town's traditional anthem hasn't stopped being in B-flat minor.

The star's key hung on the board. Gone out quite early or not come home at all, who could say; Dussouchel went into the closest bistro to dispatch a glass or two of fifrequet. He had difficulty finding a seat. His neighbors were commenting on current events. They fell silent when he sat beside them, aimed there by a waiter. Dussouchel drank his fifrequet. The others cautiously resumed conversation.

"Fine weather," said one of them without conviction, ekstinguishing a match in a small pool of fifrequet.

He drew on his pipe, tobacco crackling.

Another stroked at his beard and said, before gulping down his small glass of fifrequet: "It's curious how on Festival days one gets thirsty early."

The third smoothed his mustache and, putting his glass down empty, affirmed that what one drank on Saint Glinglin's Day was better than it was the rest of the year.

"It has more taste," he affirmed.

They turned towards Dussouchel, to engage him in conversation. Dussouchel, neglecting his scientific duty, was daydreaming.

Choumaque, after having coughed, repeated: "It has more taste."

They all three looked at the Tourist. And he turned towards them.

"It's," he said to them, "true I was with him yesterday at noon, your mayor."

Zostril, Saimpier, and Choumaque started violently at this ekstraordinary eksample of mind-reading. They began to think a bit higher of Dussouchel, who continued in these words:
"So: there will be changes, today, right?"
"Changes in what?" asked Choumaque.
"Changes," responded Dussouchel.
The notables ekschanged glances, raising their eyebrows.
"You know all about it then," whispered Zostril.
"Eh eh," spoke Dussouchel, trying to amuse himself.
One had to be wary of these ethnographers and folklorists. Saimpier cross-eksamined him:
"You were spit on last night," he said in an assertive interrogation.
"I don't confirm it," said Choumaque.
"But it's a fact," said Zostril.
"Your mayor isn't much liked by the population," rejoined Dussouchel.
"Nor are Tourists," added Saimpier.
"In any case," said Dussouchel, "there will be changes today."
He looked at them fearlessly. They shuddered.
"You sense nothing in the air?" he asked them.
"No," they responded, looking like rabbits.
Then they turned away from him to speak among themselves concerning their dishware.
"I'm sinking fifteen thousand turpins into it this year," said Zostril. "All of it fine porcelain."
"Then you'll be sure to retain your standing," said Saimpier, bitter and envious.
Tinware was doing no better this year than others.
"I've pledged three thousand teacups," he said.
Choumaque whistled in admiration.
"Well, I've managed a hundred. That's enough for me. Things are different now," said Saimpier hypocritically.
"What things?" asked Choumaque precautiously.
"Old things. People no longer feel driven to contribute to the success of this or that festival, if you know what I mean."
They turned anew towards Dussouchel, who didn't flinch, then back to themselves.
"What is *he* displaying?" asked Choumaque.
"Guess?" replied Zostril, always well informed.
"You know, do you?"
They leaned towards him.

"Fishbowls and aquariums," replied Zostril. "Empty ones."

"A-ha," uttered the others.

"Mandace's the one who got them for him," added Zostril. "Had them brought over specially from Foreign Town."

"That's not dishware," remarked Saimpier forthwith.

"Certainly not," agreed Zostril. "But according to him, if it's not man's dishware, then it's fish's."

Choumaque seemed to accept this argument. But Saimpier, cantankerous: "All the same it's not the fish who are going to break it for him."

This objection seemed well-founded. But Dussouchel, good-naturedly: "One never knows."

They turned, the three of them, towards him, all together.

"What changes?" Saimpier asked sharply. "What changes, for the last time."

"Aah," uttered suddenly someone situated on the terrace.

Hippolyte rushed over, face red and clenched. This was a poor client, one who didn't even have the right to a name in Home Town.

"Now what?" said the innkeeper. "My fifrequet not good?"

Hippolyte hadn't intimidated the client, who said again: "Aaah!"

"After all," said Hippolyte, "it's last year's vintage: when Bonjean won the Grand Prize of Springtime."

Everyone stood up. They looked at the one who was going aah. No one knew him. He was only a number, the syllabic-alphabetic registration number he'd been assigned. Still, this didn't prevent him from going aaah and everyone looking at him and Hippolyte becoming annoyed because he always claimed to have good merchandise, even the best.

Then this personage, who was still known to the watchers only as another customer, without having been identified, which is to say without being known as the one who had gone aaah, then he uttered one more time:

"Aaah."

And e raised is hand and pointd a finger to sumthing in thsky

Everyone looked up.

And they saw in the sky all blue

a cloud

a small cloud

a very small cloud

very small but rather dark.

And all those who saw it also went aaah.
And everyone rushed into the street.
And all the people in the street went aaah.
Even Dussouchel went aaah.
Just off to one side, close to the first, another could be seen, no larger, also dark. This was to the left. And two seconds later, a third came into view, a cloud, still no larger, likewise dark, but to the right this time. And then they seemed all at once to double, to become siks, bridging west to east. No one went aaah any longer. Then there were twelve, some of them much darker, all the more reason for interjective esspression. Clouds, a multitude of clouds, and noon approaching, noon approaching. Now there were twenty-four. And now there were forty-eight. And now there were ninety-siks. And now there were a hundred and ninety-two, an outright blackness. And so, a little after, there were three hundred eighty-four. And shortly three times the eighth power of two. Then, there were less, as the clouds started to aggregate, to coagulate, to harden. This celestial mayonnaise fermented and turned grey, grew purple and heavy. The site of Urbinatalien ceremonies was besmudged from horizon to horizon, and at the first stroke of noon it began to rain like cows pissing.

Sahul sighed. The water in its abundance had burst its bladder, and not a hope that it would lighten. Quéfasse laughed softly. Dussouchel was keenly interested. And now people were getting soaked. The twelfth stroke of noon sounded, the signal point, but no one knew what to do any longer, they stood dazed, afraid to begin. A few timidly broke a saucer or two. But that was all.

"It's raining," Zostril remarked, shaking himself.

"As far as changes go, this is definitely a change," Choumaque declared bitterly.

"Indeed," said Saimpier, attempting to follow from afar the trajectory of an individual drop.

His regard abandoned it to a puddle. But returned to the sky and its striations.

"You're going to get soaked," Dussouchel pointed out calmly.

He had brought an umbrella along with him in his luggage, not believing the legends.

"He told you about this," murmured Zostril.

"Yes," said Dussouchel. "He's thrown it into the Pits."

"What does Sahul think of all this?" asked Saimpier.

"One never knows," said Choumaque.

"And he wasn't there," remarked Zostril.

Before the display of fishless aquariums and goldfish bowls was the mayor's, Pierre's, station.

"Oh no," went Choumaque, "he's not there."

"Oh no," went Saimpier, "he's not there."

And everyone went "Oh no," adding: "He's not there."

People looked toward the town hall. Eyes which until then, since noon, had taken in nothing but the mounting wetness now settled on the statue there in the passageway, and everyone started going ah, ah, ah, for the statue was dissolving.

Dussouchel, fascinated by this local divinity, observed with some passion the process of dissolution. Mineral layers wearing away and no longer giving protection, they ceased suddenly to be, and the cadaver collapsed in a heap, decomposing suddenly, powerfully.

People cried out.

Pierre was seen gazing out from a window of his residence at the collapse of legends.

They howled.

Although water poured into their open mouths, they stood gaping. It didn't matter.

Nabonidus here lay, small, on a petty dais, and still quite dead, although without his crust now and quite green in the bargain. Some moved towards what was left and, courageously loading it onto a stretcher, courageously carried it towards the mayor. Others followed them.

Dussouchel followed them.

He hurried, but the notables got ahead of him all the same. And Dussouchel, swept up by them, found himself before Pierre, in his office. There were Le Busoqueux, Zostril, Saimpier, Choumaque. And Sahul, discomfited.

They looked on, in total silence.

"Very well," said Pierre. "You see: it rains."

"We see, we see," said the others, grimacing.

The door was open. The crowd paused there, stewing. It parted for the stretcher-bearers who deposited Nabonidus's corpse in the middle of the room, then withdrew respectfully, submerging themselves in the crowd.

"Well?" asked Pierre.

"It's decomposing now," responded Zostril.

"Another myth lost," remarked Dussouchel.

"You!" essclaimed Le Busoqueux.

He looked full of contempt.

"Monsieur is here by chance," declared Pierre. "The idea was mine."

"Neverthe," said Saimpier, "less, if you haven't been in Foreign Town, you would never have conceived this idea."

Choumaque with a broad gesture indicated something beyond the window.

"And your aquariums, your fishbowls," he asked. "Do you believe they'll fill themselves with fish? No."

"Not yet," replied Pierre.

"Rubbish," said Le Busoqueux.

"What?"

And Pierre frowned. "Am I not the mayor?"

"Only until it rains," said Le Busoqueux. "When it rains, there must be a change. It's our law."

Dussouchel took a notebook from his pocket to inscribe therein this practice, for the tradesman certainly seemed to know his stuff.

"Is that true?" Pierre asked the others.

The three notables signaled yes, and the crowd ratified with a murmur.

"So? Must I renounce?"

"And what's more," continued Le Busoqueux, "we must escort you from the town with great kicks in the butt."

Dussouchel went on taking notes.

"And who will be the new mayor?"

"It will have to be your brother Paul."

Dussouchel scribbled, scribbled, scribbled.

"I've wed him to a Foreigner."

There was great consternation. The notables deliberated, looking at one another.

"It can't be helped," Le Bu said finally.

Pierre paused a moment.

Then he started towards the waiting crowd. "Very well, then. Have it your way."

He took the necessary number of steps and disappeared.

Le Bu turned towards Dussouchel. "You," he said to him, "you'd do well to go too."

Dussouchel closed his notebook and pocketed it.

6

Foreigners

I never cried. Did they cry, my companions? They went on about their tiny lives like my own in silence in silence. Now and again they shook off their inactivity. Crept. Leapt. But they never cried about that. And then I didn't creep. I didn't leap. Hélène leaps. I found her beneath abandoned, moist spiderwebs. She was the smallest of all. There would have to be ten thousand of her to make a flea. A hundred thousand maybe. It hurt me to see her. She isn't white, she's the color of pale ash. She is blind. And she leaps. It's all she can do. I've never seen her eat. I've never seen her near a male. But from time to time, she leaps. She doesn't go far. Then all at once she stops. She looks drained. Mortally drained. But before too long her liveliness comes back. And she springs a step or two towards new fatigue. Towards new impossibility.

The storm is the largest of the insects flying outside. It knocks against the windowpane like the others. If the window is open, it comes right in. They cling sometimes to the windowpane to smoothe their wings, to cool or warm their bellies. They watch me. They never cry either, or at least their voices don't penetrate the thick glass. And this glass is so small. A peephole. I climb up on a chair sometimes to watch the fliers. But it's too much for me. I leave those agitated and return to my silent, my peaceful. To my dirty-dusty. To my larvae, to my pupae. To those sleeping in their whitish coats, to those awakening in such absurdities. To those who wrap themselves to live, to sleep, to dream perhaps.

Large insects. Tiny animals. All together. Scraping at the night. Small feet. Large wings. Rustling. Understanding the night. The hut has their odor. They are aware, the tiny beasts. They stir. Worms. Larvae. I watch the caterpillars. How they plait themselves into their cocoons. Coffee beans. Later they stir. Eloquent. Tiny animals. Worms. Some of them without feet. Others with feet. Some who glisten. Others who scrape when they move. Small feet. Large wings. Bodies sticky or hard. Rustling. Understanding the night. A fragment of moon. A worm sliding over the straw. I call him Jean. Gentle. Small, small. My companion. Now we sing a little. A fragment of the moon on straw. Silvery trail, breath of the night. Small, small Janot, little Janot. Ah he stops. He raises his little head. Little worm head. Little worm eyes. Nearsighted. Can't see well. He sways his little worm head. He watches with his little worm eyes. He is looking for me. Little little. He loves the moon's light. It makes him happy. The other insects sleep. Save in corners over there. In corners over there the cockroaches stir. Brawls. Cockroach squabbles. Jean seems not to hear them. Unholy roaches. He changes direction. He comes back towards me. Little little. Little worm. Little worm. Look at the moon. Look at me. It is beautiful and I am young. It is fair and I am cold. Sing for us Jean. Sing for me. He sways his head. His little worm head. He lifts it, tips it. From right to left. It looks as though he's about to sing. Silver sky. Rain of straw. Jean starts to sing.

And as Jean sings, Paul begins dancing. It makes a fine show. Paul rears onto his back feet. Hop hop he jumps. Hop hop he skips. Pow he falls down. Brave Paul. He gets back up. Hop hop he skips anew. Hop an entrechat. Hop another. Jean is singing. He accompanies him. Jean has a little voice clear as a whistle. Quicksilver he sings. Hop hop Paul. Another entrechat. He springs. He dances on the tips of his toes. Tourné. Jeté. What a repertoire, Paul. What a repertoire, Paul. You spring well, isopod. How well you entrechat, crustacean. Later the Foreigners will dance too. Some will leap. Those who have not crowded together in closed cartons where all together they make loud noise with their hands. Striking one against the other. From time to time. And others fidget. Paul, what a show. He never repeats himself. Jean sings along, the little nightingale. It is very calm. Save in cockroach corner where they go on squabbling. Paul the woodlouse continues to dance in the moonlight. Dear dear light to me, dear dear little woodlice. The worm is silent. It spits a little. The song has tired it. A drop of saliva punctuated by a thread of blood stains the straw. Paul falls back onto all fours. He goes to check on the chanting pearl. He tosses his head. I scratch the back of his carapace gently with the nail of my forefinger which is so long and so dark. The worm lies down, stretches itself out, goes to sleep. They put these things one atop another. To sleep on. The Foreigners. And they wrap themselves as well. Before. After. Then they get covered up. And they're not seen again. That is after. Before, I don't know. How still Jean lies there. I lie down myself on the straw. I stretch out and I sleep. The sky's scissors cuts out my shadow on the floor of my cell. My cell. There are those who squeal without singing. Without accompaniment. Before. This afternoon he gave me a pair of silk stockings. I walked in the mud with them. No moon. An aquarium without water. Insects tinier than ants glittered like glowworms. Their light is yellow. I washed my stockings in the lav. I walked barefoot on the straw. I walked barefoot in my clogs. I'd had cotton stockings, coarse white and torn, rolled beneath the knee. I marched barefoot on the barren rocks. He bought me a pair of silk stockings. I dragged them through the mud. I washed them tonight in the lav. The dark water left deposits in the bowl on its marble sides and the liquid went down gobbling.

The cockroaches. They are used to pastes like that. Nice and warm. Their things along their sides. Wings. They push their way into it. Remember it. They've come out now. Like me in my cell. Jean sleeps drained. A little whitish. I hung my legs on a rope at the window and they started to sway in the night's breath. Coals shining at one side of the carton went out and two embers gleamed in the dark. I cut out my place in the night. He made me go elsewhere, in our carton. He closed the window. He said the two embers will go out also. Jean sleeps. Paul walks the straw.

He slides down a stalk of wheat. He is going home. I know where he lives. Between what stones. Paul is going home. Into the wall of the house. Every wall in the house is inhabited. Without. Within. Inside. Outside. Spiders go up and down. At the ends of their fila- ments. They are considered savage. I know they are gentle. Here is one looking to pounce on Paul. She will put him in a little cocoon that she hoists up to her house. But I am here. I will stop her. She will be a little hungrier. She will not want me. And always the squab- bling cockroaches in the corner. The fragment of moon moves slowly. But no. The spider takes no interest in Paul. Paul goes on his way. He did not see the danger. Calm little woodlouse. The spider goes back to playing its guitar. Paul lifts a tiny stone. Then he wipes his forehead. It is so heavy. But he is home. Goes in. Good night.

The tiny stone falls back. He can sleep now. I get up. The sky is broken into lamellae and dawn's antennae sweep the horizon. I never cried. Never. A step. A step. A step. Door open. An enormous beast enters. A colossal dung beetle. A female rolling her pellet. This is its feeding trough. My bowl. For me. Soup. Cooked fat. Scraps. Peelings. Remains. And water. Water so pure. So lively. So precious. And packed mud. I make pellets of it. For me. Paul. Jean. Pierre. They do not eat it. Pierre was married this morning. The monster is already gone. It did not speak to me. It does not speak to me. I know the others better. It dresses like me. But it has hair completely grey. It gets angry, finds my little white rinds and scatters them on the floor. The others fall upon them. Those on the ground. The female monster knows nothing of it. Sometimes for treating those on the ground, I am angry at her. I want to go out, sometimes. I want to dance. I want to claw. I want to spit. But I never cried. Never. The pellicles fall to the ground. She disappears. So the little people feast. And me. I dig in my bowl. I roll up my pellets. I drink my water. In a corner there is a pail where I relieve myself. The huge beetle takes it by the handle. From time to time. And upturns it outdoors. There are beasts who make every sort of noise. I listen. I hear. I never cried.

I have known Pierre for a very long time. I listen to the days. The nights. Which sparkle. And dissolve. Pierre disappears. He comes back. He is many. He was married this morning. He lives under a flat stone which is there. I saw him born. Wretched. Clumsy. He was many. He had wings. Properly brown. A happy companion. A gay cavalier. Always hale and hearty. He trots trots nose to the ground. He comes up and eats from my hand. He has pretty little jaws furnished with horns. Like tiny thorns. He loves the stuff in the bowl. Likes everything. But not the sun so much. He comes to see me at twilight. He comes out from under his flat stone. He turns his head from right to left. He shakes himself. Then he comes running to me, so happy. He was married this morning, at dawn. Before the sun sent forth its cry. I never cried.

They all get married. Even the blind. Even the very blind. Even the very white. Even the very larval. Even the very sticky. They all have betrothed. And nuptials. And lots of noisy brats. I never married. There is not another like me. The old one who feeds me is like me of course. But she is female. I can see that. Male. Female. And I am not male. When we came here among the Foreigners, they laughed. They chased after us. They threw stones at us. We hid ourselves. At night they slept. But not so fiercely as a woodlouse in the middle of day under its stone. We tried to get past them. They awoke. They awoke. They started to laugh and throw stones at us. And we ran and we hid ourselves. The old dung beetle stopped near my cell. I was there too. We fled and ran and hid ourselves. But he finally learned. So we were left alone.

To live among the Foreigners, it is necessary to coat oneself with identity. A sticky substance. Messy. Indelible. The coating is done with documents. They call them papers of identity. There are Foreigners who believe the world is made up of this substance paper and have raised it to the level of essence. The Foreigners have other papers as well. For another substance. But they don't preserve this. They throw it away. There are Foreigners who believe that the world is made up of this other substance. But those are few in number. All these papers are of the same sort. For identity as for the other. One dares not confuse them. On those of identity, a face, considerably smaller, is glued. This is called falstography. The real face remains in place thanks to the sticky nature of identity. The Foreigners also take falstographs of fingers. They are very pretty. Elegant as spiderwebs. Last, flytracks beneath the falstography give the name. So then one can circulate among the Foreigners.

One isn't able yet to circulate among the Foreigners. I was given my identity and health papers. It was necessary to give him still other papers decorated with figures. With numbers. These are changed into something else. Whatever one wants. Or close to what one wants. That depends. These are property papers. There are Foreigners who believe that property is the one substance of which the world is made and have raised it to the level of essence. They debate whether the highest essence is that of identity or property. All these papers are passed back and forth among them. The property papers are necessary to get the health papers and identity papers. For the health paper we have to have a few property papers and the identity papers. The property papers are called bank knowits. They can be transformed into other things. Immediately. Hand over a bank knowit and you get an apple. Hand over a bank knowit and you get a glass of water. Hand over a bank knowit and you get a piece of bread. But it depends on where you are. He understands this. He understood immediately. Some Foreigners can transform things into other things or into nothing. Immediately. They are called magicians. The bank knowits can also be transformed into nothing. But the Foreigners themselves are not transformed. They are not caterpillars or chrysalises. They only change. And when this happens they are wrapped in a huge white bedsheet forever. What happens then no one knows. They never reappear. Or seldom. The Foreigners debate this. They talk about it. He talked with them. I never talked with them.

The Foreigners live in cartons. Cartons set alongside one another form an apartment. Cartons placed one atop another constitute a house. Openings are made so that the habitants, cold, and rain can get in. Covers of an opaque substance accomplish the sorting of a carton's habitants, provided the covers are themselves bored with a hole called a keyhole. There are different kinds of cartons. Generally the Foreigners marry in the one where they sleep and vice versa. It is rare for them to marry in a carton with another purpose, for instance the kitchen (this last carton is used to put away smaller cartons: cartons of preserves, cartons of polish, cartons of radishes). There are cartons they fill more or less with water, called bathrooms. These last are rare. Foreigners who do not have them are called the poor. The others are called the rich. One does not often see rich and poor living in the same pile of cartons. Sometimes a family of the rich complements itself with a feminine person of the poor type. Then this one sleeps in a special carton hooked on under the roof.

People who are wrapped in sheets to be kept out of circulation are put into cartons that are buried. Two cartons placed side by side and whose common wall is removed is called a theater. In the carton to the left are crammed spectators, in the one to the right, actors. Spectators are people who get together to make noise slapping their hands one against the other. Actors are people who speak between themselves in loud voices during the intervals of silence the spectators allow them. Between cartons of great size intended for people and small cartons intended for substances, there are small cartons intended for people called prisons and great cartons intended for substances called reservoirs. Cartons of intermediate dimension are designated furniture, most furnitures are grossly distorted cartons. A table is a carton set onto four feet. The chair was formerly a small reservoir complemented by a back; the container part having disappeared, as with the table, it is supported on four feet. The comb represents the last vestige of a defunct species: the fish-bone carton. Some round cartons contain polish; others, fragments of time. A small piece of time cut off from the world, locked into a prisonette, made to go around in circles like a squirrel. Foreigners put blades on the shaft and thereby cut time into precise pieces. But sometimes the small timepiece wastes away and dies. It is carried then to the gates of the town, to the small markets full of fleas, and let go. Cylindrical cartons contain substances which sometimes impede sleep and sometimes invite it. Cubical cartons when given to children are decorated with tracings the Foreigners call letters; when given to adults, with small circles whose number never surpasses half a dozen. Foreigners shake and roll them, counting the circles that come up on their cubical cartons. On spherical cartons Foreigners prick innumerable tiny circles, which they call stars, or else spread them with colored patches, which they call land and sea. Oval cartons contain a semen which hardens with cooking, with at the center an eye with no pupil. You have to break them to discover this, then eat it. In cartons whose empty face is replaced by a curtain, one rolls human beings into absolute flatness and unrolls them through a hole onto phosphorescent cloth. For a long time, this operation deprived actors of their speech without taking away their mobility. Recent progresses in Foreign surgery have returned this to them. Some Foreigners want to restore to them their size as well, but other Foreigners ask: then why bother with the rolling and unrolling at all?

Some feminine personages so rolled and unrolled receive wonderful tribute. Pinned to the wall they stir many messieurs to marry with them, but always at a distance. Foreigners also cultivate many feminine representations which are not rolled and unrolled, though deprived for all time of their mobility; they are called dolls. There are three types: giant (or above average), life-size, and small. These last are reserved for children, the second for adults, the first for communities. There are even supergiants. These are very rare. Foreigners can cite only two. One stands all alone holding a torch on a small island, the other comprises a frame of steel trelliswork and stands on four wide-planted feet; it is very tall and elegant and waves antennae. The giant (or above average) dolls are encountered in town squares or public gardens. If they are nude, their pubis is presented cleanshaven. If they are dressed, their clothes are made of bronze or marble. Some are armored and on horseback. Some are gilded. The oldest are sheltered in old houses. Sometimes their arms had to be broken off to get them in, and Foreigners call them milos. They make life-size dolls and place them behind windows, almost always dressed. When they wear only a very few garments, they break their arms as with the milos, and even the legs. They display the legs separately, covered in the serous secretion of silkworms.

Small dolls are entrusted to children of the feminine kind to teach them to be mothers. Infants of the masculine kind who dare playing with the small dolls are severely dealt with. Me, I never cried. Never. Never. I am a girl, I am. I never cried. Never.

7

Saint Glinglin

It rained hard as stone.

Paul noticed in a corner of the shop a display of those foreign rain things whose use happy merchants had begun promoting. Though he had ordained the closing of all halls of cinematographic projection, every bit as foreign as these barometers, still he felt himself from time to time attracted by Tourist customs, though never going so far as to wear an impermeable d'eaucoat, an article of clothing much prized for its eggzotic air.

He looked at the sculpture and shook his head. Pierre continued hammering away at the marble, his blows uniform and uniformly clumsy. He was laboring over the representation of a length of arm. He finally decided to greet his brother and as it rained (it rained to the left and righteously) he said to him (to his brother): "Bad weather, isn't it."

Although it was because of him that things were as they were. Other times Pierre said: "Foul weather, isn't it."

Or still again: "Not very nice out today."

Eventually he'd have to come up with something else, since now it never stopped raining, but for the time being these formulas seemed as sufficient to Pierre as to the rest of the population which, every morning, took note of the sky's porous state with the same sharp concern.

For similar reason, Paul replied: "Yes, it's raining."

He esspressed himself straightforwardly.

But he wasn't much satisfied with his brother's efforts at ekshumation and, these words said, retained the doubtful esspression he'd taken upon entering and first eksamining the work in progress.

"That's an arm?" he asked skeptically.

"This?"

"Right."

"Of course it's an arm."

"It doesn't have hair," said Paul.

"There's never hair on a statue's arms."

"Father had hair there. Almost a fleece."

"That's not done in marble," Pierre said irritably.

Paul shook his head.

"And this?"

"It's a foot."

"Really? And again no hair?"

Pierre set the mallet down, turned away from the stone and sat. "Listen to me, Paul," he began. "I'm going to ask you something very simple. Who's the artist here? Right: who's the sculptor? You? Or me?"

"Neither," said Paul. "I'm mayor, and you're a marble-cutter."

"I've been mayor, you were never a marble-cutter."

He took up the mallet again.

"What labor! What torment!"

"Hello, Eveline," said Paul. "Don't you agree he should put hair on the arms? And especially on the legs. The old man had plenty of it: you know that."

"Take your essplanations somewhere else," said Eveline.

"He's beginning to irritate me," said Pierre.

"Don't pay any attention to him, then."

She sat and slipped on boots.

"I'm going to go buy some cakes."

Paul watched her slip on her boots. She had wonderful legs.

"You don't have a rain-shield?" Paul asked her.

"They're far too ekspensive, and pretentious as well. They're not for us."

A reasonable answer. Her parents had never had one of those bumbershoot things. So, why would she? True, in their time, thanks to the cloud-chaser, it had never rained. And now the boot was on a different foot, so to speak. Walls wept, streams were forever full, the whole countryside was ceaselessly inundated, all color had washed from the sides of the houses, and vegetation sprang up on every side, in every niche, everything from lichen to cedar, fungus to trailing vines, oaks to frail reeds.

Just going to the corner grocer got one drenched.

There were many rain-shield in use. (Grammarians of Home Town had decided this didn't require the plural, since there had been, after all, only one rain since the demise of the cloud-chaser and decomposition of the great stone.) But this invention which happy merchants had begun importing from the land of the Foreigners seemed to most inhabitants an unbefitting eccentricity the mayor had permitted only from absolute necessity. As for the d'eaucoat, so far only the mayor's wife was bold enough to wear it; and she was from elsewhere.

Eveline owned neither rain-shield nor d'eaucoat.

"Do you want me to lend you mine?" asked Paul.

"No thanks."

She looks pretty in her boots.

She pushed open the door and there she was, underwater, on her way to fetching dessert.

Pierre returned to his labors.

"I," said Paul, "understand how difficult all this must be, the plastic arts. Whatever you think right, you must do, to statufy your father. The municipal demands are harsh ones, but don't let them stop you."

"I know, I know," said Pierre, who added: "All the same, this arm's not so bad, it has a certain form and substance. One senses the muscle within. It's neither a leg nor a throat."

"I won't say. A little hair, all the same, I'd say: that would help."

"I don't know," sighed the marble-cutter.

Paul shrugged. He picked up his implement and, without saying more, went out into the rain after having opened it. Eveline waited a little farther along, sheltered under a pedestrian entryway. Paul took cover beside her, closing his apparatus, smiling with satisfaction at his manipulation of the thing.

"It's nowhere near being finished, that stone of his, and it's not at all what they want either, so they're sure to protest. The notables will be in an uproar."

"Can't you do something to help? After all, he's your brother."

"I've already said a good word in his favor, many good words. But persuading them won't be easy: if only there were hair on the arms and legs."

"True. But can't you bring them around to the view that for an individual's representation in stone the down is simply left off?"

"It would be necessary to come up with a theory then."

"Go on, Paul, give it a try. For your brother."

Paul didn't respond. The rain began falling a bit more roughly than usual. Beneath the violence of the impact a paving-stone sometimes cracked.

"Don't you think my boots are pretty?" said Eveline.

Cats went by, swimming hard in the stream.

"Poor beasts," said Paul. "Their lives are so difficult, and they all end up clawless, vulnerable."

"And my boots?" asked Eveline.

"Who made them?"

"Zostril. Aren't they pretty?"

"Zostril's also begun selling d'eaucoats."

"He's an odd duck."

Quéfasse went by, covered with canvas.

He pretended not to see the mayor. His mustache poured long streams down either side of his mouth.

"I'm asking too much," said Eveline.

"They're truly pretty boots," said Paul.

"Try to persuade the notables," said Eveline.

She left to buy cakes. Paul, beside her, also left after having again engaged the unfolding mechanism of his bumbershoot. He caught up with Quéfasse.

"Bad weather, isn't it," said the urban guard. Other times, he said: "Foul weather, isn't it." Or still again: "Not very nice out today."

Today he'd decided (for whatever ineffable or unspeakable reasons) to utter:

"Bad weather, isn't it." And he added: "My mayor."

For he was about his duties.

"With the new moon this will change perhaps," he added. "If only the merest speck of sunlight would fall just then, it will give us a week of respite. Damn, that's all we need. Then plants will truly start springing up everywhere."

"I've heard there's a shrub a meter high near the Nicodemedes'," said Paul.

"Right. It's hard to miss. Before long all our hills will be covered with forests. To say nothing of moss covering the stones, of lichen on their oaken beds, of molds on bran and mushrooms in fields. And grass almost everywhere, thick and green like no one's ever seen before: a true catastrophe."

"Horrible," said Paul.

He watched the urban guard's ceremonies.

"This way you don't have wet feet?"

"No, my mayor. Thanks to the cellophane introduced at the bottom. Which guarantees to protect me from this intemperate weather."

"But your toes must run with sweat, Quéfasse, with all that cellophane."

"I couldn't say, couldn't say, my mayor, but, as I've been a bachelor since my mother's decease, it really doesn't matter, does it."

"Dirty old man," said Paul. "I wonder what ever led me to reinstate you to your duties. Pierre did well to rid himself of you."

"You're too kind, my mayor."

"I have my eye on you, pigface."

Then Paul stomped into a puddle, splashing Quéfasse's pants up to the knee. And that was how he left him.

The town hall lay before him. He went in because he was mayor and wanted to make a show of being mayor. He had decrees to sign, but they were all pulpy and soft from the rain and his pen proved useless.

There wouldn't be many decrees, then.

But there was plenty of water.

Manuel curled his mustache with a small warm iron. Robert annointed his hair with brilliantine.

"It's ekstraordinary all the same," said Manuel, "this water that never stops. What foul weather."

"It's called rain," said Robert.

He scattered sawdust on the floor where his father had made peepee. For the father, since carrying off the Grand Prize of Springtime (in the old days of good weather), had lost for the most part his mental facilities. Drained by this effort, he could thereafter no longer restrain his bladder.

"Ash would do better," said Manuel, "there's less moisture in it."

His mustaches formed the arc of a parenthesis. A slight odor separated itself from his callipilous procedures.

"How can the sky hold so much water?" said Robert, pressing his nose against the pane to avoid smelling the fraternal scorchery.

"Things are as they are," said Manuel. "I'm going to give Laodicée a bumbershoot."

"Don't be a fool. You'd both look silly and esstravagant underneath one of those things. I can see you under it now, ugh. And then the uncle'd start bawling that his daughter was turning queer."

"Leave me alone."

"He's a good man."

Manuel shook his mustaches.

"Leave me alone, I told you."

The father came in struggling with delusions here and there, fore and aft, to the right, to the left.

"Yesh shor no," he said, "Saint Glinglin's celebrated this year?"

"What the hell's he doing?" asked the younger.

"I want to win the Springtime again," said Bonjean.

"Forget it," the elder said to the younger.

Bonjean, old champion, then fell. He slid on his buttocks into a corner where he hid.

"Filthy little bastards," he said. "Filthy little bastards."

For he understood a little after all. And he added: "No Saint Glinglin. Still. No Saint Glinglin."

"Still," the elder picked up the cue, "the Springtime this year could be an odd one."

"Will be or may be?" asked Robert.

"There's going to be a Saint Glinglin," yelped Bonjean. "There's going to be a Saint Glinglin. And there'll be a Springtime. And there'll be a prize. And there'll be Bonjean who has the prize. Holy holy of holies!"

"He interrupted us," said Manuel.

"I'll go with you," said the younger.

They left Bonjean to his grumblings and, at the bottom of the stairs, outside, it rained.

"It just pours on and on," said Robert, still amazed after all this time and rain.

"I'm going to splash my way to the bumbershoot shop. Where are you heading?"

"I'll go that far with you. I'm curious."

They traversed several streets and, soaking, came up before a door that, when opened, rang a bell. To the right were two pink mannequins, pubis and backside sheathed in sleeves of a stiff, impermeable tulle. They, the mannequins, threw their chests out wantonly, leaning against anti-rains. Mandace, importer-traitor for Foreigners, traded in all these things: at the center of his shop, a brassiere pierced by an umbrella lay on a black velvet cushion. This was his trademark. It advertised his services.

"Sheath? Parasol?" he asked. "Corset? Bumbershoot? Wasp-waist? D'eaucoat? Suspender belt?"

"Parasol."

"For yourself? For a young lady?"

"For a young lady."

"Here it is then. Done."

Manuel paid. He wrapped it in a tarpaulin to keep out inquisitive drops of water.

"Till this evening then," Robert told him.

He planned on going to the municipal drying-rooms before returning home.

Laodicée lived a bit further on. Manuel went there.

"You smell like wet dog," she told him, lighting a small wood fire.

He took off his coat and trousers, which she laid out, dripping below, steaming above, by that fire. He poured the contents of his shoes into the sink. Then he crouched beside the hearth.

"I brought you a gift," he said to the young woman. "Look."

He removed the tarpaulin, displayed the bumbershoot.

"What do you say?" he asked.

She took the object, trembling.

"It's nothing special," said the young lady.

"The very height of fashion," said Manuel.

"Oh," she cried, "then it must be tried out immediately."

"Your uncle won't object?"

"Oh," she cried, "it's sure to cause comment. But your gift is so pretty."

"So it's going to get tried out immediately?"

He hurried back into trousers and jacket that he put on still soaked and steaming, and into heavy shoes that swallowed up his socks. Laodicée wrapped a wimple of cellophane around her head and they went down. Pushing open the door, they verified that weather and water were still synonyms.

"It's raining," said Laodicée.

"Coming down hard," confirmed the gallant.

The young lady shook the implement in her hand several times in vain. No opening.

"How does this thing work?" she asked, blushing wonderfully.

Manuel utilized the unfastener and freed the whalebones which, bracing themselves, inflated the black, protective canvas.

"Marvelous!" essclaimed the pretty child who, trembling with emotion, snatched the apparatus from the donor's hands.

She held it up then, the apparatus, in its vertical position and, clinging to Manuel's arm as he leaned toward her, took her first umbrella-assisted steps. Water beat at the canvas, gnawed away futilely, then streamed down to the wet paving-stones.

Laodicée and Manuel walked on in silence, entranced.

Laodicée finally murmured: this is marvelous; and then she applied her lips softly to Manuel's right cheek.

It was thus that, informally, they became engaged.

"What weather," sighed Paracole. "Water, water, everywhere."

"Looks that way."

They had arrived at the same time on the doorstep, and, following this verification of the general order, fell to discussion.

Paracole began by pointing out, quite simply, that sun and water were meteorological beings: contradictories; to which Catogan responded that the mayor surely couldn't imagine that by making all the barometers disappear he'd bring them around to believing the weather had taken a turn for the better. The general conclusion was comma by common agreement colon that the Naboniduses were responsible for all the city's misfortunes.

This discourse having somewhat improved their tempers, they blew their noses, each thinking in his heart of hearts "I have a cold."

"Looks like you've caught cold," said Catogan to Paracole.

"Probably should have a little drink," said Paracole to Catogan.

They went out from under the shelter of the roof and, finding themselves under rain instead, set off towards Hippolyte's tavern.

"You don't have a bumbershoot?" Paracole asked Catogan.

"Does the mayor have one?" Catogan asked Paracole.

It was said he did, but this had never been verified by sight.

"If ever," said Catogan, "I come across him with one of those things, I'll snatch it from his hands and break it across his head."

"You wouldn't dare," said Paracole.

"Did our fathers have parasols? Of course they didn't."

"They did have beautiful weather, though."

At which Catogan shrugged, sending streams of water down his back.

"Did your father have one?"

"No," admitted Paracole.

"There, you see. Beautiful weather has nothing to do with these things."

Taking advantage of a brief silence punctuated by liquid impacts, Paracole assimilated this reasoning.

"You have to admit," said Catogan, "that it's very ingenious, this import."

"A Tourist trick," said Paracole.

"Very ingenious, I can't deny it. The handle above all."

"It's said that they destroy whole whales just to produce these silly contraptions."

"The bone does fall into place well, I admit it, but the handle, now that's truly a wonder."

"It can't be denied," said Paracole. "But with ideas like that, you never know where they'll lead."

"True. And even the fanciest ones don't keep the rain from falling."

"That, we can thank the Naboniduses for."

"Swine. Offspring of swine."

"And the Tourists?"

"Filthy beasts!"

They came to Hippolyte's and, going ahead with their plan, went in.

Streams ran the length of the stairs they descended to the common room, where water kept a constant level (just below the ankles of an adult of average height) thanks to a pump manned all day by Albérich and Bénédict, the kitchen boys, two hours each in rotation. Several fish swam there, carp for cooking, redfish for ornamentation. A filter prevented them from being esstravasated with the water.

The two clients splashed their way to a free table. Actually, all the tables were free. Hippolyte dozed, stretched out on one of them. Mounted similarly, but on a footstool, Albérich worked the pump. Paracole and Catogan hoisted themselves onto high chairs (the patron had mounted them on stilts), emptied their boots, then their bladders, hailed finally the innkeeper.

"Hallo," they said.

Hippolyte climbed down and waded over to them: they wanted a glass of fifrequet from the year Yves-Albert Tranath won the Grand Prize of Springtime. He went off to fetch it from the attic where he had moved his wine cellar; not knowing about the invention of diving suits, he hadn't been able to find anything there. He climbed a ladder on the rungs of which grew mosses and lichen, ever more adhesive with each day. Then, coming back down, he slipped and plunged into the bath, waves sweeping to his clients' feet the requested bottle of fifrequet. They fished it out. Paracole opened it with his pocket knife. Glasses were emptied, individuals smacked their lips.

"Not bad," Catogan said to the innkeeper, who was drawing himself up out of the water.

"It's getting better," said Paracole.

They tossed off what remained.

"Everyone insists on cellars: on the whole an attic's a good enough place for the conservation of wine."

They agreed with Hippolyte.

"But none of that will restore good weather," concluded Paracole.

"You," said Hippolyte, "see how it is again today. Water, nothing but water. Water, water everywhere." And he began shedding tears. They fell one by one into the pool, each one making a soft plop.

"You do your best to hold on," said Catogan, "until finally you just can't hold it any longer. How right you are."

He laughed, dispatching tiny jets of saliva.

"Dry up, friend," said his companion.

Hippolyte sniffled.

"You have to admit," he said, "that one can't call this weather."

"Still, it must have a name," said Paracole, "since it egzists."

"It's the Naboniduses," said Catogan, "who got everything so mikst up. So now it rains, and that's all it does."

"But all the same, it can't be said," said Hippolyte, "that this was the new one's fault. He did everything he could to recover the cloud-chaser."

"A hypocrite," said Catogan.

"He's honest," said Hippolyte. "He restored Quéfasse as urban guard."

"You can't put too much stock in that. It doesn't slow the downpour."

"Alas, that's true." He resumed blubbering.

"Bring us another bottle of your fifrequet from the year Yves-Albert Tranath won the Grand Prize of Springtime."

"On the house," said Paracole.

"Gladly. For such good clients as yourselves. And then I can make it rain, myself. But wine, ah, ah. Make it rain wine ah ah ah."

He headed back toward the attic, falling again on the return trip, and the two acolytes, glasses in hand, opened the bottle when it was placed near them. Clinked glasses and drank. The bottle emptied. Outside, the downpour continued.

"There seems no end to it," said the innkeeper.

"Everything has an end," Catogan said without conviction.

"So they say," said the innkeeper. "That's some consolation."

They sighed.

A carp leapt. The kitchen boy on duty, daydreaming, had let the water rise several inches. A cry from Hippolyte set the pump back in motion.

Paracole winked sideways at Catogan. He said to Hippolyte: "You know how to swim?"

"Who? Me?"

The innkeeper was stupefied.

"The scoundrel," said Catogan purposefully, "he plays it close to the vest."

"Who? Me?"

The two clients were amused, the innkeeper out of sorts.

"Why do I go on wasting my time on you."

"Don't take offense."

"Then you don't know how to swim?"

"Leave me in peace."

"A-ha, he doesn't know how to swim?"

"Why this buffoonery?"

"Never mind," said Paracole.

"It appears that she's going to take a bath," said Catogan.

"You'll have to join her," said Paracole.

"It appears that she's going to take a bath in public," said Catogan.

"Now that there's no more cinema, she's going to give a show just for us, for Urbinataliens; she's going to take a bath for us."

"Right," said Catogan, "in a hole they're digging on the Great Square."

"She'll swim," said Paracole.

Hippolyte gaped with bliss. He blushed. "It's not quite proper that I should ask you this," he said, "it's even a bit risqué, but after all it's man to man."

"Go ahead," said the clientele.

"She'll swim how?" asked the innkeeper.

"How: how?"

"I mean: uh, it's a bit licentious what I'm hinting at. But just between us."

"Let's hear it," said Paracole.

"She'll be in a swimsuit?"

The conversation ground thereupon to a brief stop. Albérich once again had left off working the suction-force pump. A thicket of crayfish descended the stairs clumsily. A trout leapt. Arrowheads sprouted.

The two gentlemen looked embarrassed.

"Well?" asked Hippolyte in a low voice.

"Haven't given it much thought," murmured the others.

Hippolyte repeated: "It's one of those things you have to wonder about, this woman who'll go swimming in front of everyone." He bit back his words, then began to shout as he took note of the rising water level.

The kitchen boy, who had been sampling in his mind the delicacies of Springtime, got back to work.

Scratching at his privates, Paracole paid for the bottle of fifrequet. With the back of his hand, Catogan rubbed at the tip of his nose. Putting their boots back on, they departed.

There were three bells, three beats of silence, a fourth bell.

"It's Le Bu," said Zostril. "I'll get it."

The others cowered, fearing it might be urban guard Quéfasse, a traitor. Zostril, trembling, let off the catch and, latch having fallen, the notary entered. They took a breath all together and resumed their discussion.

"It's raining," said Le Busoqueux to bring them abreast of the situation. He shook himself. He placed his umbrella in a corner.

"Hold on," said Zostril.

"What?"

Zostril pointed to the object.

"This?" said Le Busoqueux.

"That."

The other aspirators had stood to greet the tradesman, this high somebody. They remained upright and silent, staring at the instrument.

"Well?" asked Le Busoqueux.

"An umbrella," said Zostril.

"Well?"

"An umbrella," said Zostril, seeing that it was one.

This remark seemed to provoke the arrivant, a stern man. But he composed himself.

"Good day, my friends," he said to the aspirators. "This? Yes! An umbrella. I confiscated it from my niece. An admirer gave it to her."

"He bought it at Mandace's?" asked Choumaque.

"No doubt," said Zostril.

"It's practical, all the same," said Le Busoqueux.

The others, though shocked, didn't persist because of respect for the elder. They sat.

"Oh yes," repeated Le Busoqueux, "I have to admit it's practical. I would not, of course, approve its being carried by young women, but after all, for a man of my years, surely it can be permitted. Look: I'm scarcely damp at all! Only the bottoms of my trousers."

He pulled them up for display. They were in fact wet.

"And naturally the shoes," he added.

He sat down.

"Yours looks quite a bit smaller than the mayor's," said Zostril, heavy at heart.

Zostril didn't like the importations now gaining such currency.

"Women," essplicated Le Busoqueux, "have been provided a smaller model."

"Let's change the subject," said Saimpier irritably.

"We have a number of issues to address," said Choumaque, who knew nothing of them.

"To work," said Rosquilly.

"To work," said Marqueux.

"To work," said Machut.

The tradesman's umbrella had indisposed them. Encouraged now by their own voices, they regained enthusiasm.

"Let's call these proceedings to order," said Zostril, raising his voice.

They fell silent, and could hear raindrops tapping everywhere against the shutters.

"Doesn't look like it'll ever stop," someone said.

They all agreed.

Outside, it rained.

"Let's call these proceedings to order," repeated Zostril.

"Ah," went Le Busoqueux. "One small thing before we commence. I take notice that I arrived last. I am late, then, and ask your pardon."

"Not at all," said Zostril, "not at all."

They all thought: what a bloody nuisance, but because of respect they kept their mouths shut.

"Now we can get started," said Machut.

"We," said Zostril, "are, I believe, all in accord: There's news."

"Is it true?" asked Rosquilly.

"We have to be sure," said Saimpier.

"The whole town's talking of it," said Marqueux.

"It doesn't make sense," said Rosquilly.

"I'm not following this," said Machut.

"Don't play dumb," said Saimpier.
"You know as much about it as we do," said Zostril.
"One can't act on rumor," said Machut.
"I agree completely," said Rosquilly.
"We're among men," said Saimpier.
"We know what we're talking about," said Zostril.
"Not me," said Machut.
"One's either a hypocrite or he's not," said Zostril.
"You're saying that because of me," said Machut.
"Don't be difficult," said Saimpier.
"Still, it's necessary to know what is actually going on," said Rosquilly.
"The whole town's talking about it," said Marqueux.
"But is it true?" said Rosquilly.
"What?" said Machut.
"Tell him," said Marqueux.
"Let's get on with it," said Zostril.
"Or into it," said Saimpier.
"Into what?" said Machut.
"Into the flesh of the matter," said Marqueux.
"No lewdness," said Rosquilly.
"No what?" said Marqueux.
"Let's not waste time," said Zostril.
Le Busoqueux struck the flat of his hand three times atop a pile of papyrus files shriveled to parchment and dating from a time the rich were buried in chariots with all their worldly goods.
"We," he said, "will never get anything done here if I don't intervene."
"With an umbrella," said Zostril.
"What?"
"Right: if you don't intervene with your umbrella."
"Umbrellas have nothing to do with this," said Rosquilly.
"What then?" said Machut. "I'm not following this."
"We'll never get on with it," said Zostril.
"Or we'll never get into it."
"Into what?"
"Into the flesh of the matter."
"No lewdness," said Rosquilly.
There were again three bells, three beats of silence, a fourth bell.
"It's my daughter," said Le Bu.
They scraped their legs and got up, from politeness. Zostril let

off the catch and, the latch having fallen, Eveline entered.

She shook herself. Leaning against the wall to keep her balance, she took off her boots. She had very good legs. The bottoms of her stockings were dark with water.

"It's raining," she said to inform the aspirators of the meteorological situation.

"Weather as usual," said Saimpier.

A chair was offered to the visitor. She sat and crossed her legs, drying first one foot, then the other with the warmth of her hands. They watched.

"So," said Le Bu. "Is there any truth to what we've heard?"

"Please," said Saimpier.

"You have the details, madam?" asked Rosquilly.

Eveline left off manipulating her little feet, uncrossed her little legs and looked at the assembled males.

"Would you like me to light a fire?" asked Zostril.

"I don't know a great deal," said Eveline. "No, thank you."

"What do you know?" asked Le Busoqueux.

"Wait, that's Laodicée's umbrella."

"If we might return to the question," said Saimpier.

"She's here?"

"I'll essplain later. Meanwhile tell us what you came here to tell us."

"What's that?" asked Machut.

"Don't be difficult," said Saimpier.

"Good advice," said Zostril.

"Well?" asked Le Busoqueux.

Eveline looked at them. "Alice?" she asked.

They blushed.

"Ah," went Machut. "Alice Phaye. I understand."

"The whole town's talking about it," said Marqueux.

"For the coming Saint Glinglin?"

"The same," said Zostril.

"Her bath?"

They all blushed harder, with the ekception of Saimpier, who grew pale; of Le Busoqueux, who turned green; and of Rosquilly, now beet red.

"Yes, yes," stammered Saimpier with a dry mouth.

Eveline thought them comic, but she couldn't understand the why and wherefore of the presence of Laodicée's umbrella. She didn't laugh.

"Very well, you want to know the program for the coming Saint Glinglin? At the Festival of Midday, in lieu of the breakage of dishware, Madame Paul Nabonidus will inaugurate the Waterhole they're digging on the Great Square. She'll swim in it."

"She'll swim?" asked Machut.

"She'll swim."

"Swim?" asked Machut.

"Right," said Saimpier, "one moves arms and legs in the water, one doesn't sink and one moves forward."

"Upright or lying down?" asked Machut.

"Lying down."

"She'll be lying down then," said Machut.

"Yes."

"That's indecent," said Machut.

They all agreed.

It was raining when they arrived at the gates of the town, gates long since reduced to a simple portal, then to a plaque and finally demolished. They found themselves in that part of Home Town stretching and thinning along the Outer Way. Through one window, open despite the downpour, an odor made its way past the watery web, an odor stale and sodden, vaguely vegetable, not quite like the odor he recalled, but still bringing pleasure to the traveler, who said to the person accompanying him: "You smell that?", and the other said: "Yes."

"That's brouchtoucaille cooking at Mame Sahul's," said the traveler.

The person accompanying him didn't know this odor.

"Yes," she said.

"We'll go say hello," said the traveler.

"Yes."

They opened the door, entered, causing behind and beneath them pools and puddles.

"We disturb you, mame?" asked the traveler.

"What can I do for you?" asked the housekeeper.

"This looks to be eccellent," said the traveler.

"I didn't do a very good job this year," said Mame Sahul. "There are just too many legumes and plants because of all this water. They spring up in every direction; the sorrel is huge, the spinach gigantic, the watercress monstrous: it's no use. There won't be any more good brouchtoucaille like there used to be in the good old days as long as we have to make it from all this greenery."

She turned towards the Bare Mountains: "Look, our mountains, they've become all green with this unending rain. Trees spring up, almost as you watch, it's phenomenal. One doesn't know even their names. They're all kinds. And that's not the end of it: the wink of an eye, and there's one more leaf than before."

"The countryside has indeed changed," said the traveler.

"You've seen it before then?"

"Yes," said the person accompanying the traveler.

"You're not a Tourist?"

"No," said the traveler.

"Where are you from then?"

"We've been among the Foreigners," said the traveler.

"Yes," said the person accompanying him.

"And you've already been in our Home Town?"

"Mine as well."

"Yours?"

"Absolutely."

Mame Sahul essclaimed: "But it's not possible! Meussieu Jean!!"

"Himself," said Jean, making a concession to the foreign spirit and feeling somewhat alienated.

"Meussieu Jean!" re-essclaimed Mame Sahul. "May I?"

And so they embraced, peck peck. And a tear came to the left eye and to the right eye of Mame Sahul, although Jean's were dry.

"It gives me such great pleasure to see you again," said the hostess. "Especially after all these changes."

"It seems to be raining," said Jean.

"Don't talk to me about it. Nothing but water, morning to night, and so on and so forth, ekcetera."

"It's wet."

"Eksactly," said Mame Sahul, "that's the word for it. Ah, Meussieu Jean, you haven't changed a bit: you always find the right word to say."

"Thank you," said Jean.

"It's only what I think, without egzaggeration."

"And Sahul?" asked Jean.

"I worry about him. He drinks."

"Good old Sahul," said Jean.

"Without stop. Big tumblers of water. He inflates. His liver is dissolving, of course, but it's so sad, a man of his dignity. Every moment of the day he has to have a big glass of water that he gulps down greedily. He's lost his good name, sad to say. And the one responsible, Meussieu Jean, is your brother who chucked out the cloud-chaser. In your father's time, meaning no disrespect, Meussieu Jean, you understand, there was always good weather and my husband stayed as dry as the mountains. Before long he'll have mushrooms on his bottom and moss up his nostrils, just like our mountains staggering under so much vegetation. Ah! stones!"

She went back to stirring her brouchtoucaille.

"It's true," said Jean, "I remember it smelling stronger."

"I know," said Mame Sahul. "But what else can you do with all these turnips, carrots, strawberry-spinaches, and Jerusalem artichokes that fall on us out of the sky ymight say! And there's so much water that our ancestral plates get washed despite us: so how can we conserve the essence of taste?"

"As far as I'm concerned," said Jean, "and despite everything, I'd be most pleased should you invite me."

"Meussieu Jean! Of course!! And your companion as well!!!"

She turned towards the companion in order that he might thank her, but he said nothing. She looked closely at him. He wore a shirt-waist, chorts, and sandals, like a Tourist. His wet hair went every which way, sometimes in curls. His look was inward.

"My companion," said Jean (he smiled), "has never eaten brouchtoucaille. This will be a happy occasion."

Said companion bowed his head politely; then he raised it to whisper something in Jean's ear. Upon a gesture from the latter, said companion walked across the room and went out into the yard.

Mame Sahul, intrigued, worked her way closer to the window on that side; glancing out, she essclaimed:

"But it's a young lady!"

"It's my sister," said Jean. "Hélène."

"Bless me," said Mame Sahul.

Flabbergasted, she sat down.

"Yes, it's Hélène."

"I'm so stupid not to have known it. But Meussieu Jean, all the same you must never dare to take her walking like that in the town, showing her legs, dressed like a Tourist."

"I thought times had changed."

"What do you mean, Meussieu Jean?"

"I came back for Saint Glinglin," said Jean, "the nautical Saint Glinglin."

Mame Sahul didn't reply. She looked out the other window and said: "It's raining."

Hélène came in; she sat back down.

"Hello, Mademoiselle," said Mame Sahul. "I didn't know."

Hélène smiled at her. Mame Sahul studied the chorts, legs, shirt-waist, face, hair. All of it quite wet.

"The stories will start up again," she muttered.

"Tell me about my sister-in-law," said Jean.

"Why? What is there you don't already know?"

"Oh, Eveline: no, of course not. Tell me about Alice Phaye."

"Things are said."

"It's raining," said Jean.

Mame Sahul sighed. "She's had a great hole dug in the Great Square. And now, water fills it."

"I told you that I came back for the nautical Saint Glinglin, Mame Sahul."

"That's all anyone speaks of."

"We'll see," said Jean. "Thanks for the brouchtoucaille, but we have far to go." He turned towards his sister and said to her: "Let's go."

Hélène got up. With thumb and indeks finger of her right hand she freed the cloth of her chorts from the cleft of her buttocks, then after a gentle flekshun of her legs she asked: "Yes?"

Then, he spoke several phrases of a special sort; certain sounds reappeared at the end of a certain number of syllables, everything was not said in the same tone, and words were combined in curious ways. When he finished, the kitchen floor was dry, the brouchtoucaille smelled wonderful.

They turned away. Mamsahul rapturously watched them go.

When she went back to stirring her pitiful stew, water again began trickling into it. The odor of the dish again grew stale and distasteful.

Germaine had pendant breasts and a barren, depleted wallet of a belly. Her brownish hair hung lifelessly from head to backside. She was the mother of three Nabonidus children, spouse of the husband Nabonidus, daughter-in-law of the grandmother of the three Nabonidus children, sister to his brothers, niece to his uncles, aunt to his nephews, cousin to his cousins, pitiable withered cow of ancient mayordoms, teacher of brats with uncommon futures, accomplice in Helenic sequestration, dessicated rind of a widow brainless and drained, deleted domestic mistress of house and nothing more, most nothing of all, gloomy watcher of rain, Germaine née Paletot widow Nabonidus without children really, since neither Pierre nor Paul ever comes to see her, even less Jean who's among the Foreigners, so when at this very moment he passes in the street it astounds her. He's not alone, he's with a Tourist in touristic uniform, they're both soaked, they don't wear cellophane or carry umbrellas. Jean has aged hardly at all. As for the Tourist, he seems familiar. Germaine, dull and slow as she is, nevertheless recognizes, imagine!, under the falling rain, her daughter. So great a surprise might have killed cardiacs but brought her a little life. She opened her window, the shutters. She received full in the face a volley of water-fire. All her parlor, all her cardigan, all her chairs, all her elm and all her oak, all her andirons and all her brass, all her knickknacks and all her statuettes, all her dishes and all her velvets, all her writing paper and all her wallpaper, all her papa drawings and all her mama drawings and all her papa-and-mama drawings and all her children drawings ran with drizzle. Leaning over the sill, she shouted their names. Her senile ringlets were soaked, and water ran abundantly down the ravines of her antiquated face.

Hélène and Jean looked up. "Well, she lives here now," said the son.

"Yes," said the daughter.

People continued on their way, for they didn't want to miss getting good spots to watch Alice's bath in broad daylight. Some would have preferred the breakage of dishware, as in bygone days. But everything else was changing, so why not that, and besides, no one really knew what this swimming was all about, cinematographic memories having faded. They'd all watched the Waterhole get dug in the Great Square, saw that it had filled with water by itself, and now they were going to see what use Alice would make of it. A few even suggested that perhaps Alice wouldn't be completely dressed when she undertook her swim, just as one had seen her onscreen sometimes in the depths of the cinematograph's artificial night.

When they knocked, Germaine made for the door and flattened it brusquely against the wall to see in a single glance half of her progeny, very soaked.

"My children," she said.

"Hélène," she said.

"Jean," she said.

"Hélène," she said.

"My children," she said.

"You've said my name one time less than my sister's," said Jean. "I'm going to leave."

"My Jean! My Jean!" she said, the mother.

Finally they sat at a battered table and drank a bit of trapu together.

The music boks reeled off its thin, shrill airs while they talked over what lay ahead and while childhood memories moved, unvoiced, about the small, damp maternal apartment. In the nekst room growls could be heard, the grandmother in her ekstremity, a penny-piece of bone and neglect, a bit of used-up flesh, an obscure wound consumed by its years and eggzhausted by its aigresistence and now awaiting only its release.

"It's almost time," said the mother, "for the Festival to begin."

"Yes," said Hélène.

She rose, her brother too. They moved quickly. They went outdoors, outside. They were in the street. The crowd pressed in on them. People began running. They splashed through the water. They were splattered. The splishsplash of their progress mikst with the others in great volleys of sound. They passed beneath the window, hurrying. Germaine lost sight of her children.

Not too much water had found its way into her room. She reshut the window, and rain went back to pecking at the pane while small cannons with their dull eggzplozions summoned the population to witness the swim of the woman who had married the current mayor.

The grandmother, disturbed by the noise, burrowed molelike into her sheets. Germaine went into the adjoining room, somewhat drier.

"Whatsit?" said the old woman, "whatsit?"

"Nothing," said Germaine.

"Whatsit?" said the old woman, "whatsit?"

She began ranting, angry at being kept in the dark.

Germaine hesitated, then essplained: "The Festival."

Hearing these words, the grandmother died. Everyone was at the Festival. They'd have to stick her in the mud later.

Germaine went back to knitting before the window. The streets were empty, ekcept for the water.

With obstinacy, cunning, and guile—in short, artfully—Pierre, following the advice of his mayoral sibling, at last succeeded, after many hours' effort (this attesting to his talent), in forming tiny hairs on the statue's arms, planning nekst to erect them on calves, thighs, pubis, and pectorals. For the first time in his life, before this redoubtable accomplishment, smiles widened the lips of the condemned. He put down his hammer. He listened to the rain fall. He scraped at bits of moss growing in a crack in the stone.

Eveline entered.

As always, she brought plenty of water with her.

"There it is," said Pierre. "I've done it."

"The bitch," said Eveline.

"Something's happened?"

"All the men have shown up for the Festival of Midday in a terrible state."

"How's that?"

"You can't imagine. There are even some making propositions to the women."

"Proposing what?"

Eveline didn't respond.

"And Paul?"

She smiled, but added nothing more.

"I'm off. The brouchtoucaille will be ready in fifteen minutes."

"Then I have just enough time to make three more hairs."

He went back to his toil. With the last hair, two people entered, scantily dressed, heavily soaked. Pierre recognized Jean and divined Hélène. And cursed inside, wrung with need to finish erecting the third hair, but after all, this was his brother, this was his sister.

"So," he said, "back from the adventure. And now" question mark.

He turned to Hélène.

"But," he said, "my sister, you're dressed like a man. And all soaked in the bargain."

She went to him, kissed him on both cheeks.

The brothers shook hands forcibly.

"We're back," said Jean.

"But for what reason?" asked the sculptor.

"Yes," said Hélène. "I never cried."

"Have a seat."

Hélène and Jean shook themselves and put their rear ends on blocks of rough rock, which were cold. But they were rough themselves, outdoorsmen, mountaineers. They didn't flinch.

"Yes," said Pierre. "Why have you come back here to our Home Town" question mark.

He looked at Hélène's chorts, and at her legs, which she held slightly apart, thinking of gentle, rolling hills in the countryside where clement sky and hospitable earth might shelter in their harmony a small singing watercourse.

"That's the statue" question mark from Jean, who indicated with a jab of his thumb the block of marble on which hair was laboriously sprouting.

"You know about it" question mark from Pierre.

"Yes," said Hélène.

"A little," said Jean.

Pierre didn't often have occasion to tell his story since the Urbinataliens all knew it and Tourists had become increasingly rare and in any case didn't seek him out for conversation. He opened his mouth and said:

"They've kicked me out of town because I made it rain. The fact is that it's been raining, you see, without interruption, since last year. I've been here like this a long time, here at the border, and foul weather continues. Carcass in stone, the father has melted. Paul's a good brother, he's been happy because of his spouse, a star known even here. Because of his ekcess of good fortune, he's come to feel pity for the Urbinataliens. I'll be able to go back to the town providing that I don't leave my house until I've re-created the father's stony form: his statue, that is; for they claim it's because of me that it's lost. I brought it to them. I took it away from them. But now I have to give it back to them again. I've worked long and hard. But look: the job's almost done."

"Yes," said Hélène.

"The brouchtoucaille is served," Eveline announced.

She was at the top of the stairs.

"Your wife?" asked Jean.

"Wait," said Eveline. "Look, look."

"Yes," said Pierre. "Oddly enough. She married me. When I began my statue."

Eveline descended to greet the arrivals and decided then and there that someday she herself would dress in chorts, like Hélène, if not a swimsuit like her sister-in-law. This, Jean had seen, Hélène too, though women never participated in the Festival of Midday, when dishware was broken, but she'd been taken for a boy. She'd thus been able to attend her sister-in-law's undressing on the steps of the mayor's office, till Alice wore only two sportive pieces, the men all going: ah. Then she dove, and staying near the surface of the water, moved within that element with grace and ease. The men, despite their skepticism, were forced to admit it: the woman swam. Finally, after three or four passes, Alice came out of the waves, and the bits of cloth covering small areas of her flesh seemed to have melted. And all the men again went: ah. It hadn't stopped raining. Alice gathered up her clothing and went back into the town hall. And all the men again went: ah, standing there.

Then they themselves started moving. Some began speaking to women they didn't know, and it was rambling, incoherent talk.

And in the inns and taverns they drank fifrequet more or less in silence. From time to time they leaned over to look at the water in which their feet steeped, they stirred it gently, and their gaze followed the motion of the waves, pale echoes of Alician curves.

"And you," asked Eveline of Jean, "you're not concerned?"

"Why should he be?" asked Pierre.

"Stay out of this," said Eveline.

"It's a common sight," said Jean, "in Foreign Town."

"A woman is a woman," said Eveline, "and she's very pretty, very attractive."

"What are you talking about?" muttered Pierre.

"Right, Jean?"

"Yes," said Jean. "She's very pretty."

Hélène raised her eyes. She too said: "Yes."

Eveline looked at her.

"Come eat brouchtoucaille with us," said Pierre. "It's ready. But Eveline already said that. We'll talk about all this over our Urbinatalien dish. It's odd, but I never used to like it much, I'd even think up esscuses to keep from having to eat it, and now I love it."

"You've finished your three hairs?"

Eveline took note of Hélène's legs and their soft down.

"They'll be done very soon now."

"She's dead," Paul said, placing in a corner of the shop, dripping with rain, one of those objects whose use happy merchants had begun promoting.

"They're waiting for you at the town hall," said Eveline.

"I only dropped by," responded Paul. "She's dead. The old one."

He shook himself. Pools splashed around him to the right and the left. He rubbed his face with an absorbent sponge and looked up, seeing his other brother near a young woman who could only be Hélène.

"You know," he said to Jean, "I don't really want to go on being mayor."

Le Busoqueux had hardly finished blowing his nose when Rosquilly knocked. Then Marqueux arrived, Machut nekst, all of them covered with dew. Zostril and Saimpier, having lunched with Le Busoqueux, were somewhat drier. They sat looking at one another, giving every indication of the most desolate desolation. They held back, avoiding speech. Finally Le Busoqueux cleared his throat. He said the following:

"We must face facts."

The others agreed, lifting shoulders, ekstending hands, raising then lowering eyebrows.

"What does the populace say?"

Again they looked at one another. Heads were scratched, eyes and faces were rubbed, eyebrows went up. What does the populace say? It says nothing, the populace. It's in no condition to say much of anything. There was a woman imprinted on the eye of every Urbinatalien, a new wonder, and it prevented them from talking.

"Where is she? What's she doing? Now?" said Zostril.

Nothing was known.

And for Springtime? Another question altogether. But no more light was shed on that than on the other.

They sighed, all of them.

And decided on a breather.

Le Busoqueux said: "Let's have a glass of fifrequet from the year when Bonjean had the Grand Prize of Springtime."

They all agreed to it, although they thought nevertheless that it wasn't such a good year for fifrequet.

Le Busoqueux got up to go find the liter. During this time the others were silent, giving themselves over to various pursuits for the most part relating to ekscavation (nails, ears, etc.). The tradesman returned with the opened fifrequet. They drank. Before their appreciations could lapse into formula, the bell sounded.

"Hold on," said Le Busoqueux.

"Ah," said Zostril.

"Oh, oh," said Saimpier.

"Eh," said Marqueux.

"No?" inquired Rosquilly.

"Who could that be?" uttered Machut.

"Hold on," resaid Le Busoqueux.

He took a sip of courage from his drink; stood, said: "I'll get it."
He did.

Two people entered, dredged from the downpour. The one who
was on top failed to bend his head in order not to strike it against
the pier. The one who was below staggered in a zigzag, jostling
the tradesman and shedding mud and water on the carpet already soaked from preceding arrivals. Then the human pyramid
disintegrated and the two cripples, recognized by the aspirators
now, picked themselves up with deep groans and a grinding of
bone.

"Drink, drink," they said, pledging bursts of spittle.

"Have a glass of fifrequet," Le Busoqueux urged them amiably.
"From the year when Bonjean had the Grand Prize of Springtime."

"Drink, drink," the poor devils responded.

They thought it was a bad year.

The blind one groped his way towards a seat, the paralytic
crawled towards the same. The others distributed themselves
among the appropriate number of chairs.

"Well?" said Nicomedes, looking around.

"Well?" said Nicodemus, tapping his foot.

"Well?" replied the others, eyeing and elbowing one another
furtively and discreetly.

There was a silence.

"As though it weren't known what's going on here," said
Nicomedes.

"What's going on here?" asked Le Busoqueux.

"Drink! drink!" replied Nicodemus.

Le Busoqueux filled their glasses. The two visitors engorged their
drinks with esspressions of distaste. They hurled the last drops on
the floor where twin globs of spittle joined them.

"It's not worthwhile talking about what's going on here," said
Nicodemus, wiping his beard on the back of his hand.

"No, it's not worthwhile," confirmed Nicomedes, making the
same gesture.

"What, then?" asked Le Busoqueux.

"Well, there is news which perhaps you've not yet heard," said
Nicodemus.

"Definitely not," confirmed Nicomedes.

"Really," said Le Busoqueux.

"Shall we essplain?" Nicomedes asked his brother, turning
towards him.

"Go ahead," responded Nicodemus, pivoting his face in his interlocutor's direction although he couldn't see him at all, for it was an old habit and he had conserved in this manner certain gestures that still gave some comfort in life.

"Very well," began Nicomedes, "Grandmother Pauline is dead." He waited. The conspirators egzamined themselves. They all had egzactly the same thought.

"Who cares," said Marqueux.

The blind one grimaced.

"Wait, wait," said Nicomedes, "there's more: Jean Nabonidus and his sister arrived this morning."

"Everyone knows that," said Zostril.

"Who doesn't!" essclaimed Le Busoqueux.

"An open secret," said Saimpier.

"And that's it?" asked the tradesman of the two veterans.

They scratched their heads.

"They'll gossip," said Saimpier.

"It's urgent that we reach a decision," said Zostril.

"Throw them outdoors," proposed Marqueux.

"They'll gossip," said Saimpier.

"Lock them up here," proposed Machut.

"Where?" asked Le Busoqueux.

They thought it over. The apartment, being sparsely furnished in modernist style with touches of foreign fashion, included a refrigerator. It was there, after having egzamined it, that the aspirators imprisoned the two invalids.

Manuel blew his nose, but his face still ran with water. He wrung out the tail of his shirt that he'd used as a handkerchief and said: "Let's go."

Bénédict, Robert, Fulbert, and Albérich looked at him and bent down. They lifted their burden.

"Shit," said Bénédict. "The old woman must have spent all her time stuffing her face. Weighs a ton."

"You're not kidding," said Albérich. "My back hurts already."

"Shut your traps," said Fulbert. "We're taking her and that's that."

They started down the stairs.

It was a bitch of a job. Fortunately, one with a stairway.

They came to the door. It was raining.

"Shit," said Bénédict, "always this soup."

"It don't ever stop," said Albérich. "Old-timers claim that it never rained in the old days."

"I don't remember," said Fulbert.

Manuel and Robert urged them on.

"Let's go! To the Pits!"

They took up their task again, lifting the litter and taking three steps. They stopped. An old frump had appeared behind them.

"You're going with us?" murmured Manuel to Dame Nabonidus.

"Family," murmured this one, "family," murmured Dame Nabonidus, "family," murmured Nabonidus's wife, "family," murmured the daughter-in-law of the ancient toothless jailer of the Bare Mountains.

The young men ekschanged glances.

"It's raining hard," said Bénédict.

"That's for sure," said Albérich.

"Truly," said Fulbert.

They glanced wearily at the form revealed beneath the shroud. Bit by bit, rain soaked it.

"Quickly to the Pits," said Manuel.

"Get a move on," said Robert.

Dame Nabonidus began weeping. She lamented: "Family . . . family. . . ."

The young men didn't want to hear any more.

Then, suddenly, the family appeared.

It appeared first in its least virulent form. These looked rather like Tourists. And one, judging from her full thighs and bulging shirt-waist, was a young woman.

"Looks like Jean Nabonidus," whispered Manuel, saying nothing of Hélène.

"Looks like," whispered Robert.

The two boys made no move to resume their burden. Having heard the whispers, they looked with respect at the third brother and, with less respect, at the sister.

"It's your grandmother," said Albérich politely.

"Dead," said Bénédict solemnly.

"She's being carried to the Pits," essplicated Fulbert.

Hélène said: "I never cried. Never."

The boys lowered their eyes, blushing.

"Good, then," said Jean.

"Let's not waste time," said Paul.

The boys turned back, another bit of family was there.

"My children, my children," bewailed Germaine.

Eveline was sheltered beneath an umbrella held by Paul. Alice, still in swimsuit, was cloaked in a wrapper of cellophane. Pierre stood there with them.

He's the one the young boys noticed.

"Pierre Nabonidus," said Manuel, "the statue's finished?"

"Being finished," replied Paul irritably. "I've authorized his coming today. Because of this."

He indicated, with an indeks finger, the litter and its body.

"Then," asked Manuel, "the statue's not finished?"

Paul turned to Pierre: "No? right?"

"No," Pierre responded. He took a step towards Manuel: "But I have special authorization to come here. Because of this."

He indicated, with a small motion of his chin, the cadaver and its carriage.

"I don't like any of this," said Alice.

"The old cow," said Eveline. "The filthy cow. She'll do no more evil."

"I never cried," said Hélène. "Never."

Thus Alice discovered who this young woman in chorts was. She studied her attentively. She thought her singularly perfect. She wondered if she herself were less. She compared noses, thighs, breasts, plus parts less remarkable, lobes of the ear, wings of the nose, furrows of the armpit, curves of the ankle, angles of the knee, points of the elbow, sheen of the hair. She wondered, she wondered, she wondered and finally Robert said:

"Don't you think she's beginning to stink?"

He was speaking of the grandmother, of course. Yet he didn't fail to take note of this vision of the star in her cellophane, and he, too, compared the other in her chorts, without knowing where to start or end, where to start or end.

And the larger family appeared, the family of aspirators. Le Buso-queux tradesman father-in-law, Marqueux, Rosquilly, Machut, Zostril, and Saimpier, they all showed up dripping with rain. And behind them, at a distance, were silhouetted Paracole and Catogan.

They all looked at one another. Le Bu identified the young woman in chorts because of her vestmental resemblance to Jean.

"Well, well," he said. "It's you, Jean."

"Listen," said Hélène. "I never cried. Never."

The aspirators said nothing.

"She stinks," said Manuel. "Let's go."

They moved on.

Manuel, Robert, Albérich, and Fulbert carried the litter containing the former jailer. And behind: the family. Mother Germaine, insignificant creature. Then sons Pierre, Paul, and Jean, each with his mate Eveline, Alice, Hélène, in the last case, mated by brotherly love. And then the aspirators, snuffling.

They walked, they walked.

They went on funereally.

It rained it rained.

Water and air were inseparable.

They descended the sharp gorge to the swampland of the Pits, and the group of Urbinataliens, looking upon the swamps through drops of water, saw them just a little distorted, enlarged by their isolation, faded by their bereavements, as though transcribed onto a slightly concave surface.

Quéfasse pushed open the gate and they entered. They waded about in the murky marmalade where those who no longer lived in Home Town putrefied. The four young men chose a spot which seemed to them deep enough and turned the litter upside down, tossing in their load. Wound in her finalest linen the grandmother splashed in, then the bundle, sullied with mud, sank slowly. The ground slurped it up and released into the open air several flatulent rumblings.

It rained.

The bundle disappeared into the sludge.

Manuel, Robert, Fulbert, and Albérich stepped back. Then Manuel said to Paul: "That'll be four turpins and three ganelons."

The mayor paid them.

Pierre said: "It's good to smell the open air."

"I never cried," said Hélène.

Pierre regarded the mud now containing new remains. "There must be strange animals in there," he murmured.

"Large insects, tiny animals," murmured Hélène. "All together. Scraping at the night. Small feet. Large wings."

"They live!" murmured Pierre. "They live! It's difficult to imagine that. To be born there, to endure and eventually die so: osscure, blind."

"In my cell," Hélène said, "I became white like them. But I never cried. Never."

"Only when I lost my old knowledge of life, life as mankind comprehends it," Pierre said, "did I see clearly the objectives of my research."

"You want to look for it in the Pits?" Manuel asked him.

But Pierre said no more.

"And the idol's still not finished," added Manuel.

The four young men eyed the young woman in chorts and the star under cellophane. Eveline told them:

"Mind your own business, don't worry about the statue."

She egzamined Hélène and Pierre.

"So. The long-lost brother and sister," she grumbled. And squinting at Le Bu: "And you, Papa, so you're still alive too. You senile old imbecile. Get out of here."

The tradesman coughed a little. The porters made off, unnoticed, unseen, into the rain.

"I no longer know you," murmured Le Busoqueux. "There's no reason, just because your husband's come here even though he hasn't finished the statue of your father-in-law, to talk to me in such a manner. I object." Provoked, he said loudly: "I object."

He shook Laodicée's umbrella above her head. Since the beginning of the ceremony, Manuel had had his eye on this object. Now he snatched it from the old man's hands and, having taken it by force, closed it.

"Agree," he declared, "that you're going to let me have this."

"But it's raining," essclaimed Le Bu.

"This is true," said Pierre.

"It's raining, it's raining, it's raining," protested the aspirators.

"Which is to say that it's pouring," added Rosquilly, wishing to esspress himself freely.

"The weather's no good, that's true," Pierre confirmed mechanically.

"You're not going to try and tell us, I hope, that it's not because of you we're drenched? and that algae's growing everywhere?"

Le Bu could feel mold sprouting on his hat even as he spoke. He grew angry. Besides, since there were so many so near the Pits, they'd begun sinking little by little into the mire, and, in counterbalance, debris had begun rising to the surface. The recent grandmother was the first of all to reappear. Eveline pointed:

"Look, we're still not done with her. She's coming back up."

They confirmed this and splashed away towards their homes. And Pauline disappeared again into the mire.

"It doesn't really look finished," Le Busoqueux finally said, having circled the statue several times.

"There's still some work to be done on top," replied Pierre. "You'll have a glass of fifrequet? Eveline, bring your father a glass of fifrequet."

"Many thanks," said Le Busoqueux. "But I don't understand. The other one was clearly more natural."

"That's a leg," said Pierre, following the notary's scrutiny. "It's not quite finished. The hairs are missing. I've only made three so far."

"And this?"

"The eye."

"Why the eye? Why not: an eye? Your father had two eyes, it seems to me. Where is the other?"

"There."

"I don't see it."

"I'm showing you the location. I haven't actually made it yet."

"This is taking a long time. It seems to me it's not going very well at all."

"Papa, leave him alone," said Eveline, pouring fifrequet generously.

"How insolent you've become."

Eveline shrugged. The two men drank.

"You're envious?" asked Le Busoqueux.

"I'm loyal to him," Pierre replied passionately.

"That's not what I mean. She must want to show off her legs like your sister in her chorts or your sister-in-law in her swimsuit."

"I do have pretty ones, don't I?"

She tucked up her skirt, causing a small flood around her.

"What slush," she sighed.

Le Bu inspected his daughter's thighs.

"All the same," he said, "Hélène has rounder and Alice firmer ones."

"You've tried them out yourself, have you, you old viper?" asked Eveline.

"As far as Alice's are concerned, I studied them closely some time ago when I went to the cinematograph. Even on a flat surface like that, one can tell if a woman's thighs are firm or not."

"Since then, she's gotten older," said Eveline.

"I think you're jealous."

"As for me," Pierre said, "I have no interest whatsoever in Alice's thighs."

"Do you love one another? Both of you?" Le Bu asked suddenly.

"Not often enough," replied Eveline.

"Of course," said Pierre.

"Don't make trouble," added Eveline.

"Well. Well."

The tradesman looked vaguely at the window of the workshop, on which flowed, in a heavy downpour, more rain.

"And this little rabbit Manuel's stolen my bumbershoot."

"It wasn't yours. It was Laodicée's."

"Well, well."

He shifted his weight from one hip to the other. Pierre clapped him on the back, spattering geysers from his father-in-law's coat.

"So, tradesman, what do you think of my statue?"

"Hmm! Hmm!"

"Frankly?"

"So, old man," Eveline said, "give us your opinion, even though it's worth about as much as what's trickling from your nose."

"Well," said Le Busoqueux. He hesitated. "It's not finished."

"That's all you have to say?" asked Eveline.

Pierre made a gesture of weariness: "Trust him to murder language with his commonplaces."

"I'll have plenty to say when it's done," cried Le Busoqueux, ekcessively annoyed. "Things cannot go on like this. Your sister-in-law showing herself worse than naked, and at the Festival of Midday, of all things. Your sister returning from living among the Foreigners, without a word of warning. And you, leaving here without authorization. Things cannot go on like this."

"This idiot speaks to me rudely," Pierre said to Eveline.

Le Bu shouted: "Things cannot go on like this."

"You're talking about events," remarked Pierre, "that took place only once. How can they go on?"

"As though you think you're going to make him understand anything," intervened Eveline.

"But it's what comes of it!" essclaimed the tradesman. "What comes of it!"

"Something's keeping him?" asked Eveline.

"The rain!" added Le Busoqueux wearily.

"Especially since you don't have Laodicée's umbrella anymore."

"The rain," repeated Le Busoqueux in a whisper. "The rain, the rain."

"So what," said Eveline, "it's just water after all!"

"And these women showing themselves naked! Is that just your water? your water! your water, that makes all this possible! This Alice rampant on the surface of the lake, this Hélène with her wet buttocks in her chorts. You, Pierre, you're responsible for all this, you with your fish and your aquariums, this is what it's all led to, this is where it's taken us."

"So what?" said Eveline.

Pierre stepped close to the tradesman and said the following: "What do you want from me? after all. The statue? It's not finished. The rain? it's here. Me? I don't know how to stop it."

"Right. Now go, Papa, don't bother us anymore with all your pompous chatter. And don't ever think for a minute that you'll become mayor now, with the help of your aspirators."

"And why not, little girl?"

"Get out of here with your babbling. You? Mayor? No one would look twice at you. Dried-up old biscuit, get out."

"Don't stand in my way."

"You're dreaming, Papa. Everyone will put you out to pasture. Even the aspirators."

"Who else would you want then?"

"What about Paul?"

"What about Paul?" asked Pierre, half-hearing.

He again took up his hammer and chisel and set to working with minute care, first here, then there, on the half-begotten statue of Nabonidus.

"Paul!" responded Le Bu. "After the scandal?"

"There's been no scandal."

"Really?"

"It's no scandal that all the men should have erections."

"No? You think so?"

"I do," said Eveline. "It must be a great pleasure to a woman to be the reason for a whole town's erections."

"You're raving, little girl. Such ideas sound like things your two whores of sisters-in-law would think. They've put such notions in your head, I don't know how. Or why."

"Collusion?" suggested Pierre with utter indifference, going on about his work.

He bustled about, working suddenly now with great precision and speed. Particles of marble flew from beneath his hands. His smock became imbued with creative perspiration. Le Bu paid no attention to him. Le Bu went on, still addressing his daughter:

"But these notions amount to nothing. The proof of it is that soon all those who have squandered their time trying to bring about such changes will have no recourse but to flee and live among Foreigners."

Pierre listened, shrugged his shoulders, then turned his attention back to his work. Eveline aimed a kick at her father's tibia to emphasize her question: "And, tell me, what do you intend to do?"

"I'll make decency prevail. By brute force, if I must."

"What force?" asked Eveline.

Le Bu tore out a tuft of hair. It was wet.

"My Eveline!" he creaked, "you've been turned into a sensualist!"

They were discussing the proposition brought before them by Jean Nabonidus. There were in attendance: Jean Nabonidus of course, since he'd come to address them, his sister in chorts named Hélène, his brother Paul with wife Alice Phaye the star, urban guard Quéfasse, and aspirators in indeterminate number, as well as professional grumblers Paracole and Catogan, all now called to order.

This small aggregate of intellects began humming, rippling, phosphorescing, ekcepting, speculating. Shortwave, ultrasound, subtle lights transpiercing the present matter, how singular, how very singular, was the proposition brought before them by Jean Nabonidus, youngest of the sons of the deceased mayor.

He stood and made his proposition to them, speaking in a clear, firm voice.

The meeting was thrown open to discussion.

They scratched at the skin of their skulls, digging from it, under ploughing nails, a kind of grayish humus whose teksture they egzamined absentmindedly.

"I can't see what we have to lose," Rosquilly finally said.

"Perhaps," replied Machut. "But better the devil we know than the one we don't. . . ."

"We've had more than enough of this devilish rain," essclaimed Marqueux.

"It's a serious thing, tampering with the future," said Zostril.

"Let's suppose things do change," reprised Machut. "Nothing guarantees it will be for the better."

"To be sure," said Saimpier.

"But this rain," said Marqueux, "surely we've had enough of this rain."

"Oh yes," said Saimpier, "rain, we've seen enough of that."

"And then," said Rosquilly, "it's hard to imagine how anything could be worse."

"Well," said Machut, "for eggzample: snow."

"What?" asked Marqueux.

"Snow," Machut cried in his face. "There aguesists a thing called snow, according to travelers' stories. And even in the cinematograph, sometimes."

"What is it?" asked Marqueux

"Water, solid and white, in flakes," shouted Machut.

"Not possible," said Marqueux.

Machut indicated Hélène and Jean. "They know. They've traveled."

He pointed to Alice. "And the Foreigner as well, she must know of it. Coming from Holy Wood."

Paracole intervened: "Of course he knows, the young Meussieu. It's probably because of this very thing that he proposes his project to us. He loves snow. Just as his brother loves rain. If you listen to him, soon you will be in water up to your necks—but in icewater this time."

"Well said," bellowed Machut. "That's it. Icewater. Icewater. Icewater."

"But," said Rosquilly, "there's really no reason to believe that."

"It's pure nonsense, this story of frozen water," said Marqueux. "No such thing achesists. Whereas fine weather: I can remember that. I can almost bring it back, in a manner of speaking. How I'd love to have it again, that fine weather, every day, all day. . . ."

Machut spoke sharply to Alice: "Yes or no, tell us in all honesty, Madame: doesn't snow aguesist?"

"Of course," responded Alice. "And hail as well."

"What?" asked Marqueux.

"Hail."

"I know nothing of that," admitted Machut loyally.

"It's water that's become solid," essplicated the star. "In small hard pieces. Like small stones."

"What did I tell you!" essclaimed Machut.

"Not possible," murmured Marqueux, overcome. "What a world."

Zostril took the floor: "If we take time to touch on every possible perturbation in the air around us, we'll never finish. The fact remains that because of our previous mayor's acquiratic ideas, we're subjected to a continual rain. OK. Some don't want to tamper with that. Some want to do something about it. I think there's even a certain approval for all this water among some, and then the swimming, that's truly a fine thing to see."

He smiled blissfully. The others reddened.

"Then too, I like the greenery," he added.

"Pah," went Paul.

"Ah!" said Paracole. "You promised that you would not involve yourself in the discussion."

Everyone was silent.

Catogan took the floor: "His proposition makes no sense."

"It's just as I've essplained it," replied Jean.

"We're here to discuss it," essclaimed Paracole.

Everyone was silent again.

"It might well come to nothing," said Machut. "But there's a chance."

"And then one brother after the other," said Paracole. "No. We know them for what they are, these Naboniduses."

"But finally," creaked Marqueux, "if all the same we have a chance of fine weather, even a tiny one? You've forgotten how it was. This snale, this ho, we know nothing about. Whereas fine weather, what if it could return, what if there were even a chance for its return."

"This man is an adventurer," shouted Zostril.

"Me?"

Marqueux, surprised, ran his hands over his face, then, looking at his palm, discovered there several drops of a liquid that he identified as sweat. It was certainly not rainwater. He looked Zostril straight in the eye and pronounced these words:

"Me an adventurer? Who's never left this town? Who's never wanted to leave? Who's never bought port wine, nor an umbrella, nor any other foreign product? Who's always deplored any such initiatives when they were made? And who nevertheless never complained when initiatives were passed, even the first, concerning Pierre Nabonidus? who has brought us this rain? and I deplored the second aswell, I must avow: that of condemning Pierre Nabonidus to the sculpture. But I do approve this third, which comprises wanting to restore fine weather. Bring back fine weather? yes! agreed."

Zostril began shouting: a dog intent that some creature stop moving out there. He waved his arms grandly and sat back down, egzausted. He opened his mouth several times without managing to utter anything other than pauses and sighs.

" 'Sdone," he finally said, "then, see, if."

"If what?" asked Marqueux.

"If the rain won't simply stop, once Pierre's statue is finished."

"What!" he essclaimed fiercely. "And no one thought of it!"

"We'll see," said Rosquilly, troubled.

"That's not sound," said Choumaque, taking the floor finally.

"Your deliberations are taking forever," said Paul.

"Silence!" bellowed Catogan. "Let us reflect!"

"There's a solution to all these problems," Rosquilly blared.

"That's right," said Marqueux. "That's right."

"The statue's a hoaks," said Choumaque.

Zostril and Saimpier regarded him with astonishment.

"That's why you've kept quiet since the beginning of the meeting," they said in unison.

"This man is an adventurer," shouted Zostril.

When the last echoes of his voice had faded, sounds were heard on the stairs, as of many people running at full speed. The door flew wide, pushed open vehemently without a knock, and Le Busoqueux appeared, breathless, soaked, tongue hanging. He collapsed onto a chair and stammered:

"Itsfufuh, itsfufuh. . . ."

He was followed closely by Pierre and Eveline, who soon hove into view, no less wet, no less breathless.

Le Bu struggled on the chair, like one in the throes of bad health.

"Yes," he said in a breath, "it's true. It's true. The statue is finished. Finished."

Outside, it went on raining.

"Now," said Paracole, "we have the whole family close at hand."

With great patience, Jean essplicated to them once again his project.

The importer was charged with finding the eel-basket. There weren't any in the countryside, nor in the town, nor in the suburbs. Fishing had been little practiced by Urbinataliens, as much from the rarity of icthyic materials (increasing now, it's true) as from lack of means. Sometimes urchins might go after cats swimming in gutters, offering, grafted to the end of a string, a bit of twisted sharp iron adorned with morsels of some substance or other. As far as catching fish in quantity, such ambition had never arisen.

In these days of anticipation, the rain of course didn't cease falling. Paul resigned office and left for the Foreigners with Alice

Phaye, who discovered she was pregnant. They were never seen again. They had bunches of kids. It became necessary to choose a regent. Some (the aspirators) proposed Le Busoqueux, others (Paracole and Catogan, for eggzample) put forth as their choice Nicodemus and Nicomedes who gradually reconciled themselves to their residence in the refrigerator. But after due deliberation, it was Manuel Bonjean who received this charge. Laodicée immediately married him, this restoring some confidence in the notary within the family politic. Pierre worked his marble, fashioning hairs, giving curves to calves, pulling up the paunch, doing away with superfluities. Eveline respected this endless painstaking labor, but the chastity made her suffer greatly.

Finally the eel-basket arrived and Mandace, in a fit of civic responsibility, himself paid all fees. Actually this eel-basket was a wind sock, white and red, like those one sees on foreign airfields. But who, among Urbinataliens, could tell porpoise from propeller? The entire population rejoiced.

Nekst morning at break of day, the hour when wet roosters go *kwha kwha kwha*, they assembled on the Great Square. The Water-hole had been filled in hurriedly with mud, broken tile, and gravel. It rained still, and those concerned quickly selected a spot and made their way there. Mast, rigging, and hoists were ready. Jean Nabonidus embraced his sister, then shook hands with Bénédict, Robert, Fulbert, and Albérich. It was time. He climbed into the eel-basket. The four young men pulled hard and the mast rose, some seven leagues in height (the Urbinatalien league being about a meter and a half). When it looked to be vertical, the perch was anchored in place. The crowd then thoughtfully withdrew. Hélène remained at the foot. Pierre, laboring away in his workshop, had been unable to attend the event.

The rain, of course, didn't stop at once. At first, though it fell every bit as abundantly as before, it seemed somehow less wet. Perhaps this was only an illusion, but there was general rejoicing. Hélène attended her brother, sending up to his heavenly perch sponges imbued with vitamins. About that time, Pierre delivered the statue. The notables were shocked, but Manuel approved it. It was set up on the Great Square near Jean's post. It greatly impressed the populace.

Then the water, instead of just falling, stiffened, and rippled, like a shaken tapestry. A light wind came up and began blowing continuously. Taken by this wind, the eel-basket filled and billowed out, waving above them there in the sky. Pierre went often to observe it, and it always brought back to him many memories of his youth and bygone days. More than thirty years had passed since he'd left Foreign Town (the Urbinatalien year had no equivalent in the others' chronometric system). He was passionately dedicated to sculpture now, and made love sometimes with Eveline.

Finally the rain reached an end. The wind, doing its job, methodically swept away the water. The sun came out, dull at first, then ever sharper. The wind blew, blew, blew, and water fell no longer. Jean remained apart from life there in his perch, the wind itself after a time ended, and fine weather settled in for good. It was even somewhat warm. The statue began to dissolve and, collapsing, to caramelize: apparently, statues couldn't be long preserved here in Home Town. Its crumbled debris was thrown into the Pits, where Pierre, disgusted, went to rejoin it. His widow remarried many times, consequently.

Jean's body dried to parchment there in his perch in the sun. Mast and mummy together were called chaste-clouder, then by a kind of spoonerism, cloud-chaser. Hélène, driven to despair among her useless sponges imbued with vitamins, fled into the Bare Mountains; at any rate, she disappeared in that direction.

Festivals were established in Jean's honor and called Saint Glinglin (probably because, in putting a stop to the rain—and it rained all the time—he "gleaned the glen"; but how is it that such a rustic term ever came to this town?). In the morning, dishware was broken; afternoons, men made stroking motions to simulate the growth of eksotic plants; at night, fireworks brought on no atmospheric perturbations at all, for fine weather was now firmly established. And the people were happy, thinking they knew how to make or unmake it, should they so desire, when they so desired, with no trouble at all, the weather, this fine weather, this weather of everlasting excellence.

![logo]

DALKEY ARCHIVE PAPERBACKS

DALKEY ARCHIVE PAPERBACKS